BEAUTIFULLY
Broken

MICHELLE HEARD

Original Title Published 2016: Predator.

Cover Designer: Cormar Covers

TABLE OF CONTENTS

Dedication

Sometimes life sucks.
Sometimes you feel like death might be the better
option.
Sometimes you reach the end of your rope only to
find no ground beneath your feet.

In those darkest moments of your life, I want you to
remember one thing – it's okay...
It's okay to cry.
It's okay to break.
It's okay to scream.
It's okay to stay in bed until you feel like your body
has become a part of the mattress.
It's okay...
Because you are human, and you need time to just
breathe.

Please remember that you are not weak when you
break. You are beautifully broken and so much
stronger when the storm passes.
Please remember that you are not alone.
Please remember that you are worth a chance at a
beautiful life.

Remember that once you let go and you break to pieces as you hit the bottom of that dark pit, there is only one way to go, and that's up.

Songlist

Click here - *Spotify*

Real World – Ryan Star

Darkness Within – Michael Logen

Head Above Water – Avril Lavigne

Rescue – Lauren Daigle

Grace – Rachel Platten

Beautifully Broken – Plumb

You're Gonna Be OK – Brian Johnson, Jenn
Johnson

Bird Set Free – Sia

Unbreakable – Jamie Scott

Hush Hush Baby – Lxandra

My Escape – Ravenscode

Falling – Oh Gravity

Safe – Alisa Turner

Synopsis

I've been on the run for the past seven years until there's no corner on this god-forsaken planet left for me to hide. No one with Ellison blood in their veins is allowed to live, and I'm the last one left.

Captured, I'm kept in a container waiting for my death sentence to be carried out. I'm tortured and beaten within an inch of my life when *he* walks right into my hell. No one knows who he works for, only that he leaves no one alive. But for some unknown reason, he doesn't end my miserable life.

Instead, he takes me, and I don't know which is worse... the death sentence hanging over my head or being at his mercy.

BEAUTIFULLY BROKEN

Suspense Romance / Dark Romance
COMPLETE STANDALONE.
Previously published as 'PREDATOR.'

WARNING:

This book contains subject matter that may be sensitive for some readers. There is dark and triggering content between these pages related to rape and violence.
18+ only.
Please read responsibly.

This is Cara's story.
Her trauma and her journey of healing are the main focus of this book.

Prologue

CARA

The Past... 18 Years old. South Africa.

"Cara," Dad calls out to me, "do you have the blanket?"

"Yes, Dad." I pull the blanket out of the car, and shutting the door, I set off after my parents. Unlike most teens, I love spending time with mine. We have a great relationship, and I can talk to them about anything.

Dad starts the boat's engine and steers us down the river. It's a sunny day with a light breeze to cool the worst of the heat. We always come out here after lunch on a Sunday. This is our family time together.

Once we get to the wide-open space of the dam, Dad starts to slow the boat down.

I spread the blanket open and laugh happily as Mom and I lie down, trying to get comfy. Once Dad's satisfied with the spot we're in, he turns off the engine and comes to lie down on my other side.

"Look at that one," Dad says, pointing to a cloud. "It looks like a car."

I laugh. "Everything looks like a car to you."

"No, seriously," he chuckles. "Look, those are the wheels, and there's the frame."

We talk about the silliest things before we eventually grow quiet, just listening to the birds chirping all around us. I'm going to miss doing this with my parents once I'm away at college. I only have a few precious weeks left with them.

Feeling lazy, I drift off to sleep like I always do.

A sudden loud crash yanks me out of my peaceful sleep. My parents' screams fill the air, and my body instantly turns cold with shock.

The boat tilts sharply, tossing my body to the side and ripping a panicked cry from me. I try to claw at the floor, searching for something to grab onto. My left side slams hard into one of the chairs, and it jars my body, making a sharp pain shoot through my hip and chest.

Horror fills me as the boat breaks apart with a thundering crack, and water swallows the pieces with greedy gulps.

"Dad! Mom!" I cry desperately. My eyes dart wildly over the chaos, searching for any sign of them, but there's nothing but the boat breaking apart and the awful noise.

What's left of the boat rises sharply into the air, like a beast gasping its last breath. I start to slide down and grab for the chair, but I'm too late. Something knocks hard into my shoulder, only speeding up my descent into the water.

"Dad," I scream as I claw for anything to stop my fall. Splinters of wood stab at my palms and fingers, and then the water swallows me.

Desperately, I struggle against the water to reach the air while an ice-cold fear spreads through my body.

I don't want to die!

I hear a louder sound, nothing like the boat splintering to pieces. This time it hits at the water, hammering its way closer to me.

Thud. Thud. Thud.

The water won't let me go, its bloody fingers dragging me further away from the precious air my lungs need.

White-hot pain slices through my back, and I begin to swallow the water as agonizing cries are torn from me.

I keep swallowing blood until it drowns the life from my body.

———————————

Waking up to a blinding light, I have to blink a couple of times before the light stops stinging my watering eyes, then confusion crashes through me.

Where am I?

I try to say the words, but they come out sounding like a garbled groan.

My eyes dart around the room, and then a sharp pain starts to pulse in my back.

Where are my parents?

What happened?

Dazed and confused, shuddering sobs begin to ripple from my chest, making the pain so much worse. Hot tears spill from my eyes, slipping into my hair.

"Cara." My eyes jump to the voice, and I see it's Uncle Tom, Mom's brother. "I'm sorry," he says while getting up from a chair in the corner of the room.

I frown, not sure what he's sorry for.

He rubs tiredly over his face and then sighs heavily. "There was an accident. Your parents... they didn't make it."

My parents ... they're dead?

No.

No.

A crippling emotion fills my chest until it feels like I'm being torn open from the inside out. My heart squeezes painfully, a sharp ache impaling it.

I suck in an agonizing breath, but the feeling keeps growing until I'm hollowed out and only filled with the loss of my parents.

On my next breath, sobs start to build in my throat, thick and suffocating.

They can't be gone.

No, it's too soon.

I didn't get to say goodbye.

This isn't happening.

It's a nightmare.

My thoughts start to race, and panic sets into my bones.

They can't be dead ... not my parents.

The reality of never seeing my parents again hits hard, an ache so deep it shatters me. An empty feeling overwhelms me, something I've never felt before. It's like a wave that washes all my happy memories away, leaving only a harrowing heartbreak behind.

I'm too devastated to say a word, and my eyes beg Uncle Tom to tell me it's not true. I keep looking to the door expecting Dad and Mom to come rushing in at any moment.

They'll make it all better. They'll take the emptiness away.

"The nursing staff will take care of you. Once you can walk, you should leave the country." My eyes widen on my uncle, not understanding what he's saying.

Why would I leave South Africa? This is my home.

He lifts the mattress right under my butt, and the movement jars my body, sending a wave of pain through my back. I watch as he shoves a thick envelope under the mattress before dropping it down again.

"Keep that envelope safe. It has a new passport and some money in it for you. I've arranged a visa for you to go to America, but it's only valid for three months. You can't stay here. Once you're in America, stick to the small towns and never use your name again. Forget where you come from, or they will find you."

They? Who are they?

Why would people come after me?

I don't understand any of this.

I want to scream as a helpless feeling overwhelms me.

Uncle Tom gently caresses my cheek, a sad expression giving his face a worn appearance. "Leave South Africa, Cara. As soon as you can." He leans over me and presses a chaste kiss on my forehead. "Run, Cara. Run far away and never stop."

I watch him leave, and then I'm alone in the hospital room with only the envelope and a heart filled with sharp pieces of emptiness, stabbing at my insides with every panicked breath I take.

For a moment, I can only blink and breathe before reality starts to squeeze at my insides again.

My parents are dead.

I'm alone?

I start to weep, grief-stricken and distressed by all that's happened to me, not able to process any of it.

I'm only eighteen. I don't know what to do. I want my parents.

A nurse comes into the room and smiles sympathetically at me, but I feel none of the warmth. She gives me something, and soon it soothes the pain that's clawing at my heart.

I know the relief is only temporary, but I welcome the blissful sleep with open arms.

Chapter 1

CARA

7 Years Later. Present Day.

"Time to close up," Mr. Johnson says with an eerily quiet tone.

In the beginning, it used to freak me out, but you get used to things like that if you need money. Since coming to America, I've done many different jobs, but selling dead stuffed animals must be my least favorite and weirdest.

Mr. Johnson offered to teach me the tricks of the trade, but there's no way I want to learn how to be a taxidermist. I just need another hundred dollars, and then I'm out of here.

I've already stayed here for too long.

I live a lonely life, but I've grown used to it. It's just the way it is. It doesn't help to question something you can't change. It's better to just accept that it's the way my life is going to be.

I now go by the name of Cassy Smith, my mother's name. Cassy is short for Cassandra, and Smith was her maiden name. It was nice of Uncle Tom to arrange that when he had the fake documents made. I feel closer to her that way.

I still don't understand any of the things that happened to me when I was eighteen. No, I'm lying. I understand the pain because it's the only thing that was real and constant.

I don't understand what happened on the boat or to my parents. I don't know why I had to leave or why Uncle Tom left me.

I've come to the conclusion life is not meant to be understood – trying will only drive you insane. Life is just meant to be lived, every day a new day with its own problems.

I've been in the US for seven years. *Lucky number seven ... right?* I can't use my passport anymore. It was only valid for three months, but it's all I needed to find my first job, which was cleaning restrooms at a truck stop. It was a shitty job, but that's why they let me work there in the first place. Cheap labor.

I keep moving from town to town, just like Uncle Tom said. I don't stay longer than two months in one spot. I've been here six weeks, and already I'm feeling the familiar itch to run.

I don't make friends, and I sure as hell don't grow attached to anyone. When you're on the run, getting attached to another person is like carrying a dead weight around your neck.

I only hooked up with Steven for one night, seeing as he was traveling through Scappoose, and I wouldn't see him again. He came to hunt some deer, then he'd head back home.

We had sex, nothing spectacular, but it soothed the craving for another human's touch.

But he hasn't left.

I've seen him hanging around at the local bar and have stopped going there. It makes me feel apprehensive, so my guard is up.

It's time to leave. I can feel it in my gut.

———————————

I shrug on my jacket that's seen better days and make sure the heater we keep under the counter is off. This store is already an icebox, and it's not even winter yet.

While Mr. Johnson locks up in the back where his workshop is, I quickly take out my food for the day. The water in the thermos is still warm, so I just pour some over the cup o' noodles and then wait for Mr. Johnson.

He comes shuffling out of his workshop, and I open the front door so he can keep shuffling by me. I don't want him to slow down, because he'll find a hundred things to do, and I'll be stuck here longer.

Using my foot as a doorstop, I quickly turn the open sign, so it shows closed. When we're both out of the store, Mr. Johnson locks the door. He waves tiredly at me before he slowly shuffles down the sidewalk.

Time to go home.

I let out a sigh at the thought.

Home.

There's no such place for me. I move from shady motel to even shadier motel. That's been my life since I ran away from that hospital. I had to run, not only for fear of my life but because I had no way of paying the insurmountable bills. I snuck out like a thief in the night.

Another heavy sigh leaves me as I begin to walk while testing the heat of my dinner with the tip of my finger. It's cooled down already. I stick my finger in the cup and stir until it looks good enough to swallow. When you've been living off cup o' noodles for years, you don't chew. You just swallow so the stuff can fill your growling stomach.

Chewing, now that's reserved for tacos, or pizza, or burgers... sigh.

"Hi," I hear someone call behind me. Glancing over my shoulder, I see Steven jogging toward me.

"Well, this sucks," I mutter, wishing he'd leave me alone.

Steven catches up to me and throws his arm around my shoulders, making me feel annoyed and even more guarded than usual. "Where are we going?"

"We?" *Oh, buddy, you have high hopes.* "We aren't going anywhere. I'm going home."

"I'll walk with you," he says way too cheerfully as if he'll be getting lucky tonight.

"I'm fine by myself." I shrug his arm away from my shoulders and walk faster.

Damn, I wish he'd get the message I'm not interested.

"Oh, come on, babe. We had a good time the other night."

I stop dead in my tracks and glare at him. "One. Night. Stand," I spell the words out for him, holding up one finger for emphasis. "That's not happening again. I have zero interest in you."

He takes hold of my hand, his grip way too tight, and starts pulling me into the street.

"I said no, asshole," I snap, trying to yank my hand free. Alarm bells start to sound through me, and nervous tension washes over me.

The cup o' noodles spills over my hand, and it has me angrily snapping, "You're spilling my dinner!"

Steven doesn't seem to care about the loss of my food and just keeps yanking at my hand, forcing me to move faster.

My stomach tightens painfully with apprehension, and for the first time, I actually start to feel scared.

How well do I really know this guy?

Shit.

"Okay," I say a little breathlessly. My heart is racing as panic floods my veins. "You can go to the bar, and I'll meet you there in half an hour. I just want to go shower the day away."

My voice is pitching. Fuck, he can hear I'm scared.

"Hell no, babe. You're not going anywhere," Steven says with a dark undertone to his voice.

He drags me across the street, his grip on my hand now bitingly painful. I hear the squealing of tires, and before I can glance over my shoulder, it's too late.

Arms grab me from behind, and a piece of cloth is shoved over my mouth and nose.

Harrowing fear instantly ripples over me as it sinks in –
I'm really in danger.

Oh, God.

A terrified scream tears from me as I'm thrown onto a
hard metal surface. I hear a door slam shut, and an
overwhelming sense of fear and panic stuns me for a
moment.

My heart lurches to my throat as prickles of shock
spread over my skin. My senses heighten until it feels as if
I'm having an out-of-body experience.

I manage to yank my face away from the sickly-
smelling cloth. "Let me go!" I scream while I start to
blindly kick and hit at anything in my reach.

I try hard to push myself up with my arms, but I keep
getting shoved back down.

"Go. Go. Go," I hear Steven yell. "We've got the
package."

Something slams hard against the side of my head, and
then there's a sharp prick in my right arm. I try to yank
away, but it's too late.

My whole world wobbles and spins.

Chapter 2

CARA

The world blurs, and at first, I think I'm still dreaming, and I'm underwater, but then I taste the sweetness on my tongue. I always taste the metallic hint of blood in my nightmares, and this is not it. This is sickly sweet.

My eyes feel heavy, but I pry them open, squinting around me. It's dark and whatever I'm on makes a hollow banging sound as I push myself into a sitting position. I wait for my eyes to adjust, but they don't.

Crap, it's really dark in here, as if I've been dropped into a pot of ink.

"Hello?" I whisper because I'm too scared to say it out loud. There's no answer, only the harsh echo of my own pathetically frightened voice.

Slowly I get up, carefully testing the ground beneath my feet, and again it makes the hollow banging sound. I must be standing on some sort of metal sheet... I think.

Trying to reach for anything around me, I bring my arms up, but there's nothing but the darkness. It feels as if my balance just up and left me, and as my fear intensifies, it throws my senses totally off.

I'm too scared to move, but I know I can't just stand here.

God, I'm in trouble.

My body begins to tremble uncontrollably as the thought hits hard.

"You're okay," I try to calm the panic growing in my stomach. "Find a way out. You just need to find a way out. Stay calm. Don't lose it."

I take small steps forward, my hands shaking terribly. When I walk into a solid wall, my breathing turns to rapid gasps of terror. "Shit, where am I?"

I feel my way along the wall but find nothing but another wall, and then another… and another.

"No. No. No. No," I gasp fearfully as desperation and horror erupt inside my chest, sending a shockwave through my body.

This… box is small.

Claustrophobia sets in, making my heart pound frantically against my ribs and a fine layer of sweat form on my skin.

26

Fuck, I'm so deep in shit.

Was I found by the same people who killed my parents? Did they somehow manage to track me down?

But how?

I was so careful?

Shit. Shit. Shit.

My panic increases, numbing all common sense. I feel my way to a corner and slide down until my butt hits the floor. I press back against the cold, hard metal wall until, and bringing my knees up to my chest, I wrap my arms tightly around my legs.

God.

Please.

Dread makes the dark reach at me with clawing fingers, only making the shivering in my body a million times worse. It makes time slow down and the air thin. The horror of my situation makes my insides quiver and my mouth dry.

Shit. What's happening?

Where am I?

Who has me?

Why?

Seconds tick over into bloodcurdling, terror-filled minutes.

Minutes slither into what feels like unnervingly scary hours.

I don't know what time it is. I don't know if it's night or day outside. I don't know who has me or why.

I know nothing but the naked terror that keeps growing... and growing until it's impossible to form a coherent thought.

I begin to go through stages – panic, fear, and then I'll start to reason with myself that I'll find a way to escape until I'm able to take a deep breath.

Anger comes last, where I begin to plan ways of defending myself until I'm filled with rage, and I'm imagining ways I'm going to kill whoever has me.

It all happens in a matter of minutes, and then the panic overwhelms me again.

I go from feeling hot to cold in seconds, from crying hysterically to just rocking myself like some crazy person.

Please, God...

Paralyzing fear, unlike anything I've felt before, seizes my soul.

I keep thinking any second can be my last second. I keep worrying I'll run out of air.

What if I'm buried, and I don't even know it?

I keep imagining dying in this black hole, and no one will ever know. A sob escapes my parched lips, and I grip my knees tightly to my chest, rock myself.

——————————

More unnerving minutes pass, and then I hear a loud bang against one of the metal walls. I shriek and press further back into the cold sheet behind me.

What's that?

Oh, God.

This is where they kill me.

I'm going to die.

No. No. No.

Please.

I hear keys clinking and something like a lock being turned, and then light spills into the box. A frightened yelp slips from my dry lips. I quickly scan my surroundings, noticing I'm in a freaking shipping container.

Oh, God. They have me in a box.

My chest starts to tighten, and it gets harder to breathe. My skin breaks out in a cold sweat, and my body starts to shake harder.

I don't want to die like this.

God, help me. I'll do anything you want. Please help me.

Hot tears spill over my cheeks, but I'm too scared to wipe them away.

The man standing by the open door just stares at me doesn't move, and it's terrifying the crap out of me. As my eyes adjust more to the light, his features become clearer until I can make out rough beard and shaggy, salt and pepper hair. He's larger than the average man. Tall and broad, with a stomach that tells me he lives a comfortable life.

It takes me a moment, but then recognition sets in, and a tidal wave of relief washes over me.

Thank God.

"Mr. Tredoux?" I croak, and then the tears come.

I struggle to climb to my feet, using the wall for balance. My legs are a trembling mess, threatening to give way any second.

Mr. Tredoux used to come over to our house all the time. He, Dad, and Uncle Tom were really close before the accident.

But then Mr. Tredoux scowls at me, and he looks far from friendly. It makes my moment of relief short-lived, and the tears dry right up as dread washes over me.

No.

"Cara," he says as he steps into the container. He closes the door, and I'm plunged into darkness again.

My heart rate spikes, and I flinch when a match lights up the small space for an instant. The tiny flame makes eerie shadows jump and dance against the metal walls.

He lights a cigarette, and then all that remains is the glowing red coal.

"Imagine our surprise when we saw you walk down the road near Easy's bar. You look so much like your mother. May she rest in peace." He takes a drag, and the coal glows brighter, lending a creepy quality to the room. "Stupid changing your name to your mother's."

He takes another drag, lighting up his face in a scary red glow.

"Yeah, that was a really stupid thing to do," he mutters unnervingly, making cold chills race up my spine. "So, unfortunately for you, we have a score to settle with your father."

I've forgotten how deep his South African accent is. I don't understand why he would be here, though, or what he wants with me. I start to shake my head, and fear swells in my chest until it begins to suffocate me again.

"I don't understand any of this," I whisper when the fear becomes too much to bear.

"I know, my girl. I'm sorry, but it's just the way things are. You know how it works. Children pay for the sins of their fathers."

The door opens again, and three men come in. For a moment, I can only make out their silhouettes against the sharp sunlight that's streaming in behind them. When my sight adjusts, I notice one of the men is holding a camera. He sets it up on a tripod, and after he presses something on the camera, a red light starts to flash.

What do they need a camera for?

The other two men move closer to me, and my eyes dart to them. Then a fresh wave of shock ripples over me.

Steven?

Steven's one of them?

The shivering in my body stills, and I can only stare as my already worn mind tries to process the new shock.

God, they've been watching me.

"Say your name to the camera, girl," Mr. Tredoux snaps, yanking my attention back to him.

"Cassy Smith," I blurt out. I don't want to make them angry. Lord only knows what they'll do to me then.

32

"Your real name!" he snaps irritably, and I cringe back from the hostility in his voice.

"Cara Ellison." My heart pounds in my ears, my breaths too loud in the small space.

"Who is Ralph Ellison to you?" he growls, and my stomach churns with dread.

"He's my father," I whimper anxiously.

"Only for ten minutes, men. We only need enough on tape to let that piece of shit know we're serious." Mr. Tredoux's eyes drift over me. "After the boys are done with you, your uncle will come running to save you, just like he did when I killed your parents." He lets out a heavy breath. "This is just the way things are done. No hard feelings."

What?

With wide eyes, I watch as Mr. Tredoux hands the cigarette to the man next to him. "Here you go, Henry." And then he walks out, leaving me with the three men.

The door closes, and a bright light flickers on from the camera, spotlighting me and making eerie shadows stretch against the walls.

My body starts to shake, and I press back against the cold sheet behind me.

Shit.

No.

A million horrible scenarios begin to race through my mind, tightening the cold grip of panic on my insides.

The man called Henry moves first and comes right at me. He looks like a hulking mass, and it has me letting out a startled scream as I duck to the side.

But Henry's fast and manages to grab hold of my arm, yanking me back. His voice is a vicious growl that agitates every nerve and leaves my insides quaking. "Don't just stand there! Get your ass over here and hold her down."

The other man darts behind me, and then I'm forcefully dragged to the middle of the container. Losing my balance, my knees slam against the floor, making my teeth clatter. I accidentally bite my tongue from the force, and then I'm forced onto my backside.

"Get the jacket off," Henry barks.

"No!" I shriek while trying to yank free from the hold the other guy has on me.

"Please don't." I don't know what I'm begging for, but it's all my mind can come up with, too shocked to think clearly.

My movements grow frantic with panic, and the air becomes hot and stuffy with all of us in the small space. The smoke from the cigarette makes me want to gag.

Steven moves in front of the light, making it disappear. For a second, I sit shocked before all my senses rush back to me, and I try to scramble away from them. Henry's fingers dig into my shins, and he yanks me toward him. I fall over backward, and my head slams into the hard steel floor, making another hollow banging sound vibrate through the floor and into my body.

A suffocating feeling settles heavily over on me, tensing all my muscles until they feel like they might snap.

In a moment of frantic panic, I cry, "Fuck you!" I start to kick with every bit of strength I have in my legs. I manage to kick Henry in the chest, and he falls back on his ass.

I use my moment of victory to scramble to my feet, so I can defend myself, but then they pounce on me, and the fright rips a petrified scream from me.

I yank and hit, but it feels like I'm getting nowhere. All I hear are harsh breaths, definitely my own and theirs right by me.

For an awful moment, my arms are yanked painfully back, and then my jacket's ripped from my body. My ass hits the floor hard as I'm shoved down.

I keep hitting, kicking, and growling like a possessed person. Dread has taken over every part of me, and my survival instinct has taken over.

I have to survive this somehow.

Fear makes my mind terrifyingly crystal clear, and I take in every single thing that's happening around me. It feels as if my body's running purely on adrenaline with not a drop of blood pumping through my veins.

The air shifts as Henry pulls back his arm, and I swear my skin stretches tightly over my face as I wait for the blow to come.

Not knowing what's going to happen next makes it so much worse.

Fear makes pain worse.

Fear makes time stand still.

Fear turns people into monsters and every sound into a warning of what may come.

A fist slams hard into my cheek, and my head whips back from the force. A cry escapes me, and it sounds desperate to my own ears. Pain engulfs the whole left side of my face, making it pulse with a heartbeat of its own.

Then Henry's menacing voice ripples through the dark. "Get the shirt off." The growl comes in raspy breaths.

I try to crawl away, but they're so much faster than me. Steven moves behind me, and bile burns up my throat.

I wish I could vomit all over them. Maybe then they'll stop.

But I don't vomit, and my body convulses the second Steven grabs hold of me.

I can't just let them beat me.

Shit, what if they rape me?

Oh, God, I won't survive it.

Just the thought of one of these fuckers bringing his dick near me is enough to make me turn into a wild beast. I try to swing my elbow into Steven. But the movement throws me off balance, and I fall to the side.

Steven grabs hold of my shirt, and then he yanks it up against my neck. For a blinding moment, it tightens horribly around my neck, cutting off my air supply. He yanks again, and the force snaps my head back. The material bites at my skin, and then it's gone. Clammy air sticks to my torso, and I feel horribly exposed.

Then Steven grabs hold of my shoulders, his fingers digging painfully into my skin.

"No! Fuck you," I scream until my throat burns. "No!"

"Hold her in place," Henry orders. I see the coal of the cigarette burn red, and as Henry takes a drag, it lights up his face.

Fuck, he looks evil – like the devil himself.

"Let me go!" I shriek as a fresh wave of panic and fear breaks over me. I start to thrash and kick, trying to worm myself out of this impossible situation, but it only makes Steven tighten his hold on me.

Henry places a knee over my thighs, and his left hand comes down hard over my breasts. He forces me back to the floor, and then he kills the cigarette against my stomach. The burn is intense, but nothing compared to the fear of not knowing what they're going to do next.

Henry flicks the cigarette away, and then his fist comes at my face. The blow makes my eyes bulge with pain and forces the air from my lungs. The world instantly begins to spin as a coppery taste explodes in my mouth, causing my throat to burn with bile.

The next blow feels like he's trying to rip a hole through my face. The third punch makes the bright light fade, and pain takes over until it feels like even my teeth are aching.

All the fight is sapped from me, and I give up fighting, my body going numb. Blood fills my mouth, dribbling out the side and down my aching jaw.

The last memory I have is a sharp pain in my chest as a foot connects with my ribs.

Chapter 3

CARA

The incessant pain and dark are killing me slowly. But the blinding light scares me even more.

Four days. That's how long I've been stuck in this hell hole.

It doesn't sound long, but they make a recording once a day for Uncle Tom. Every day, Mr. Tredoux adds five minutes to the beating. Yesterday, the twenty-five minutes felt like twenty-five years. I thought it would never end.

I'm dreading the next beating. Every sound makes me cringe with fear.

Every day, they remove an item of clothing. First, it was my jacket and shirt, then my sneakers, then my socks, and yesterday my jeans. They keep taking my clothes away, leaving me with less and less of myself.

I can't stop shivering, and I don't know if it's from the cold or fear. I only have two items of clothing left. My underwear.

At first, I was in shock and didn't eat when an old man brought food. On day two, I forced myself to move and pushed through the pain after they were done beating me, but it was a struggle to keep the food down. Day three was worse, and yesterday I couldn't keep the food in at all.

I think my ribs are broken, or at the very least cracked. My right hip hurts as if someone is constantly shoving a fist into my side.

The tiny space reeks of vomit and blood.

It smells like death.

A sob begins to build in my chest, and like all the others, it gets stuck, making the pressure build.

Whenever the old man comes with food, he never looks at me. He just puts down the plate and water, and then he leaves in a hurry.

It has crossed my mind to try and overpower him, but I have no strength left for a fight.

Suddenly I hear the lock rattle, and I press harder into the corner. My body screams with pain from the movement, making air burst over my bruised lips.

The door opens, and a low growl builds deep in my throat, making me sound like nothing more than a beaten dog.

When Steven comes in alone, a frown forms on my forehead because he's alone.

I watch him set up the camera on a tripod, and then he presses record, and the blinding light falls on me.

Swallowing hard on the deep ache, I push my torso up off the floor, my arms shaking from the effort it's taking. "So now you're going to beat me? You finally grew a pair of balls, asshole?" I mutter, angry that I've let the monster touch me.

Angry that I didn't move on from that town sooner.

Angry that I caved and had a one-night stand.

Angry that I let myself be taken.

"No, Henry does the beating," Steven says calmly.

He begins to fiddle with his belt, and my lips part as my eyes widen.

What the hell?

I shake my head and struggle through the pain to climb to my feet.

Steven's cruel gaze settles on me, and then his mouth lifts in a smirk. "It's been a while."

No.

No.

Ice pours through my veins, making every bruise come alive with a heartbeat of its own.

I'm too shocked and scared to snap at Steven and instead whisper, "I'm not letting you fuck me."

"Come on, babe. It will be like old times," he chuckles darkly, the sound grating at my ears.

He unbuttons his jeans and then drags the zip down, exposing his boxers.

God, no.

Please. Not this. I can handle anything but this.

A fresh wave of adrenaline surges through me, and I dart toward the door. I don't even get halfway when I'm taken down by Steven's body slamming into mine. I fall down face first, the intense ache shuddering through my body, ripping a scream from me.

Before I can push myself up, Steven grabs hold of my thighs, dragging me back. My fingers claw at the steel floor like a feral animal, trying to get some sort of grip so I can pull myself away from him.

Then Steven crawls over me, using his full weight to press my body harder into the metal.

"Get off me!" I try to elbow him, but he yanks my right hand away, pinning it to the filthy floor. He uses his knees to spread my legs wider, and I try to kick. I try to fight back, but lying on my stomach makes my attempt useless.

In a desperate attempt to get free, I use my whole body to throw him off, but his weight pins me down, making my injuries throb relentlessly.

"No!" For a desperate moment, I resort to begging. "Please don't. Please."

My lungs are on fire from my panicked breaths. Anger and dread flare through me, and I scream to let some of the hopelessness out.

Steven doesn't even bother removing my panties. I feel his dick press between my legs, and a wave of disgust makes bile burn its way up my throat.

His fingers shove the filthy cotton to the side.

"No!" I let out a distressed cry as I feel his dick ram against my entrance, but all my struggling and protesting only seems to excite him more.

Steven keeps ramming against my vagina as he struggles to get his dick inside me while holding me down.

I try to clench my legs together, but his knees stop my attempts.

With a grunt, Steven enters me violently, and I can't hold back the inconsolable and horrified screams that are ripped from my soul.

"No." In this moment of absolute depravity, it's the only word my brain can come up with. The burning ache is sharp as Steven begins to aggressively thrust into me.

"Don't worry, babe," he chuckles savagely. "I'll be quick. You won't remember this for long." He keeps pounding into me, each thrust a scorching stab at my body. At my soul. At everything that made me human.

My mind begins to separate from my body until I'm only aware of my body jerking.

"Tomorrow, Henry gets to shoot your brains out," Steven grunts again. As if my impending death is the biggest turn-on for him, he comes hard, jerking against me.

When he catches his breath, he chuckles, the sound filled with depraved amusement, "You didn't think you were going to live, did you?" His clammy breath sticks to the skin beneath my ear, and then he whispers, "But first, we all get to have a bit of fun with you. You'll be begging Henry to put a bullet right between your eyes by the time we've fucked you raw."

Exposed and debased, I shut down.

Steven grabs a chunk of my hair and yanks me up from the floor as he climbs to his feet. I feel the stickiness of his cum dribble down the insides of my thighs, and somehow it makes it all so much worse.

I feel filthy and empty, like a piece of discarded trash.

He shoves me closer to the camera and then talks directly to the blinding light. "There's nothing left of her, Tom. You should have given us the money when we asked."

Steven shoves me to the side, and I fall hard to my knees. I don't even bother getting up, but instead, curl into a fetal position.

I don't notice him leaving. I don't take in anything but the wetness between my legs that makes me sick to the pit of my stomach.

Emptiness stretches and grows inside of me, consuming every part that ever made me human.

It's quiet in my soul as if there's nothing left but a devastated wasteland.

It feels like I'm already dead because they killed my will to live.

Chapter 4

CARA

"Cara," The whisper comes from the old man on the other side of the door. It's too early for him to bring me food.

Maybe it's my last meal.

"Get ready to run," he whispers urgently.

The door creaks open, and I lift my head, but he's already gone.

Did he say run?

The door stands wide open, and sunlight streams in, but I can't make myself move a muscle.

Last night the men all took turns, and the horrors they inflicted on me drove me to the brink of insanity. The terror that's been embedded in every inch of me keeps me rooted to the spot.

I hear gravel crunching under a heavy footfall, and then a dark figure appears in the doorway, making me instinctively recoil.

"Please," I whimper brokenly.

Yes, I'm begging for the scraps of my worthless life.

I don't know how many times I've said that word in the last five days. *Please. Please. Please.*

They've degraded me until all that's left of me is... a beggar, pleading for the shreds of my life scattered around me.

A man I haven't seen before stalks toward me, and I whimper again, shrinking back like the coward I am.

When he crouches next to me, I anticipate a blow, but instead, he shrugs out of his jacket.

I press harder against the wall, not able to cope with being raped again.

Revulsion wells up inside me as flashes of the past twenty-four hours torture me. It feels as if my mind has fractured, the cracks filled with the depravity of what the men did to me.

The true nightmare is the memories I have to face when I'm awake. Every time it feels like I'm able to take a breath, they just drag me down deeper, suffocating me more.

"Move forward," the man snaps icily. He doesn't wait for me to move but instead grabs hold of my shoulders, pulling me into a sitting position. I cringe away from his touch, but then he pulls me up onto unsteady legs and forces my arms into the sleeves of the jacket.

I hear the zip go up, and then I feel his fingers close around mine, taking hold of my hand in a really tight grip.

What kind of rapist dresses his victim?

Maybe he's not going to rape me but kill me?

God.

I'm not sure how I feel about dying.

There were times during the night I wished they'd just kill me. I'm not scared of dying, but rather where I'll end up afterward. I'm not sure where I'll go, and that makes a whole different kind of fear bleed into my soul until I'm a shaking, sobbing mess.

"Stay behind me at all times," the man orders. "Don't scream, and stay behind me." His voice is unnervingly emotionless.

What?

It takes a second for the meaning of his words to sink into my terrified mind. I'm not sure why he's telling me this, and I don't have time to ponder his words, because he's already moving and pulling at my arm.

I take my first unsteady step forward.

Is he here to help me?

Dare I hope?

The second step hurts so much I struggle to breathe. My chest is on fire, and every inflicted wound throbs.

With every movement, the stickiness and raw ache between my legs remind me of the vile things they did to me.

As we reach the door, my breaths are nothing more than desperate gasps as I try to swallow down the pain and harrowing memories.

"I'll set the room on fire. You do your job," the old man says to the stranger holding my hand.

The man pulls me after him until we're out of the container, but then he lets go of my hand.

Shit, this is it!

Oh, my God.

I'm not ready to die.

My heart pounds in my ears, and I'm well aware of the fact that each of those heartbeats might be my last.

But then he reaches out to me with his left hand. "I need my right hand free."

My eyes dart to his face, and I'm filled with a fresh wave of horror. This man is easily the scariest thing I've ever laid eyes on.

Every line on his face is pronounced as he pulls a gun from behind his back. I didn't even see the weapon where it was tucked into the back of his pants.

My throat and mouth dry right up, and I can't swallow the thick spit coating the inside of my mouth.

The man nudges me a little until I'm right behind him, and then I remember what he said – I have to stay behind him.

Please let him be here to help.

Please. Oh, God, please.

Desperately, I grab hold of his left hand, not caring that I have to touch him as long as he's here to help me.

When we walk toward a simple-looking house, I wrap my other hand's fingers around his wrist, clinging to him because I'm scared shitless.

My legs are numb, but somehow, I keep from dropping to the ground. I inhale the fresh air, but it only makes agonizing pain tear through my chest. Quickly glancing around us, I take in the mostly empty property. There's only the house and a yard surrounded by tall grass and trees.

Heat flares up behind me, and I glance over my shoulder. The old man has set a shipping container alight.

"I'm going to kill them, and then we can leave," the man says, his voice filled with anger and vengeance.

He's so focused I can feel the intensity coming off him in waves.

Gathering what's left of my courage, I ask, "Are you here to help me?"

"Glad to see you're still thinking straight enough to ask a question," he mutters gruffly. The corner of his mouth twitches. "Yes. I'm here to help you."

Intense relief hits me so hard my insides shudder from the force.

Thank God.

Oh, thank God.

He tightens his grip on my hand when we near the house, and I see a muscle jumping in his jaw. It only makes me more nervous.

As we climb the four stairs to the porch, my vision tunnels on the front door.

Why the fuck aren't I running in the opposite direction?

Why am I just letting him pull me along?

I should be fighting, kicking, and screaming, not freaking walking to the house where my torturers are.

My mind races from absolute panic to the void filled with the emptiness I found during my darkest hours.

I see the man lift his arm, but nothing can prepare me for the loud bang as he kicks the door in, leaving the wood squeaking at the hinges.

And then it all happens faster than my mind can process.

Flashes and loud bangs.

Shouts and blood.

Men lunge at us, and my rescuer lets go of my hand, moving fast and with precision as he takes out one man after another. As if he's done this a million times.

All I can do is stand rooted, my eyes wide with shock and my heart racing like a wild horse trapped in a burning barn.

The world slows down around me, yet everything races inside of me.

Every shot he takes hits a target, and then red blossoms, exactly like I've seen in the movies. Only this isn't a movie. These are real bodies dropping to the ground, real blood, real screams of terror, and for a change, I'm not the one screaming.

"Stay there," my rescuer growls.

He doesn't have to tell me twice because I can't make my body move as I watch him shove open a heavy-looking door to my right.

"Fuck!" someone yells, and then there are more shots.

Any sane person would run from this nightmare, but I stand frozen as I watch them die.

I imagined many ways for them all to die, but not this, not such easy deaths.

I wish they were burning, just like the container outside.

My rescuer comes back into the living room, his features grim and his eyes constantly searching for a target.

He looks like a predator. Wild and powerful.

Then his eyes settle on me, and just a look from him makes my heart leap to my throat.

Suddenly he trains the barrel of his gun on me, and before I can take another breath, he pulls the trigger.

I can't make myself duck for cover, and I don't even flinch as I feel a slight burn on my cheek. Then something heavy drops behind me.

I exhale a quivering breath as terror makes my blood race hot through my veins. Pins and needles spread over my skin, making my wounds ache terribly.

"Good girl," my rescuer murmurs. He closes the distance between us and takes hold of my hand again in a tight grip.

When he pulls me toward the front door, I do my best not to look at the bodies. But my eyes are drawn to them, drinking in the gruesome scene with a crazy sense of relief.

We're almost to the door when my eyes land on the camera where it's lying on a coffee table. Tugging against the hold my rescuer has on me, I get his attention.

"The camera," I manage to whisper.

His gaze falls on the camera and memory cards, then he says, "We need a bag. Touch nothing but the bag."

We find a paper bag in the kitchen, and as we rush back to the living room, my foot slams into something hard, and I almost trip. My eyes dart down, and I see blood.

Shit, there's so much.

Then recognition sinks hard to the pit of my stomach. *Steven.* I instantly recoil back as revulsion surges through me.

"We need to get out of here," my rescuer snaps at me. He nudges me forward, and with shaking hands, I help him shove the camera and memory cards into the bag.

He grabs my hand again and pulls me out the front door. The moment I step outside, something snaps deep inside my soul and yanking my hand from his, I rush forward as if I've finally been set free.

Once I'm off the porch, I run as fast as my numb legs and aching body can move. But I don't get far before my legs give way beneath me, and I crumble to the ground.

I hear the gravel crunch behind me as a sob tears from my chest.

"Cara." My head snaps up at the sound of my name. It's the way he says it as if he actually cares. It sounds comforting. "It's time to go. You're safe now."

When he crouches next to me, I get my first good look at him. His dark brown hair is short and neat, shaved at the sides. His face is grim and hard, with a beard that only makes him look grisly and dark. He looks like he's made of stone.

Then I see his eyes, gray and ferocious.

I quickly drop my gaze from his, unable to make eye contact because I'm scared he'll see everything, just like the walls I was trapped between saw everything.

For a moment, emotions threaten to bubble up, to drown me in the horror of what's been done to me, but I close my eyes and focus on the emptiness that's blackening my soul. I'd rather take the empty feelings over the memories of the nightmare I've been put through.

"Can you walk?' he asks, ripping me from my dark thoughts.

I try to get up, but whatever adrenaline I had is gone now.

"Okay, no walking then," he murmurs. His arms slip beneath me, and he lifts me effortlessly to his chest, making me feel small in his arms.

Not because he's so much bigger than me, but because there's nothing left of the person I once was.

When he begins to walk, I find myself not caring where he's taking me – as long as it's far from the container… the house… the torture.

Again my mind begins to shut down because every fiber of my being is tired of fighting.

"You're safe. I have you now," are the last words I hear.

Chapter 5

DAMIAN

At least everything went smoothly.

I let out a heavy breath as my gaze scans over Cara.

Jeff was already knee-deep in with the group we were watching when they brought Cara to the property. It threw a spanner in the works, and we had to move in quicker than initially planned.

My day job is rescuing kidnaped victims for payment, where it's a hobby of sorts bringing down illegal syndicates. It was pure luck that we already had eyes on the group when they kidnapped Cara, or she'd probably be dead by now.

I only trust Jeff because he's the one who gave me my first job. We've been working together for twelve years.

Fuck, it feels like a lifetime.

Jeff's old and looks harmless, but the man can still hold his own in a fight. Since he's retired from the FBI, he's been working with me. He loves to get his hands dirty by infiltrating the groups, to dig his way right into the heart of the hell hole. He checks how many men, the layout, how hard it will be to extract the victim if there is one. Then, when he has all the info, he gets it to me so I can go in for the kill.

I watch as Cara slowly comes to. I've done this so many times, it should be second nature by now – but it never gets easier.

When it's a paid job, I usually only stay with a victim for a day before handing them over to the person who sent me in to get them.

But not this one – not Cara Ellison. I have to keep her for a while and ensure she's safe until I figure out what's going on.

We're still putting all the pieces together where Cara is concerned. All I know is that the mafia was using her to lure her uncle out of his hiding place.

I'll have to teach her how to be a ghost so she won't get caught again while Jeff and I try to find out more about Tom Smith and the mafia.

Cara's eyes flutter open, and they look foggy with confusion and pain. Her ginger hair is wild and dirty, and her green eyes are haunted by the hell she endured the past four days. The red of her hair only makes the color stand out more.

But it's her face that makes her easy to spot. Even with all the bruises and blood, she's still beautiful.

Rage simmers in my chest as I shake my head.

Cara has a fragile kind of beauty. The kind that makes you want to protect her... but still, they beat the shit out of her.

Christ.

It's easy for me to kill because the fuckers I take out don't deserve to live, but fuck, I'd never be able to hit a woman.

There's a flicker of satisfaction in my chest that I got to kill the bastards who hurt her so badly.

I used to feel a high every time I saved someone, with every bullet I fired, and with every dead body that dropped to the ground. But after doing this for too many years, the high has faded, and a coldness has taken over. It's become a clinical thing to do. Go in, get the victim or take down the group, and leave no witnesses alive.

Cara clears her throat, and it brings my attention back to her.

There's another punch to my gut as my eyes settle on her.

Christ, they did a real number on her.

There's a twinge of regret in my chest when I see the burn on her cheek. That bullet was way too close.

As soon as we reached the motel, I checked her wounds and tried to clean them, but she needs to shower so I can treat them. She definitely has broken ribs, and her dire state had me contemplating taking her to the hospital.

But then they'd just find her again. It's too much of a risk.

I take solace that she's alive.

"You're awake," I murmur, drawing her eyes to me.

"You're the man…" She clears her throat again. "You helped me?" She frowns, and it looks like she's in a world of pain. "Who are you?"

"Damian," I give her the name I've been using for the past two years. I watch as a look of confusion flashes over her bruised face, then I say again, "My name is Damian Weston."

I watch her closely, and then understanding crosses her features.

"Damian," she whispers, testing the name on her bruised lips.

"You're talking today. That's very good." I say as I get up from the chair I've been occupying in the corner of the

61

room for the past sixteen hours. "It's time to get you clean, so we can treat your wounds. I also got you painkillers and antibiotics."

Cara just stares at me before I head into the bathroom to open the faucets in the shower. When I walk back into the bedroom, she's struggling to sit up. She whimpers and slumps back to the bed, closing her eyes.

Seeing her struggle grips my heart in a tight fist.

"No sleeping," I say. "You need to get cleaned up."

I grab the painkillers and a glass of water and walk to her. "Lift your head, Cara," I say, and her eyes fly open on my command.

She listens and lifts her head. I drop two tablets in her mouth and then move my hand behind her head to help her keep it up. I bring the glass to her lips, and she takes a few sluggish sips.

"It's going to hurt when you shower, but if you don't, you'll get an infection, and we need to try and avoid that," I say while placing the glass back on the table. "You'll feel better afterward."

When I throw the covers back, Cara's body tenses, and the little color she has left drains from her face. She's so scared I can almost taste her fear.

Fucking bastards.

It makes me wish I could kill those fuckers again.

Moving slower, so I don't startle her, I gently take hold of her upper arms and pull her into a sitting position.

"There you go," I murmur encouragingly. "Just shower so I can check your wounds, then you can rest again. Okay?" I pull her to her feet, and this time there's more strength in her body. She sways on unsteady legs, and I quickly place an arm around her waist, but it has her flinching as she tries to yank away from me.

"I can walk. I'm fine," she slurs through the pain.

I nod and step back, not wanting to make things harder for her.

Watching Cara make her way to the bathroom is difficult. I fist my hands at my sides, so I don't give in to my need to help her.

CARA

There's something about losing yourself, being hollowed out and stuffed full of relentless pain and degradation. All I have on is Damian's jacket. It doesn't look like he did anything but put me in bed. It must be because I smell like a sewer, and I look like shit.

I'm tired, not just physically. I'm shattered to the bone. It feels like my soul weighs a ton, dragging me under the wave of emptiness that keeps crashing over me.

I press my hand to the wall and use it to keep my balance. When I reach the bathroom, steam is billowing from inside. On trembling legs, I walk to the basin so I can use it to keep myself up. There's a little square mirror hanging above it, but it's misted over.

"This is how it's going to work," Damian says from behind me. "You're going to shower. Once you're in clean clothes, you'll eat. After that, I'll look at your wounds, and then you can sleep. This is all you have to do today."

I wonder if this man has any feelings. He sounds as dead as I feel.

"Who are you?" I ask, wanting at least one of my million questions answered.

"I'm just someone who cleans up other people's fuck-ups," he answers without any emotion.

"Did my uncle sent you? Tom Smith?" I ask, not able to think of another reason Damian would've saved me.

He hesitates for a moment before answering, "Yes."

Uncle Tom didn't leave me?

He sent someone for me?

Thank God.

I cover my mouth with a trembling hand to smother the sob. Swallowing hard, I force the tears back down.

"I have two rules," Damian says, and he takes a step closer to me.

Instantly my muscles tighten, sending a wave of pain through my body. He might have saved me, but I feel far from comfortable around him.

"Don't look at yourself in the mirror, and don't lock the door." There's a clear note of warning in his voice.

Nodding, I glance at the faded pattern on the tiles to avoid looking at him. The tiles are peach and brown, and the colors make my stomach churn. Then my eyes jump to the faded towels that have bleach stains on them.

But I can only avoid him for so long, his presence demanding my attention, and my gaze slowly creeps back to Damian.

Again he reminds me of a grizzly bear. With the beard, I can't make out much of his facial features. But his eyes... they're sharp and cold as if they've been carved from an iceberg.

"You have fifteen minutes, Cara. I don't want you on your feet for too long." Damian leaves the door slightly ajar as he heads back into the room.

Honestly, I'm relieved. I think I might die if he closes that door. I couldn't stand small spaces before I was taken. Now, they terrify me.

I take a slow breath, as deep as I can, before an ache seizes my chest, and then I exhale.

Just focus on one thing at a time.

Shrugging the jacket off, pain pierces through my left side, making it hard to breathe for a moment. I place my hand against the wall as I step into the shower, so I don't topple over and then grab hold of the little rail.

When the warm water sprays over me, my lower back stings, where Henry kicked the shit out of me.

I turn my face up to the water and let it wash over me for a while. My cheek, jaw, and mouth start to throb as life returns to the wounds, and then the pain spreads down my body, relentless and raw.

It's too hard.

Everything's too hard.

With zero energy, my movements are sluggish. All my strength has been drained from me and replaced with this harrowing nightmare that fills every part of me with suffocating darkness.

I reach for the bar of soap. It's hard and cracked, and I have to rub it under the water to soften it a bit. Then I keep my eyes on a cracked tile where the one corner is chipped away, and biting my tender bottom lip, I slip the bar of soap between my legs.

The moment the soap touches my skin, it stings like fire, so much that my legs start to quiver under my weight.

God.

I can't.

Why didn't I just die?

I can't deal with this.

A sob breaks through my feeble barrier, and I quickly cover my mouth with the back of my soap-covered hand. One tear slips from my right eye and disappears into the water.

I try to take deep breaths, but it makes my chest feel like it's going to split open any second.

One step at a time, Cara.

Don't think about what happened. Just focus on this second... then the next.

As I fight for control over the devastating feelings, I keep my breaths shallow and stare at the cracked tile until I feel a little calmer.

I wash my left arm next, making sure to cover every inch. Even though I want to scrub my skin off, my movements remain ginger. The pain is a sickening reminder of what happened.

Once I've washed my whole body, I start the process again. Every bruise is pulsing with pain. But I don't stop, my need to find some semblance of feeling clean again, forcing me to ignore the pain.

Using the soap, I do my best to wash my hair, and then I rinse the suds out.

When I'm done, I gingerly lean back against the tiles, totally exhausted and consumed by the unrelenting pain.

Letting out a sigh, I turn off the faucets. My legs tremble beneath my weight as I reach for a towel. I wrap the rough fabric around my aching body, and the instant I step out of the shower, I see Damian standing by the door.

My heart leaps into a turbulent battle to not let the terror drag me under.

I freeze and clutch at the towel as if it can protect me while watching Damian with an apprehensive gaze.

He points to the counter. "Clothes. Get dressed and come eat."

He leaves again, and out of fear he might come back, I move as fast as I can. I endure the pain as I drag clean panties up my legs. I skip the bra and grab the cotton shirt. It's brown and old, but I tug it on.

Next is the brown sweatpants, and I'm thankful they're comfy and soft, especially between my legs.

For a moment, I hesitate, fear threatening to overwhelm me, but then I cautiously move closer to the door.

My heart begins to beat faster as I peek into the room, and when I see Damian sitting on the chair in the corner, I slowly inch out of the bathroom.

Panic grips my insides in a merciless fist, but then Damian's gaze flits over me with zero interest, and it makes me feel a little safer.

"There's a burger and fries on the bed. Eat it so you can take your antibiotics."

I notice he changed the bedding while I was in the shower. I gingerly sit down, and picking up the paper bag, I take the burger from it.

I have zero appetite, but I force myself to eat half so I can at least get some of my strength back.

Damian doesn't say anything when I place the leftovers on the bedside table.

I hear him move and glance over my shoulder. He has a small bag with him. When he nears the bed, my body instinctively tenses.

"Let's make this quick," Damian murmurs.

I watch as he places the bag on the bed before taking out some antiseptic wipes. When he presses one of the wipes to my cheek, I hiss from the burn and yank my head away.

Destructive emotions rush through me, and I quickly wrap my arms around my waist, hunching my shoulders.

Damian moves slowly as he sits down next to me. It makes my anxiety spike, not liking that he's so close to me. Then he leans even closer, making it hard for me to breathe as the air evaporates between us.

My breathing speeds up, and I close my eyes, not wanting him to see my panic and fear.

This time his touch is much softer. It still burns like hell, but the gentle way he's dabbing at my face makes my throat close up.

The minutes creep by, each one intenser than the one before as Damian cleans all my bruises.

When he applies some sort of balm to my bottom lip, it becomes too much. I pull away, scooting back on the bed so I can put some distance between us.

I can't bring myself to make eye contact as I fight the tears down.

I can feel Damian's eyes burn over me. "I need to look at your ribs."

God, no.

Quickly I shake my head, wrapping my arms tighter around myself. "I'm fine."

"I doubt that," he murmurs, a compassionate tone lacing the words. My gaze darts to his, and again, I'm hit with the intensity of his ice-blue eyes.

Damian slowly exhales. "Let's get this over as quick as possible so you can sleep."

I sit still, my eyes trained on the opposite wall, and then I nod.

When Damian takes hold of the shirt, I shut my eyes tightly, and my heart explodes into a violent pounding. I don't move a muscle as he tends to the cuts and bruises scattered over my ribs.

"You have a couple of broken ribs. I'll get an ice pack for you," he mentions.

I can't even nod.

When he's finally done, and he gets up from the bed, I let out a burst of air.

Opening my eyes, I watch as he places the first aid kit on the table.

Keeping his back to me, he murmurs, "Sleep, Cara. You're safe with me."

Am I?

Am I really safe with this man?

I stare at him, wishing I could believe his words… but I don't. I don't think I'll ever trust another human ever again.

Lying down on the bed, I curl into a small bundle, and then I pray the numbness of sleep will come quickly.

Chapter 6

CARA

We've been at the motel two days when Damian leaves to get food. I climb out of bed and gingerly make my way over to the window. Every movement hurts like hell, but I can't stay in bed, and I have to get better so I can get out of here. Carefully I nudge the curtain to the side and peek outside.

There's a parking area with only two cars in it. We're at a Village Inn. I've stayed in one plenty of times, so the experience is nothing new.

I spot Damian as he comes walking around the corner of the diner. He's carrying a brown paper bag. I stare at him as he comes closer, his steps firm and every movement calculated.

Damian keeps his head down, but I get a feeling he sees everything around him, including me, even though I'm hiding behind the curtain.

Once again, I wonder who this man is. The first day I was terrified out of my mind, but he's done nothing but help me since he saved me.

My eyes drift over his muscular body.

He could easily kill me. Instead, he takes care of my wounds and feeds me.

Uncle Tom sent him, but still, who is Damian Weston?

Am I really safe with him?

Letting out a sigh, I go to the bathroom, not closing the door all the way. When I'm done relieving myself, I wash my hands, and then my eyes settle on the mirror. It's out of habit.

Damian told me not to look at myself, so I expected it to look bad, but the thing staring back at me can't possibly be me.

God.

I lift a trembling hand to my cheek and gently press the pads of my fingers to the ugly burn.

The trauma I suffered rushes to the surface, and it fills my empty gaze with desperation and horror.

"I told you not to look," Damian snaps, almost giving me a heart attack. I yank my hand away from my face as my body jerks. "Come eat."

I quickly follow him into the bedroom and sit down on the side of the bed.

Dark memories swirl around me, like sharks waiting to attack. I try to take a deep breath, but the ache in my chest stops me.

Shh... it's okay.

You're okay.

Don't think about it.

I take the paper bag Damian left on the bedside table and open it, but then I just stare at the sandwich.

My throat swells impossibly thick with unshed tears, and my breaths start to come faster.

Shh...

Don't think about it.

I can't deal with what I just saw in the mirror. It's not that I'm black and blue, but rather the stark reminder of my time in the container that's dragging me under.

God.

I fight to keep control of the volcano that's threatening to erupt inside of me while just staring at the food.

You're okay.

Finally, I reach into the bag, and taking the sandwich out, I bite into it. It's tasteless and thick in my mouth, but I swallow the food down, along with the destructive emotions threatening to drag me under.

I focus on finishing the food, and then I crawl back under the covers. Closing my eyes, I concentrate on the black behind my eyelids to keep my mind from wandering.

We've been at the motel for almost a week. Damian locks the door behind him whenever he goes for food, and he's never gone for long. He reads a lot. I don't ask what.

The TV's always on, murmuring in the background. I don't ask where we are. I ask him nothing, and he says nothing. He's just there to bring me food and tend to my wounds, and for now, I'm okay with it. I don't think I have it in me to do anything more than the absolute basics.

"Time to go, Cara," Damian breaks the silence during the early hours of the morning. He sounds different. His voice is deeper, and the neutral tone he's been using is gone. I open my eyes and glance at him where he's stuffing things into a bag.

"We're going home," he adds.

Home?

What?

It's still dark out, and glancing at a clock on the wall, I see it's almost three am.

Damian's eyes meet mine. "You're strong enough for the trip home. Come on. Let's go."

I haven't looked at Damian's face since the first day in the bathroom. I think it's the way he wants it, too. But today, my eyes have a mind of their own, and they take in his rough features.

I remember dead gray eyes. That's why I've been avoiding his face, plus it made the past week easier. They're still gray, but it looks like there's a storm brewing in them, something deadly and sharp.

I'm scared Damian can see too much, and I drop my gaze to his neck. A tattoo peeks from the neckline of his shirt. It almost looks like some sort of claw as it disappears beneath the charcoal fabric.

Home.

"Ah… home?" I ask.

Damian nods. "My home. We'll be safer there."

Oh.

Right.

We can't continue to stay at this motel, but… home?

It's been years since I thought of a place to call home, and it reminds me of everything I've lost, my grief, my trauma.

I quickly push myself up off the bed, not wanting to think of the hell I've been through.

Damian grabs the bag, and I watch him leave the room, unsure how I feel about leaving the motel to go 'home' with this man. I'm not sure about anything anymore.

I quickly go to the bathroom, and when I'm done washing my hands, I walk out into the sleeping area and wait, unsure if I should just go outside.

I wring my hands together and wonder what would happen if I tried to make a run for it. I know Damian said Uncle Tom sent him, but that doesn't mean much. He could be one of them, babysitting me until Uncle Tom shows up, and then they kill both of us. It could be a trap.

My body is seized by panic as one unrelenting dark thought after the other flashes through my mind.

Damian comes back into the room, and then he heads right for me. My mind screams at me to move, but I stand frozen like a deer in front of an oncoming truck. He lifts his hands, and I flinch, but then I see the sweater. He pulls it over my head, and I quickly shove my arms through the sleeves. Then he takes hold of the hood and covers my head.

"Keep your head down out there. There's no one outside. It's a two-hour drive home." Damian lifts a hand to my face, and placing a finger beneath my chin, he nudges me to look at him.

"After today, this is all over. You get to disappear."

I swallow hard, not sure I understand.

"We just need to blend in as best we can so no one looks at us. Almost home." His mouth twitches at the corner, and then he lets go of my chin, and he moves to the bed. He grabs a pair of shoes from the floor. I didn't even see them there.

Walking back to me, Damian crouches in front of me. "Foot," he mutters. I lift my left foot, and I have to grab hold of his shoulder, so I don't fall over. He slips the shoe on, and then I quickly push my right foot into the one on the floor before he can pick it up. I let go of his shoulder and move away from him, my pulse racing from having to touch him.

I don't think I'll ever trust another human being or feel safe again.

Damian rises to his full height, and then he starts to strip the blankets and sheets from both beds. I watch him wipe the room clean – everywhere, and with such precision, it's unnerving.

I don't move as he works his way through the room and bathroom.

Shit, this guy is meticulous. He's making sure we leave nothing behind.

When he's seemingly satisfied, his eyes snap to me. "Let's go."

My heart leaps to my throat as I slowly turn to the door. Only then does it hit me that I have leave the motel room.

Shit.

My legs feel numb as I slowly make my way out of the room. It's dark outside, the cold air stealing my breath. I wrap my arms around my waist for some extra warmth.

When Damian's arm falls over my shoulders, my body jerks, and I let out a startled squeak. "It's okay," he murmurs, then he pulls me against his side. "Just stick close to me."

My insides shrivel with apprehension, my muscles so tense it makes every inch of my body ache.

Ducking my head, I keep my eyes on our feet as we walk away from the room where I didn't have to think about what happened to me. It was a safety bubble.

We reach a white sedan that's seen better days, and Damian nudges me into the passenger seat. My eyes dart around the area before I watch as Damian climbs behind the steering wheel. He starts the engine, and then his left arm suddenly moves in my direction.

I recoil against the door, turning my face away from him and bracing myself for the blow as a breath of air bursts over my lips. A broken sound escapes me as my wide eyes lock on Damian.

His arm stops midair, his icy gaze snapping to mine. "It's okay. I'm not going to hurt you."

All I can manage are the breaths rushing from me, setting my chest on fire.

He moves slower, placing his hand on the headrest, then he looks behind us as he backs the vehicle out of the parking.

My body slumps in the seat as a flicker of relief eases some of the tension coiling in my body.

DAMIAN

Fuck. I didn't mean to scare Cara.

I hate the naked terror in her eyes, and it makes me clench my teeth.

Watching over Cara this past week has been both the easiest and hardest thing to do. She's fucking strong, trying to hide her pain from me. But she's broken.

They fucking gutted her soul, and it's starting to chip away at my heart. Compassion's a foreign emotion for me to feel. Whenever I have to deal with a victim, I always focus all my attention on the job. It's what I've been trained to do because emotions will get you killed.

But it's becoming harder and harder to see Cara as just another victim. Especially because she'll be staying with me. It's not something I've done before, always passing the victim off to whoever hired me. Cara's situation's different, though, because she's not a paid job, and leaving her to her own defenses will only get her killed.

I glance at her, and once again, an intense protective feeling bleeds through my chest.

No, I can't turn my back on this woman.

When Jeff told me about Cara, we sped up our plan to take down the group and free her. Remembering the state I found her in, there's a ripple of regret that I didn't get to her sooner.

Steering the car down the highway, my thoughts turn to the group we took down and Tom. I need to find out what's going on and how big the threat is to Cara.

All I know is the mafia kidnapped Cara to get to her uncle.

My gaze flicks to her, where she's squashed against the door, trying to put as much distance between us as possible.

The lie I told her about her uncle sending me to get her seems to have set her a little at ease. I'll keep going with that story until I've found out exactly what's going on.

Knowing Cara might have all the information I need, I ask, "How old are you?"

She startles from the sudden sound of my voice, her fear-filled eyes darting to me. "Ah... twenty-five."

I've picked up on her accent but asking where she's from might give away the fact that her uncle didn't hire me. Instead, I ask, "Do you know anything about the group that took you?"

The color drains from Cara's face, raw terror tightening her features. Her body begins to tremble like a leaf in a shit storm. It's on the tip of my tongue to tell her I'm sorry for asking the question when she stammers, "Mr. Tredoux... used to work with... my dad... and Uncle Tom."

A fine layer of sweat begins to bead on her forehead, and she swallows hard. "I don't know why… th-they took me."

Nodding, I turn my attention back to the road, and knowing she needs to hear the words, I murmur, "All that matters now is that you're safe."

I can feel her eyes on me, and I know she's trying to figure out if there's any truth to my words. It's going to take a while before she learns to trust me. Until then, I'll just keep reassuring her.

The intense desire to protect her creeps up on me again. It's been a fucking long time since I felt a connection of any kind with a woman. Although I've been with my fair share, it was always just to fulfill a need, like scratching an itch.

There was never the desire to get to know one of them, to take care of the shit threatening them, to keep them close so nothing could ever hurt them again.

Once again, my gaze finds Cara, and taking in her fragile beauty that's become more prominent as the bruises begin to fade, I try to pinpoint why I feel different about her.

Because she's broken?

Because I found her in the bowels of hell that's my everyday life?

Christ only knows at this point.

Chapter 7

CARA

After the questions Damian asked, we drive in silence with only the buzzing of other cars and the hum of the wheels breaking the stillness of the night.

When Damian asked if I knew the group, it scratched the frail scab right off that's managed to form over the trauma.

It makes me remember, and I don't have tears to ease the flashes away. I have zero strength to fight off the demons.

It's as if the motel was a cocoon of safety from my memories, and now that we've left, I'm assaulted from all sides.

I remember the smell of the car when Damian placed me in the back seat. I remember the blankets he covered me with. I don't know how long I was unconscious until I finally woke up that day in the motel room.

I also remember the look in his eyes when he killed them all.

He killed people.

"They're all dead. You killed them all." My voice sounds as neutral as his has been the past few days.

"Yes," he says.

"Why?" I don't know why I'm asking. I don't want to think of them. I don't care whether they're breathing or not.

My stomach knots painfully, and I start to feel claustrophobic as the traumatic events whirl around me like a deadly tornado. It's like I'm in the eye of the storm.

"Do you really want me to answer that?" Damian asks. I feel his eyes on me for a moment before he turns his attention back to the road.

I glance at his strong fingers gripping the steering wheel, his other hand resting on his thigh. His whole demeanor is casual. Everything – but his eyes.

"Yes," I whisper. I want to know why Damian does what he does and what exactly it entails. I want to know who this man is.

"I do various things, mostly I track and clean," he starts.

I keep my eyes on his hand, the one on his leg.

"Part of my job is to retrieve kidnapped victims."

What about the other part? What is he leaving out?

"And you just kill the kidnappers?" I ask the trembling in my body echoing through my voice.

"Careful what you ask, Cara."

I don't know if I'm scared shitless of him or whether I feel safer knowing what he does. All I know is I'm tired, and I feel old, so very old.

And maybe… just maybe, it doesn't matter if Damian kills people. As long as he doesn't hurt me, right?

If I'm really safe with him, does any of it matter?

As the miles slip away behind us, I stare into the night. My mind is a chaotic mess of memories, all vile, all crippling. Then there's the gnawing uncertainty of whether Damian's a friend or enemy.

I can't take any more.

Please let him be a friend. I could really use one right now.

Please.

When Damian finally stops in front of a house, I can't see much of it in the dark. I can make out it's big and old, but that's it.

Climbing out of the car, my body aches from sitting still for so long. I follow Damian to the porch, but I make sure to keep a safe distance between us. He unlocks the door, and then he disappears inside.

A light goes on somewhere inside, and then I take a step closer. I peek into the house and can only see a glimpse of what looks like a living room, a set of stairs going up, and a hallway to the right.

I glance over my shoulder and peer into the darkness.

Can I trust this man to not hurt me? Should I make a run for it?

For a moment, the urge to run is overwhelming, and I panic. I turn away from the front door and move as quickly as I can. I rush down the porch steps and almost miss the last one.

That's about as far I make it. The quick movements and panic deplete my energy like starving leeches. I take a couple of deep breaths, and then a hopeless sound escapes over my lips. I have no choice but to stay. I'm in too much pain to be on the run.

Please don't let him hurt me.

I glance back at the open door, and I'm startled when I see Damian leaning against the wall right at the foot of the stairs. His eyes are on me as if he's patiently waiting for me to decide whether I'm staying or running.

He saved me.

He's done nothing but take care of me the past week.

He doesn't even touch me unless it's necessary.

I'm torn between my need to find a safe place where I can piece myself back together and running.

I'm in no state to run, and I've lost the meager possessions I had. The motel I was staying at has probably thrown my belongings away.

My shoulders slump wearily, and I take the stairs slowly back up to the porch. I suck in another deep breath and then step into the house where I'll either be able to lick my wounds or… where I'll be killed.

My heart starts to race at the thought, and I keep my eyes cast down.

I'm so tired.

My chin begins to quiver with tears as the hopeless feeling suffocates me.

"Let me show you around, and then you can get some sleep," Damian murmurs softly as if he's being careful not to startle me, and it makes my gaze slowly lift to his.

The intensity from his ice-blue eyes hits hard, and I instinctively take a step backward.

For a moment, a slight frown flits over his forehead before something close to compassion softens his features a little.

90

"You've been through a lot, and I get that I'm a stranger. It's going to take time before you trust anything I say, but I'll say it anyway – I won't hurt you, Cara. You're safe in this house."

Feeling anxious, I nod. I want to beg him to mean the words.

My eyes dart around us while my tongue slips out to wet my dry lips.

The tightness in my chest increases, reminding me of my broken ribs. I wrap an arm around myself and then lift my eyes to Damian's again.

When I nod, he turns and begins to head up the stairs. He moves slowly so I can keep up with him, but halfway up, sweat starts to bead on my forehead from the effort it takes. When I reach the top of the stairs, my head starts to spin, and I feel nauseous.

Damian glances at me. "Need help?"

I shake my head and push through, not wanting him to touch me.

I just want to sleep and never wake up.

It looks like there are three bedrooms, and Damian opens the door to the middle one. Gesturing to a set of stairs leading up to what could be an attic, he says, "My office is up there. It's the one room that's off-limits."

I nod as I step into the bedroom where I'll be staying. It's sparsely furnished, with only a bed, bedside table, and lamp. There's a closet against the left wall.

Using the last of my energy, I walk to walk to the bed, and I sit down. I can cry from the relief of finally being off my feet.

"Cara." I look at the faded blue bedspread. It reminds me of water. "Cara," Damian says a little louder.

My eyes dart to his.

He looks at the bed and then at me. "There are other covers in the closet down the hall. Change it if you don't like these. There are some clothes in that closet," he points to it. "They might be a bit big, but it will do for the time being."

Damian turns around but stops midstep, then, after a couple of seconds, he says, "I have a question."

"Yeah?" I fold my hands together on my lap and interlace my fingers tightly.

"You said Tredoux worked with your father and uncle. I'm assuming your parents have passed away?"

The grief I never dealt with mixes with the fresh trauma, making my emotions spiral out of control. While it feels like I'm being suffocated, my voice is strained as I manage to answer, "They were killed... right before I left

South Africa. Uncle Tom gave me a passport... and told me to run, and that's what I've done for the past seven years."

Damian absorbs the information, then asks, "Is there anyone here who will be looking for you?"

I quickly shake my head and then realize my mistake. I just told him no one would notice if I disappeared or if he killed me.

Oh, God.

Panic flairs through me. I can't stay here. But... shit, it's either the death sentence hanging over my head – or this man's mercy. I don't know which is worse right now.

Damian instantly picks up on my distress. "That's not why I asked. I need to know if there's someone I should contact. That's all. You're safe here, Cara."

With wide eyes, I watch as Damian leaves the room, and then I numbly sit down on the bed. Unable to control anything, I let the tears flow. I don't move as the trauma shreds through me until all that remains is the empty shell.

DAMIAN

Leaving Cara to get some rest, I head out to the car to grab my bag, along with the camera and memory cards we took from the syndicate.

It's time to start putting all the puzzle pieces together.

From what Jeff overheard while he was guarding the container, we have some information about Cara, but not enough to go on.

I now know Cara's from South Africa, and her parents are dead. She's been on the run for seven years. Which means she was eighteen when she was left to make it on her own with the fucking mafia hunting her.

Anger surges through me as I walk into my office. I drop the bag and place the camera on the desk. Looking at the four memory cards, I take a deep breath, and then I open my laptop. I insert the memory card marked number one and then press play.

It seems to start at the end of a conversation, giving me not much information. My eyes flick over the men, then lock on Cara.

Christ, the naked terror on her face delivers a blow to my gut that makes it hard to breathe for a moment. She's still fully dressed, not a mark on her face.

I suck in a deep breath at seeing just how breathtaking she is, and then the men close in on her. I only manage to watch two minutes, then I have to pause the footage, so I can breathe through the intense rage burning inside me.

Fisting my hands, I close my eyes and focus on my breathing until the rage becomes controllable.

I've only felt like this once before, and it was when Leah, the only girlfriend I ever had and Jeff's daughter, was killed.

Not able to deal with the demons in my past, I open my eyes and focus on the laptop's screen.

You have a job to do.

Every new detail I learn is a step closer to finding out exactly what's going on, so I can deal with the problem.

Focus.

Pressing play again, I clench my teeth as I force myself to take in every detail, searching for anything that can help.

By the time the footage ends, my hands are shaking with anger.

Fucking bastards.

Minutes pass as I fight to regain control over the vengeful emotions watching Cara get beaten elicited in me.

Once again, I wish I could go back so I could give those fuckers painful deaths.

When my anger cools a little, the protectiveness I feel for Cara becomes fiercer than anything I've experienced before.

My eyes land on the other three disks.

Christ, it's going to kill me to watch them.

In my line of work, you'd think I'd be used to seeing the brutal side of life. I can kill a man without giving it a second thought or feeling anything. I've saved countless lives while still being able to keep an emotional distance between the victim and myself.

But not with Cara.

Shaking my head, I try to figure out why she's different, but again the question remains unanswered. I shelf my thoughts and turn my attention to the job.

Pulling my phone from my pocket, I send Jeff a message.

Damian: Safe at home. Learned Cara's parents died, and she's been on the run the past seven years. We need to find out what the connection is between Tom Smith and Tredoux. Arrange a new identity for Cara…

My fingers pause as I think about the identity.

… Karen Weston. Make her my wife.

I read the message, and before I can start picking apart why I'm making her my wife, I press send and put my phone away.

Chapter 8

CARA

I hear the key rattle in the door, and my insides turn to stone. I try to switch off, to take my mind to a safer place, but it's becoming impossible.

I can't see anything. This time there's no blinding light, and I'm thankful for it. It only makes everything more real, and my swollen eyes water and burn.

I hear movement, and I stiffen painfully. I press harder into the cold floor, and it makes a relentless ache seize my body.

I can't take another beating or being raped again.

I have nothing left to fight with.

"Oh, Cara," I hear Steven mutter resentfully, and I squeeze myself harder against the floor. "Why do you have to be so damn fuckable?"

I place a hand over my mouth to keep from breathing too loudly. I will my heartbeat to slow down, to not pound, scared he'll hear it.

"Just remember," he whispers darkly, and then I hear him move closer, "this is all your fault."

My heart stops.

I try to suck in a breath of the pungent air, but then Steven's suddenly on top of me. A scream is torn from my burning chest, and I start to fight with strength I didn't know I had.

I claw at him until I have his skin under my nails. When he tries to kiss me, I bite until I taste his blood.

His hands are all over my torso, and when he handles my breasts roughly, I can't think as the fear I thought I've gotten to know so well thickens, blackens, and oozes into me.

As Steven's hands move lower, I start to heave and bile pushes up my throat. He rolls me over as I begin to vomit. I feel him press into my back, and as he moves the filthy panties to the side, I choke on the bile.

Steven rams into me, and at the same time, he grabs a fistful of hair, pressing my face into the vomit. I keep choking as I fight for air until the familiar darkness sucks me under.

Shooting up, I roll to the side of the bed only to fall to the hard floor. The sheets tangle around my legs as ragged, short bursts of terror burst over my lips.

Suddenly the door swings open, and light spills over me.

For a moment, Damian's eyes flit over me, then our eyes lock. The air begins to tremble with the intensity coming off him. "I made dinner. Come eat."

It's not a question, and with wide eyes, I watch him leave.

My body aches from the fall, and I clench my teeth as I climb to my feet. I press a trembling hand to my stomach, and closing my eyes, I fight to bury the memories.

Just breathe.

Don't think about it.

Just breathe.

I don't look back at the bed as I walk out of the room. When I step into the kitchen, Damian gestures to the plate of food on the wooden table.

When I give him a questioning look, he says, "I've already eaten."

I watch as he takes two bottles of water from the fridge. He sets one down by the plate, then moves back until he's leaning against the counter.

Casually, with his legs stretched out in front of him, he looks relaxed. I watch his throat work the water down until I see the black ink of a tattoo.

"Your food's getting cold, Cara," he says, yanking me out of my fear-induced stupor.

I clear my throat, and with a trembling hand, I brush some hair from my face. Cautiously I move closer and shooting Damian another glance to make sure he's still standing by the counter, I reach for the plate of mac and cheese.

I still have zero appetite, but just like before, I shovel half the food down.

Damian watches as I eat while he slowly drinks his water.

When I can't force any more food down, I nervously glance at him. "Thank you."

"You're welcome," he murmurs, his eyes still locked on me.

An uncomfortable silence fills the kitchen, and it has me reaching for the bottle of water. I take a couple of sips, my eyes darting from the light brown cupboards to the clean sink to the back door.

Lowering my eyes to the table, I ask, "Did my uncle really send you?"

"Yes."

I catch myself from drawing my bottom lip between my teeth. My fingers tighten their hold on the bottle, and then my eyes dart to Damian.

He keeps still, as if he knows any sudden movement will scare the living hell out of me, and it gives me the courage to look at him for longer than a couple of seconds.

Swallowing hard on the emotions running rampant through me, I whisper, "Thank you for saving me."

Damian nods, and for the first time, his eyes seem to soften with something close to compassion. It makes a lump jump to my throat.

"Wanna tell me what happened?"

The traumatic memories stir, and my hold on the bottle makes it crackle. I set it down on the table and swallow hard. "I got careless. I forgot for one stupid moment I wasn't allowed to have a normal life."

"There's no such thing as normal," Damian murmurs. "People like us, like you and me," he waves a hand between us, "are far from normal, Cara. We blend in until we become nothing more than shadows. You have to make people look the other way." As he takes a breath, I wonder if this is my first lesson from him on how to survive without an identity.

Will Damian show me how to become a shadow... like him, so I won't get caught again?

Then it hits me that I have to depend on a killer, a cleaner, whatever he wants to call himself for my survival.

"How long will I stay with you?" My voice is thick in my throat. I've never stayed with someone, not since my parents.

"Unfortunately, life dealt you a shitty hand," Damian murmurs.

One thing about Damian is that he loves eye contact. It's hard, but I force my gaze to meet his.

"You have one of two choices, Cara. You either stay here or take a chance out there on your own." He doesn't elaborate on what staying here would entail. "I'm arranging a new identity for you. The papers will be here in two weeks. If you decide to do this, to stay here," he adds quickly, "you're not gonna bail on me one day. You can't wake up and decide this is not the life you want."

What does that mean?

Damian pushes away from the counter, and it feels as if the air rushes to give way before him. I blink once when he gets close to me, and then I keep dead still. Damian's eyes hold mine, and my heart starts off with heavy beats until it's bouncing wildly in my chest.

Slowly he lifts an arm, and I shrink, my shoulders hunching, when he wraps his fingers around the back of my neck. The touch makes the air rush from my parted lips.

Fear for this man coils deadly inside my stomach, waiting to be released.

Damian's features soften a little. "You're safe with me, Cara. I'll never hurt you, and I'll do everything in my power to keep you alive."

His words make my emotions spiral out of control, and it causes tears to sting my eyes.

Damian tilts his head as a muscle starts to jump on the side of his jaw, right above his beard. "You're safe."

Staring at this man who has the power to end my life in a second, I hear him inhale.

I hear a bird call somewhere.

I hear the ticking of a clock.

I hear a lot, but I only see that jumping muscle. It looks like a bomb that's ready to blow at any second.

Overwhelmed and unable to process much, I whisper pleadingly, "I want to believe you."

His features soften even more until compassion is clear on his face, and his icy-blue eyes don't look as cold anymore. "It's going to take time, but we'll get there."

Somehow, I manage to nod, and it makes me more aware of his fingers on the back of my neck. Just then, he pulls his hand away from me and takes a couple of steps back.

Nervously my tongue darts out, swiping over the scab on my bottom lip.

I have two choices; one, I stay with him, this killer, and only the Lord knows what will happen. Or two, I take my chances out there, and I know they will find me again. I'll die this time because he won't come for me again. I also have no money, and finding a job while I look and feel like hell will be next to impossible.

Damian's my only chance at staying alive.

It sucks when your life depends on a total stranger. I drag in a deep breath, and my lungs protest with a sharp ache.

"I guess you're stuck with me." I don't sound very convincing, but instead, I sound petrified out of my mind.

"Good." Damian glances at the doorway. "For now, just focus on getting better."

There's a flicker of gratefulness, but it's quickly drowned by the trauma of what happened and uncertainty of what my future holds.

Fidgeting, I walk out of the kitchen while praying this house will really be a safe haven for me.

DAMIAN

I watch Cara leave the kitchen and then finish my bottle of water as I check my phone for anything from Jeff. So far, he's only acknowledged that he'll arrange Cara's new documents.

I tuck the device back in my pocket, then think about the interaction I just had with Cara.

She's like a wounded deer, her fear still palpable in the air. I couldn't stop myself from touching her, needing to offer her some form of comfort.

At least she's processing what I say, which is a step up from the trance she's been stuck in since I rescued her.

When I go upstairs, I hear the shower running, which I take as another good sign. As I pass by the bathroom, I notice the door's not closed all the way.

I get the first aid kit from my room then go wait in Cara's room. Soon she'll be able to do this for herself.

I stand by the window when I hear the bathroom door creak open. Her footsteps are soft, and I can feel her eyes on me, but when I turn around, she lowers her gaze to the floor.

"How do you feel?" I ask. Walking to where I left the first aid kit on the bed, I take in the bruises on her face that have faded some more. The burn on her cheek might leave a scar, which is a pity.

I watch her cheeks grow pink under my inspection.

"Confused, scared, ashamed…" she mutters honestly to my surprise. Her shoulders slump, and then she whispers, "Okay." She clears her throat and then louder, "I'm okay."

"You'll get there." I gesture for her to come closer. "Let me look at your wounds." She inches closer and cautiously sits down on the side of the bed. When I crouch in front of her, I ask, "How's the pain?"

Cara hesitates at first, but then she lets the word out with a harsh breath, "Better." She fidgets uncomfortably, and I know it's because of me. I'll have to watch the other memory cards to see what else happened to her, so I'll know how to handle her.

Cara's different from the other women I've saved. Usually, they cling and they need comfort, but she's the total opposite.

Maybe she has some fight left in her.

"Remove the sweater." I keep my voice neutral. It seems to put her at ease when I keep my tone emotionless.

I open the first aid kit. "From tomorrow, I want you to do this yourself until your wounds are healed."

I'm hoping it will give her back some of her independence.

I watch as Cara takes hold of the sweater that's two sizes too big for her. Her fingers dig into the material, and her knuckles go white.

"I...," she clears her throat again, and then she hugs herself, "I can manage. You don't need to do it."

Her whole body is tense, and she's hunkering into herself as if she's trying to make herself a smaller target.

"Okay," I say, and rising to my full height, I leave the room. When I reach the door, I glance back at her. "You're safe, Cara," I say the words because I know she needs to hear them, and at some point, I'm hoping they'll take root and drive some of the fear from her.

I close the door behind me, and then I stare at it, waiting to see what her reaction will be.

Within a couple of seconds, the door's yanked open, and Cara's eyes widen when she sees I'm still standing here.

"I... I," she takes a step back and mumbles, "don't close it."

Just like I thought, she's claustrophobic. It's a good thing the house is big because it's going to be a while before Cara's okay with small spaces again... if ever.

I'm also noticing she's showing more emotion, which means she's starting to feel. Now the hard part begins. She's either going to deal with what happened to her, or it's going to destroy her.

Only time will tell how strong Cara is, but I'll be there to help her every step of the way.

Chapter 9

CARA

I've lived with Damian for almost two months, and another morning comes, gray and miserable. The wind howls around the house, and it makes it feel big and empty.

I was too freaked to take in anything, but now that some time has passed, I'm starting to see. I'm beginning to hear and... feel... way too much.

I'm too alive for all the pain inside of me. It gives the trauma something to feed on, something to destroy.

When the walls of my bedroom begin to close in on me, I go look for Damian and find him in the kitchen. He's usually either in here or up in his study, which is the one place in the house I'm not allowed to go. I haven't been outside yet because I'm not brave enough to take that step yet.

"I'd give you something to help you sleep, but I don't want to struggle to wake you up if shit comes knocking on the door and we have to run in the middle of the night," Damian says, giving me a once-over like he always does.

I stop halfway into the kitchen and turn to him. "It's okay," I reply, my voice lacking strength.

I've fallen into a routine of cleaning and cooking, not that there's much to clean, and cooking consists of either heating up frozen dinners or making something simple like mac and cheese. It's one hell of an upgrade from the cup o' noodles I used to live off.

I haven't had a whole night's rest since we left the motel. I know it's because Damian now sleeps in his own room. I was shocked when I realized how safe I felt with him watching over me.

It's something I've been clinging to – feeling safe with Damian. It's also probably the only thing that's kept me from losing my mind.

I'm too scared to sleep for long, so the nights go by slowly, stretching the darkness in me to breaking point. It's a constant battle to keep the memories buried.

The days are easier, the light chasing the shadows and hearing Damian move around the house gives me comfort.

I'm not alone.

For the first time since my parents died, I'm not alone.

These are the things I focus on instead of trying to process everything that happened in the container.

"You okay?" Damian asks, drawing me out of my thoughts.

I nod and then begin to prepare a cup of coffee for myself. I've learned Damian only drinks water, so I don't bother asking if he'd like some.

When I take a sip of the coffee, Damian gestures to the kitchen table. "Take a seat."

Slowly I'm becoming more comfortable being around him, and even though I'm still wary, I'm not terrified of him any longer. I don't know when it happened, but it just crept up on me.

I pull out a chair and sit down, placing my cup on the table, then I meet Damian's gaze that's still as intense as when we first met.

The corner of his mouth lifts, and the sight of Damian grinning, robs me of my breath. It makes him look younger. He almost looks normal until I see the black ink snaking up from beneath the charcoal t-shirt he's wearing. Instantly everything snaps back into place.

This man is far from normal.

His smile disappears as fast as it came when I don't smile back at him. "It's been two months. It's time for you to go out."

"Where to?" My eyes widen, not liking the sound of leaving the house one bit.

I'm not sure I'm ready to do that.

"Shopping for clothes while I take care of something," he answers vaguely.

My curiosity makes me ask, "Take care of what?"

"A job," Damian replies, his eyes sharpening on me. "I still have to work."

Right.

I'm not sure I want to know what the job entails, so instead of asking, I pick up the cup and take a couple more sips.

Silence stretches between us until I muster up the courage to ask, "How... uhm... how did you get into this line of work?" Then, feeling awkward for asking, I begin to stammer, "It's just... it's not every day a person meets a..."

"A cleaner. I'm referred to as a cleaner." Damian leans forward, resting his forearms on the table. "Someone close to me was taken while I was away on tour. When I came back, it was too late. I killed the person who took her, and since then, it became my job. Jeff is the only person I trust.

He was the old man who stood guard outside the container you were held in."

Container... Old man.

The memories I've been fighting to keep buried shudder through me like shockwaves. My eyes snap shut as the flimsy wall I've managed to erect between myself and the trauma begins to give way.

No, don't think about it.

Just breathe.

Don't think.

Just breathe.

"Sorry," Damian whispers.

I shake my head, slowly opening my eyes and focusing my gaze on the almost empty cup of coffee.

How much does the old man know of what happened in that container, and did he tell Damian?

My cheeks grow hot with shame, and the scabs that have managed to form over the wounds inflicted on my soul crack open.

"Shit happens to the best of us, Cara," Damian murmurs. "It's how you deal with it that counts. You have to fight for what you want. Otherwise, this life will chew you the fuck up and spit you right out. You're either a fighter or a nobody, and I'm sure as hell, not some nobody. You don't look like a nobody, either."

I latch onto the sound of Damian's voice, letting his words sink deep.

"I want to be a fighter," I admit, my tone battle weary.

"Then fight, Cara," he says. I lift my eyes to his, and seeing the strength in his pale blue irises makes me feel a little better. "I'll be there every step of the way to help you."

Why?

I can't bring myself to ask the question, so instead, I just nod.

"Cara, we're leaving," Damian calls out.

I'm hiding in the hallway, trying to scrape the courage together to walk out by myself.

"Cara," he calls again, and I have to force my feet to get moving. I take one step at a time, but halfway down the stairs, my chest closes up.

As the front door gets closer, I can hear my panicked breaths. They sound distorted and way too loud. I wrap my arms around my waist when a dizzying wave washes over me.

"You're doing good," Damian says as he comes to stand at the foot of the stairs. He lifts his arm, holding his hand out to me.

I stare at his strong fingers, and needing whatever strength he can spare me, I instinctively grab hold of his hand. His grip is firm, and I manage to take the last couple of steps down until I stop next to him.

Feeling panicked, I tighten my hold on his hand.

"Take a deep breath," he says, his voice filled with patience. My eyes dart up to his, and I do as he says, filling my lungs with a mixture of air and Damian's cologne. It has an earthy smell that has a calming effect on my frail nerves.

The corner of his mouth lifts slightly. "Ready?"

Knowing I have to take this step at some point, I nod quickly as I grab hold of Damian's wrist with my other hand, practically clinging to him. Just like I did when he pulled me out of the container.

The thought shudders through me, and I squeak, "Wait." I suck in a panicked breath. "Wait."

"It's okay. Take your time."

My breaths keep coming faster, and it has Damian crouching a little down, so he's face to face with me. "Shh... you're safe. Focus on taking deep breaths."

Where Damian's eyes used to frighten me, they now calm me. I just keep staring at him as I work to slow my breathing.

He lifts his other hand to my face, and cupping my cheek, his thumb brushes over the scar the bullet left. "I've got you. Okay?"

I nod, slowing my breaths even more.

"Good girl," he murmurs when I've managed to work my way through the panic attack.

There's a burst of emotion in my chest as I stare at the man who saved me. It's powerful and akin to hero-worship because that's what Damian is to me – my hero. My safe place.

The realization makes me look at him with new eyes that aren't tinted with fear, and I don't see the man, but instead... my protector.

"Ready?" Damian asks, tugging me out of my thoughts.

Turning my gaze to the front door, I nod. "I'm ready."

With my hands clinging to Damian's left arm, I follow him out of the house and into the sunlight. I watch as he locks the door and activates the alarm system, and then we head to the car.

Damian opens the passenger door and waits for me to climb in before he shuts the door. My eyes stay locked on him as he walks around the front of the vehicle, and when he slides in behind the steering wheel, I relax again.

Damian glances at me as he starts the engine, and then he grins. "You did well, Cara. I'm proud of you."

His praise warms my heart, and feeling a little self-conscious, I quickly pull on my seat belt.

When Damian steers us down the driveway, I stare back at the house. It's old and shabby looking, with the paint peeling off in places. The yard is scattered with dead leaves.

But it doesn't matter because somehow it's become home – my safe haven from the cruel world.

Chapter 10

CARA

After driving for twenty minutes, Damian stops outside a smallish mall. He turns off the engine, and then we sit in silence as I glance around the parking area.

It's just a mall.

Damian moves, and when I turn my head to him, I watch as he pulls a phone out of his pocket. He holds it out to me, but when I take hold of it, he doesn't let go, and it has me looking up.

"Don't talk to anyone. Only call the number programmed on the phone if anything happens. Do you understand?" Damian asks.

I nod.

Worry tightens his features until he looks deadly. "Will you be okay by yourself?"

I glance to the mall entrance and watch as people go in and out of the double doors, and then I nod again.

Fear ripples up my spine, but I do my best to force it back down.

This will be good for me. I need to get out there, or I'll never be able to cope on my own again.

I take another breath as my eyes latch onto one person and then the next. A woman with a toddler. Two teenage boys. An elderly couple.

All normal people.

Letting out a deep breath of air, I swallow down the thick spit that gathered in my mouth.

I can do this.

I have to do this.

It will be one step closer to being able to stand on my own two feet again.

I glance back to Damian, and his lips are set in a hard line. "I need to hear the word 'yes' from you, Cara," he says, and his eyes darken to a deeper blue.

He seems worried about me.

I've been alone for so long, and seeing how concerned Damian is about me makes the warm feeling I had earlier return.

"Yes," I answer clearly. "I'll be okay."

Damian nods, and then he pulls some cash out of his wallet. "Get decent clothes… stuff you like. I'll be back in exactly sixty minutes." His eyes hold mine. "One hour, Cara."

"Okay," I say to appease him as I take the money from him. "And thank you."

Damian stares at me for a moment, and then he lifts his hand to my shoulder, giving it a light squeeze. "Keep your head down," he says, and the muscle starts to jump in his cheek. "If anything happens, find a crowded space and call me."

I nod again, and then it hits me. Damian's not ready to let me go alone into public, never mind me not being ready. This is a huge step for both of us.

It's odd, thinking Damian can feel fear, just like the next person.

My lips curve up into an encouraging smile. "Go, Damian. I have your number. If something happens, I'll go to the most public spot and phone you. I'll be okay."

He pulls his arm back as his eyes drift over me, and then he nods. "One hour."

Opening the door, I get out of the car and quickly walk away before I can change my mind. As I enter the mall, my eyes dart to every person in my near vicinity, assessing whether they could be a possible threat.

My heart begins to beat faster, and everything around me seems overly bright and loud. Then a wave of panic starts to build inside of me, making me wrap my arms tightly around my waist.

Shit, calm down, Cara.

It's just a mall.

You're okay.

I focus on taking a couple of breaths and lower my eyes to my feet.

"You can do this." My voice is nothing more than a desperate whisper.

An elderly woman shuffles by me, way too close for comfort, and I cringe to the side before scurrying away from her.

"You can do this," I let the words out on a harsh breath.

Shit, so many people, so many sounds.

I suck in a deep breath and whisper to myself, "I can do this."

Only after ten minutes of aimlessly walking around do I start to relax a little, enough to notice the different stores. I dart into the nearest one and go for a display of shirts.

They are more for summer, but I take two anyway. I just want to get this whole shopping trip over with as quickly as possible.

I mix and match, trying to create some sort of style, seeing as all my stuff was left at the motel in Scappoose when I was taken. I make sure to get comfy underwear, too, and some much-needed toiletries.

I keep an eye on the phone, watching the time, and then a pretty pair of jeans catches my attention. I wander closer, and on impulse, I take them. I also buy a pair of sneakers, boots, and two sweaters.

By the time I'm done and back outside, I have ten minutes to spare. There are no missed calls or text messages from Damian, so I hope it means everything is going okay with the job he had to take care of.

Guilt slithers into my chest because I didn't even tell him to be careful. I was so focused on myself.

With my teeth tugging at my bottom lip, I glance at the entrance, watching for Damian's car.

I wonder what the job was? Did he kill more people? Did he save someone?

Before more questions can fill my mind, Damian pulls up in front of me.

When he climbs out of the car, his features are tense, and his worry-muscle is jumping aggressively. He helps me place my purchases in the trunk and then ushers me to the passenger side, practically shoving me into the seat.

I watch as he rushes around the front of the car, and after climbing behind the steering wheel, he drives slowly away as if nothing is wrong. His fingers grip the steering wheel hard until the tips go red.

"What's wr–" A groggy-sounding groan stops me from finishing my question. Goosebumps spread over my skin as I glance over my shoulder to the back, and then I quickly cover my mouth with both my hands.

God.

There's a girl covered with a blanket lying on the back seat. She has a split lip and a bruise on her left cheek.

My eyes snap to Damian just as he glances at me. "Don't worry about her. She's okay." My eyes creep back to the girl, then Damian adds, "We're staying the night with her before her father will come to get her."

Slumping back in my seat, I think to lower my hands from my mouth, and then I stare out the window while my heart thumps crazily in my chest.

It's okay.

"Are you okay?" Damian asks.

Even though I'm not sure what I'm feeling, I nod.

"Did you get everything you needed?"

I nod again, willing my heart to calm down.

We don't go back home. Damian drives for hours before he finally pulls over at a shady-looking motel. I kept quiet during the drive, not having the guts to talk first.

As soon as we stop, I scramble out of the car.

"Stay with her," Damian orders, and then I watch as he goes to the reception area.

My eyes dart back to the girl, and I notice she's still unconscious. She looks younger than me, and I feel a twinge of compassion for her.

Instead of being swallowed by my own trauma, I take in the fact that Damian saved another life. I don't care who he had to kill to help the girl. I only care that he rescued her, and soon she'll be home with her dad.

There's a stab of grief when I think of her dad coming to get her.

A car pulls into the parking lot, and my heart stutters with fear. My eyes are glued to the driver when she gets out and walks toward the reception area, just as Damian comes out.

"Unlock the door to number nine," he says as he hands me the key.

I watch him lift the girl out of the car, and my mouth is bone dry as I hurry to room number nine. As I unlock the door and push it open, I hear Damian murmur, "Everything's going to be fine, sweetheart."

Tilting my head as I step into the room, I search my memory, but I can't find that tone or words anywhere. Damian never spoke so kindly to me.

He's almost cooing at her as if she's a baby, something precious. "Let's get you all cleaned up."

I close the door behind us and watch as Damian gently lays the girl down on one of the beds.

'Maybe I'm just not remembering it all,' I start to defend him, but then that little voice that likes to cause pain pops up and sneers at me, *'You're nothing but a fuck-up he has to clean up.'*

"Get me the towels from the bathroom. Wet one of them," Damian orders, and I stare at him for a second before I'm able to make my legs move.

Hurt blossoms in my chest because, with this girl, he's gentle, but when it came to me, he was like a robot.

I walk into the bathroom and grab the bath towel, throwing it over my shoulder. I hold the hand towel under the water until it runs hot, then wring it out as best I can before going back to the sleeping area.

Damian's sitting down on the bed, with the girl's head resting on his thigh. There's another unwelcome stabbing sensation in my chest, but I shove it away and hand him the wet towel.

I take four steps back when he starts to wipe her face, removing the excess blood on her bottom lip and chin. She flinches away, and he pauses. Then, leaning over her as if to shield her with his body, he murmurs, "Shhh... everything's going to be fine, sweetheart."

I stand as if entranced and watch as he cleans her, and only when he's done does he look up at me.

"Hand me the towel." His eyes flit over me. "Sit down on the other bed."

I give him the towel and move back until I feel the other bed bump against my legs. I slump down on it and scoot backward until I'm pressed tightly against the wall.

I watch Damian hold the girl while every couple of minutes, he repeats the words. *Everything's going to be fine, sweetheart.* Words I now know with a desperate certainty he never said to me.

I must've drifted off at some point because I'm startled awake by a pounding on the door.

Although I slept in a sitting position, I still slept through the night.

My eyes lock on Damian as he peeks through the curtain before opening the door. An older man almost falls

127

into the room, and I scramble to get to the corner. I bring my knees to my chest and try to make myself as small as I can while my heart begins to thunder against my ribs.

Damian comes to stand right in front of me. It looks like a casual move, but I can't see the man now, and that means he can't see me.

"My sweetheart," the man coos at the girl.

Tears start to burn in my eyes at the emotion weighing heavy in the room.

"Daddy?" The girl's voice sounds broken, and I press my mouth against my knees to keep from making a sound.

"Everything's going to be fine, sweetheart," he repeats Damian's words to her, and she starts to cry. Huge relieved, heartfelt sobs.

Then it feels like something dies in me. I'm not sure what it is, but I feel lost without it.

Chapter 11

CARA

I don't realize I'm rocking myself until Damian touches my shoulder. The man left with his daughter, and it's just the two of us again.

"Cara."

My emotions are out of control, my grief at the loss of my parents cutting through me like sharp shards of glass.

"We have to go," Damian says as if it should matter to me.

"No one came for me," I whimper against my knees, my breath hot on my thighs.

"Cara, look at me." I don't, not until Damian's hands clamp around my shoulders and he pulls me up, and I'm flush with his body. His face is inches from mine, and his breath is hot on my skin, then his eyes seize mine. "I came for you." His voice is filled with emotions I've never heard before, and it makes my breath hitch.

"I came for you," he says again, and this time his voice is hoarse, filled with an emotion I can't place.

Damian's arms wrap around me and lock me to his chest. I breathe in his cologne mixed with his sweat, and it somehow has a calming effect on me.

He doesn't hold me for long, but it's still comforting. Then he gently pushes me back until his eyes can lock on mine. "Better?"

I nod as I slump down on my knees, my hands falling numbly in my lap.

He came for me.

I needed the reminder, and unable to tear my eyes away from Damian, I watch as he starts to clean the room and bathroom.

Once we're in the car, Damian stares at me. At first, I used to look away, but now the intensity in his eyes eases the turbulent storm always threatening to overwhelm me.

"Bruises are almost gone," he whispers.

"Yeah."

His eyes drift over my face again, and then he starts the engine. This time when he lifts his hand to my headrest, I don't cringe away.

During the ride home, I try to make sense of what happened. Why it even matters. Why everything in me calmed the moment, Damian hugged me.

I don't find any answers, though.

When we get home, Damian goes straight for the shower. I hang the clothes I got the day before. I should wash them, but I couldn't care less at the moment.

I go stand in front of the window and stare outside, trying to figure out why it feels like I lost something back at the motel.

Was it hope?

My eyes drift shut as I realize I lost hope that I'd belong to someone again. I lost hope that I'd see my parents again.

I know they're dead, but for some reason, I always had hope until the stark reality was staring me right in the face.

No one came for me back in that hospital. Sure, Uncle Tom stopped by, but then he left me all alone in a world I didn't understand.

No one is coming for me, and it's the saddest realization.

I know Damian said he came for me, but that's not the same thing. Damian's just another person passing through my life, here one day and gone the next. I am a mess Uncle Tom is paying him to fix.

I have no friends, no family, and the thought leaves a wasteland where my heart should be.

I'm alone.

DAMIAN

Stepping into my office, I take a seat, and then I stare at the laptop.

I hugged Cara.

There's nothing I could do to stop myself, and I'm fucking lucky she didn't freak out.

The moment my arms locked her to my body, it felt like my heart was flayed wide open, and she crawled right inside.

It felt right.

Christ, it felt more right than anything's ever felt in my life.

The past two months, I've watched Cara grow stronger with every passing day. I've also heard her screams in the dead of night.

It's as if my life was on autopilot until Cara. Since I found her, there's been unbearable pain, compassion, affection, and bursts of light with every step she takes forward.

Affection.

There's no use in trying to deny it. Physically I'm attracted to Cara, and emotionally – it feels like I already care too much.

Not that any of it matters because Cara's still healing and far from ready for any kind of relationship.

To get my mind back on the job, I decide to watch the fourth and final memory card.

I could only stomach watching one every couple of weeks and seeing Cara being beaten like that, I have no words for the rage I feel.

One thing I did pick up on is that she put up one hell of a fight every single time they beat her. But with each beating, she got weaker, and that was hard to watch.

I'm relieved it's the last memory card as I press play. I lean back in the chair and take my phone from my pocket to check my messages and emails. There's one from Jeff saying Mr. Graham paid the rest of the fee for us retrieving his daughter.

I killed the two fuckers who tried to get a five million dollar ransom from him.

Listening to the footage, I hear the familiar sound as they set up the camera. There's another message from Jeff saying there's no movement from Tom Smith. We found out he practically lives at his club in South Africa and is always surrounded by two guards. He's made no effort to try to find Cara, and it makes me wonder what kind of uncle would leave his niece to suffer the way Cara has.

A fucked up one.

'So now you're going to beat me? You finally grew a pair of balls, Steven?' I hear Cara's voice echo through the speakers. The anger in her voice makes me look up from my phone. As always, the light's on her.

'No, Henry does the beating,' a new voice says. It's not the fucker who usually does the beating and talking. I can't see him yet, but Cara must see something because she strains to get to her feet.

I lean over and turn the volume up a notch.

'It's been a while,' the fucker says, sounding amused.

'I'm not letting you fuck me.'

'Come on, babe. It will be like old times.'

My heartbeat speeds up as I realize why there's only one fucker in there with her.

Cara darts out of the camera's view, but seconds later, I hear her hit the floor with a desperate scream.

'*Get off me!*' she cries, and I quickly lean forward to turn the volume down before she hears it. I stay close to the speaker, so I can listen.

For a few seconds, there are only scuffling sounds and then a clear, '*No.*'

'*Please don't. Please*' Cara pleads, sounding frantic, and it makes my blood burn through my veins.

'*No!*' she cries, and this time it's a hopeless sound that guts me.

Closing my eyes, I lower my head to my hand while my other fists the phone in a crushing grip.

Fuck. Fuck. Fuck.

'*No.*' The word sounds hollow. The fight's gone from her voice, and it makes something primal rip through my chest.

Christ.

Fucking Christ.

'*Don't worry, babe,*' the fucker grunts. '*I'll be quick. You won't remember this for long.*'

I can clearly hear the sound of skin slapping on skin, and it's the most fucked up sound I've ever heard. Bile burns in my stomach as every muscle in my body tightens.

135

My breaths begin to rush over my lips, and it feels as if the very blood in my veins is turning to ice.

'Tomorrow, Henry gets to shoot your brains out.' I listen to him grunt as he finds his release, and the sound makes the bile push up my throat. Grabbing the trashcan, I empty my stomach while my body continues to shake from the rage.

Motherfucking fuck.

Setting the trashcan down, I take a couple of deep breaths while my heart thunders in my chest.

Christ, I can't imagine how Cara must have felt – how she must still feel.

'You didn't think you were going to live, did you?'

I hear movement, and then the fucking asshole shoves Cara into the light.

'There's nothing left of her, Tom. You should have given us the money when we asked.'

The fucker shoves her hard to the floor, and seconds later, the recording stops.

Staring at the dark screen, I try to process that Cara was brutally raped, but I can't. I can't fucking accept that a piece of shit violated her even though I heard it with my own ears.

Fuck.

You need to get your shit together.

Cara needs you.

Focus.

I rewind the footage to where the bastard is holding Cara up in front of the camera, and then I press pause play.

'There's nothing left of her, Tom. You should have given us the money when we asked.'

So it was a ransom?

I rewind again, listening once more, then I pause on Cara's face. I stare into her wild eyes, taking in the fight, still reflecting in her green irises.

No.

No. No. No.

My breathing speeds up again as I realize something else happened off-camera, something that extinguished the fight in her eyes.

"Christ, baby, what broke you?"

I keep staring at her eyes, sparkling with tears and the will to live.

I think back to when I found her. She was filthy as shit... and she reeked of vomit and piss. Yet, not once did she puke on any of the memory cards I've watched, not even with the last one when the fucker raped her.

Sure, she could have puked afterward, off-camera.

But something else must've happened to kill the life in her eyes.

There's a crack right down the middle of my heart because what the fuck else could've happened after she was raped?

Slapping the laptop shut, I get up and leave the office. I lock the door behind me and then walk to Cara's room.

I hesitate for a second before knocking softly, but there's no answer. Nudging the door open until I can see the bed, I'm surprised to find it empty. Cara's always in it.

I open the door all the way and see her standing by the window.

I flip on the light, and it startles Cara, making her swing around, a clear look of terror on her face.

"Fuck, sorry," I say quickly, walking in so she can see me clearly. "I didn't mean to scare you."

"You didn't," the words rush from her, and I just nod.

This woman has so much pride. It's the one thing they couldn't take from her. Not once has she complained about the pain and horror she had to endure.

Admiration swells in my chest, making it a little easier to breathe.

I walk closer and then stare down at her. Her eyes do a dance around the room before she finally looks up at me.

Dull, green eyes. Sometimes I see a spark of anger, but it's rare.

I want to tell her I'm sorry for not getting her out sooner. I haven't felt this emotion in a long time… failure.

I've failed Cara the same way I failed Leah.

Chapter 12

CARA

Another two months have passed since Damian rescued me. I'm well aware I'm a month over the allotted time I usually spend in one place, and the familiar itch to move on is slowly creeping beneath my skin.

I'm washing the dishes while once again forcing the itch to the back of my mind because I don't want to leave.

I feel safe with Damian.

And I still don't have any money.

You could find a job.

I'm not ready to interact with people.

"Go make yourself pretty. We're going out," Damian suddenly drops a bomb behind me.

"Huh." I glance over my shoulder to where he's leaning against the counter. My hands still in the warm water as I wait for him to explain.

"We're going out," Damian says again.

"For a job?" I ask, not sure I want to go along on one of those again.

Damian shakes his head. "To a bar for a drink. It's been two months since you've left this house."

Shrugging, I finish washing the fork and let the dirty water drain out of the sink. As I dry my hands, I can still feel his eyes on me, so I turn around to face him.

"I like staying home."

The corner of his mouth twitches. "I'm glad to hear that, but I really think it's time for you to get out there again. We'll only stay for one or two drinks, then leave."

One or two drinks won't kill me, and Damian's right, I need to get out there, especially if I have any hope of finding work again.

As he walks out of the kitchen, he says, "We're leaving in thirty minutes."

It's just two drinks. I can survive an hour or two at a bar. Heading up to my bedroom, I take a pair of jeans and a long-sleeve shirt from the closet.

After getting dressed, I put on my boots before pulling a brush through my hair. Not looking in a mirror, I leave the bedroom.

I don't have to wait long in the kitchen before Damian comes in. For a moment, I stare... actually, I gawk at him because he's all dressed up.

Damn, he looks really good.

He's wearing faded blue jeans, a charcoal button-up shirt, and boots to round off the look. Then I catch a faint scent in the air. He even smells different, a good kind of different.

Damian's eyes lock on mine, and then his lips part as he stares at me. I suddenly feel very conscious of the jeans hugging my legs and butt tightly.

"Change." The word rushes from my dry lips. "I should change, yeah." I ramble, used to only wearing sweatpants and t-shirts.

"No." The word is hard and fast. Damian shakes his head as he leans against the counter. "But I'll be taking my gun with," he says casually, "and you're not leaving my side."

His words make the apples of my cheeks heat up, and for a split second, I feel beautiful. But then ice pours through my veins, and I quickly glance out the window.

I don't want to look beautiful because it will attract unwanted attention, and I can't deal with that.

142

Damian pushes away from the counter and closes the distance between us. He waits until I finally glance up at him, then says, "You're safe with me."

"I know," I whisper.

"What's upsetting you?" I shake my head, and it has Damian crouching a little down to catch my eyes again. "I can't fix it if you don't tell me what's wrong."

"I don't want to attract any attention," I admit.

Damian takes a deep breath then lets it out slowly. "You're a beautiful woman, Cara. Whether you wear sweatpants or a gown, people will notice."

Panic trickles through my veins, and I can't stop myself from giving Damian a pleading look.

I don't want to feel like a woman.

As if Damian can hear my thoughts, he nods. "I understand." He moves slowly as he lifts his hands to my shoulders, and then he tugs me against his chest. "I'll kill anyone who tries to hurt you." His voice is deep by my ear.

I take a deep breath, filling my lungs with his scent. "Promise?"

"I promise," he replies without any hesitation. Pulling back, he catches my eyes again. "Don't worry about what other people might think. Tonight it's just you and me having a drink. Okay?"

I nod, even trying to smile a little.

"Good girl." Then his hand slips to my lower back, and he nudges softly. "Let's go."

I'm starting to seriously doubt myself as Damian parks the car outside a bar.

He gets out, and I just can't bring myself to open the door.

Shit, am I ready for this?

Anxiety grips my chest in a painful hold. The last time I was at a bar... I met Steven. I fucked up, and I paid dearly for it.

My body starts to tremble at the horrible memories.

I can't do this.

My eyes dart around the parking area, and then they jump to Damian, where he's walking around the front of the car. He opens my door, and when I glance up at him, he must see the panic on my face because he takes hold of my hand and helps me climb out.

Damian moves in close to me, and our bodies brush as he shuts the door. Cornered between the car and Damian, I feel safe for a moment, and it makes me inch closer to him, wishing I could just hide from the world forever.

Damian doesn't pull back but instead turns his face to mine. His warm breath chases the cold air from my neck.

Being so close to him makes conflicting emotions erupt in my chest. It makes me shiver with both fear and comfort. It's bewildering.

"You'll be fine in there, Cara. I'm here. I have your back."

When I nod, he pulls away, but then he places a finger beneath my chin, nudging my face up. "You're safe with me."

I don't think I'll ever tire of hearing those words from him. Every time they leave his mouth, it calms me.

I nod again and keep my head up when he pulls his hand away from my chin.

When we begin to walk, I stay close to Damian, and I have to resist the urge to grab hold of his hand. I try to regain control over the rampant emotions wreaking havoc in my chest.

You can do this.

The sooner you get used to being around people, the sooner you can get a job.

The air is stale with cigarette smoke before we even enter the bar. The smell makes me hunch my shoulders, and I wrap my arms around myself, grabbing my sides tightly.

As Damian opens the door, laughter and music hit me full in the face. It's overwhelming.

Dimmed lights. Moving bodies. Constant laughter and loud voices.

Then there's a sharp-pitched scream as a huge man slaps a waitress on the ass, and I stumble back from it all.

The smoke is thick, and it presses against my face until I feel sick.

Shit, I'm going to vomit. I can't do this.

Panic flairs hot through me, and my breathing speeds up.

Damian's arm wraps around me, and he pulls me to stand right in front of him. His solid chest presses to my back, and his hand slides to my hip, then he nudges me slightly.

I take an uneasy step forward, my eyes darting everywhere. I know Damian will keep me safe, but it doesn't ease the overwhelming feeling of being out in public.

I walk where he steers me, but then a huge man staggers in front of me, and he grabs for me. I shriek and

146

jump back, slamming into Damian. Before I can stop myself, I spin around and grab hold of his shirt while burying my face against his chest. "I don't think I can do this," I admit, feeling pathetically weak.

I feel Damian's breath skim over my hair, and then his arms go around me, locking me in a protective hug.

I fear everything around me, but not Damian. I don't know why, but I trust him with the sliver of life I have left. I trust him more than I trust myself because I almost got myself killed. It's my fault they raped me because I put myself in that horrid situation.

But Damian... he saved me. He protects me, and that's much more than I have done for myself.

"I have you. You're safe." I can barely hear him, but the words sink deep into my broken soul.

I look down at my fingers, digging into his shirt, not even aware that I was holding on so tightly. I pry my fingers loose and suck in a deep breath. The thick smell of smoke is not so overwhelming anymore. Mixed scents fill the air, making it easier to breathe.

Slowly, Damian lets go of me, and then he reaches for my hand. I grab for my lifeline and stay glued to his side as we make our way to the bar. I keep my eyes on his hand, his strong fingers wrapped around mine.

I'm safe with Damian.

I can do this.

I listen as Damian places an order and take the glass when he hands it to me. Bringing the drink to my lips, I throw my head back, letting the liquid burn down my throat. The alcohol chases the chill from my body, and after a minute, I relax enough to focus on Damian.

He sits down on a stool, and it almost brings him to eye level with me. My gaze lands on the black ink curling from beneath his collar. Then I lower my eyes to his forearm, where there's more ink.

When Damian reaches for me, I instantly move forward, knowing safety is with him. No one can touch me as long as I'm with my protector.

His arm slips around my waist, then he leans in close so I can hear him. "Listen to me."

I nod.

"I'm here, and nothing will happen. They're only people. You'll probably never see them again after tonight. Focus only on me. Take deep breaths."

I do what he says while pulling back so I can look at him. A slow smile curves his mouth, and it sets me at ease.

This time I lean closer so I can reach his ear. "Just don't leave me alone." I don't care that I sound needy. I'll die if he leaves me here.

"Not a fucking chance in hell of that happening." Damian's voice is deep and reassuring. "Another drink, then we dance."

While Damian orders another round of drinks, I glance around us. We're standing at a horseshoe-shaped bar, the wood worn through over the years. Bowls of peanuts are spaced over the counter, and it reminds me that I once read it's one of the dirtiest things on the planet next to a public toilet.

The bar is not as full as it felt when we first came in. Only half the seats are taken. My eyes keep taking in everything, and then I see the dance floor, and I realize why the bar looks empty. Most of the people are there, swaying to the song I haven't even been listening to.

I don't down the next drink. I make it last four huge gulps, and it has Damian chuckling, "I charge a fee to carry you home, but dancing is for free. Come on." He takes my hand as the first piano notes of a song drift through the air.

"I can't dance," I tell Damian.

"I've got you," he replies as we reach the dance floor, then he turns to me and pulls me to his chest.

He doesn't hold me like some of the other couples are holding each other. Instead, he takes my hand and holds it over his heart. His other hand presses lightly against my lower back, securing me to his body.

It feels comfortable making a smile tug at the corner of my mouth.

I place my other hand on his bicep, and then he starts to move. He doesn't make me do some elaborate dance. Instead, he just holds me and moves us slowly in a circle.

As the seconds tick by, I start to relax more until I'm actually enjoying the dance, even though I'm super aware of every single person close to me.

Damian's breath is warm on my forehead, and I try to focus on it. I close my eyes to block out the world. It's only us and no one else because no one else matters.

I'm safe. No one can hurt me.

When the song ends, Damian leads me back to the bar, and once we're seated, my eyes keep darting to his face.

Seeing him in a social setting makes me really look at him. Damian was always just my rescuer, my safe haven, but now... I'm starting to see the man, and it wipes the smile from my face.

I watch as he takes a sip of his drink, his eyes scanning around us before locking with mine. For a moment, we stare at each other, and it makes more confusing emotions trickle into my heart.

This man has seen me at my worst.

This man came for me when all hope was lost.

Damian came for me.

Since my parents were killed, I haven't felt any semblance of safety... until Damian.

I wonder if he would let me stay with him forever. I can find work in a nearby town and contribute to the household.

Startled by the direction my thoughts are going in, I break eye contact with him and focus on finishing my drink.

Don't even go there.

Trying to distract myself, I glance at the other women. Some are visibly staring at Damian, and it doesn't sit well in my gut. Then it hits me he's never brought anyone home, and I don't know how I'd feel if he did.

The house is my safe zone. I don't want anyone else there. Damian is my shield, and another woman will only endanger that.

"Have you come here before?" I ask.

"Yes." He doesn't offer more on the topic.

Curious about Damian, I ask, "How old are you?"

His mouth lifts at the corner, and I quickly glance around me again so I don't have to look at him.

"Thirty-six," he says, and I can feel the burn of his eyes on me.

Thirty-six. Wow.

Doing a quick calculation, I realize he's eleven years older than me. Because of the beard, I couldn't tell his age.

Damian orders another round of drinks, and while the bartender prepares them, I sit down on a stool.

I glance at the stage where the band's playing, noticing how beautiful the singer is. She has dark brown hair curling wild around her face.

When the song ends, she smiles and talks seductively into the mic, "Thanks, folks, we're taking a short break."

I turn my attention back to Damian, only to find him also looking at the singer. There's a twisting in my chest when my eyes jump back to the stage, and I see her smile at him. A frown forms on my forehead as she makes her way toward us, and my hands grow clammy.

God, is she the real reason we came here tonight?

My world stills when Damian hugs her. Her fingers splay over his ribs as she presses a kiss on his cheek. Then they smile at each other, and the sight makes bile suddenly build up in my throat.

I push myself off the stool, but before I can dart past them, Damian grabs hold of my arm to hold me back.

"Where are you going?" he asks.

I pull my arm free. "The restroom." Not waiting for a response, I rush toward the toilet sign.

I just need a minute... Maybe ten.

Thoughts race through my mind in a crazy blur.

What if Damian likes her? What if she comes to the house?

I push through the restroom's door and go stand behind the four women who are already waiting, then I catch a glimpse of myself in the mirror.

God, I look like shit. I've passed albino, and I'm heading for translucency.

Maybe that's what I'll become – a ghost.

"Are you going?" a woman behind me asks.

I hurry into the stall and close the door behind me. When I turn to face the toilet, there's a sudden stab of alarm, and then horror rips the breath from my lungs.

All I can smell is urine and vomit.

All I can feel are the four walls closing in on me.

My whole world tilts to the side, and wave after wave of terror makes my heart hammer painfully.

Flashes of my hellish time in the container bombard me, battering my mind and soul until I sink to the floor. Horror-stricken, I scoot back until I hit the toilet. I squeeze my body into the small space between the toilet and wall, and I press my face against my knees.

"No," I croak. "No."

I keep saying the word over and over, trying to fight the nightmare enveloping me in its tormenting claws. Depraved and ruthless memories rip through me, and I can't fight them off, just like I couldn't fight the men off.

I hear a loud bang, and I cover my head with a shriek.

Chapter 13

DAMIAN

I keep one eye on the restrooms and the other on Jane.

"Who's the girl?" Jane asks.

"A friend." I take a sip of my drink as I take a good look at Jane. She looks tired. This way of life is starting to catch up with her.

"So... listen," she says as she moves closer to me. "There's something I need your help with. Is it okay if I come by tomorrow?"

I've known Jane for a couple of years. We fucked once, but I stopped it dead in its tracks before a relationship could start. Now that Cara is living with me, I don't feel comfortable letting Jane come around.

"I need your help with a problem," she explains.

I never turn down work, and I can't stop working just because Cara will be around. We need the money.

"I'll come by your place," I mutter.

Jane reaches for my hand and gives it a squeeze. "Thanks." She nods to the stage. "I gotta get back."

She downs the rest of her beer and then makes her way through the crowd. My eyes go back to the restrooms, and I frown. Cara's been gone a couple of minutes.

Getting up, I make my way to the restrooms. I don't care what the women might think as I go inside.

"Take a shit at home!" a woman hollers while slamming a fist against one of the stalls.

"Yeah, we all gotta piss!" another one yells.

I scan the small space, but there's no sign of Cara.

Fuck.

There are only two stalls. The one closest to me opens, and a woman comes out.

"The bitch still in there?" she asks the woman who's banging on the door.

"Yeah, the cunt thinks she can take her sweet motherfucking time!" the woman shouts, her face going red with anger.

I stalk to the stall, and it's only then the women notice me. "Hey, get your dick sucked somewhere else!"

I shove her out of the way, not caring where the fuck she goes, as long as it's away from the door.

"Cara," I call, but there's no answer. I slam my shoulder into the door, and the flimsy piece of wood gives way. Shoving the door all the way open, my heart sinks.

"Fuck, Cara," I breathe.

She's somehow wedged her body into the small space between the toilet and door. I rush in and crouching in front of her, I wonder how the fuck I'm going to get her out.

I touch her jerking shoulder lightly, and it sets her off. She lets out a petrified shriek as she rears back even further. Her arm swings out, her fist connecting with my chest. Her face is wet with tears, her breaths nothing more than strangled gulps of terror.

My heart shrivels at the heartbreaking sight and framing Cara's face with both my hands, I try to get her to look at me, but she only pinches her eyes shut.

"Open your fucking eyes," I snap, and they instantly fly open, but there's no recognition in them, only terror.

"Cara, it's Damian," I try a different tactic, but it doesn't seem to work.

Her gaze jumps wildly around the small space, and the pain I see on her face flays me to the bone.

"Cara," I say in the neutral tone I used when I first found her, "you're safe. I've got you."

Two seconds pass before her eyes flick to my face. "Damian?" she squeezes my name out in a pathetic whimper.

"Come to me," I say, my tone now gentle. "Come to me, baby."

She starts to struggle in the small space. Fuck only knows how she got herself in there. Grabbing hold of her shoulders, I yank hard to get her out. Rather the quick pain than another panic attack because she's stuck.

Cara comes free, and with a broken cry, she slams into me. Her arms go around my neck, and she clings with all her might. Climbing to my feet, I pick her up, and when I turn around, the women scatter back. I give them a dark glare. If they were men, I'd beat the shit out of them for what they did.

I stalk out of the restroom, and I don't stop until I reach the car. I quickly unlock the passenger door and place Cara in the seat. She doesn't let go of my neck, and I have to pull her arms away from me. After putting on her seatbelt, I shut the door. Running to the driver's side, I start the engine, and I don't care about speed limits as I race home.

My heart is pounding hard, and anger burns through my veins. I'm angry at myself for pushing Cara to go out. It was too soon.

Fuck, I'm an idiot. I've just undone all the hard work of the past four months.

I glance at her petite frame, where she's curled up on the seat. Her whole body shudders, and lost sobs drift from her.

"I'm so fucking sorry, baby," the words spill from me.

Fuck, seeing her break down and reliving the trauma keeps lashing at my heart with brutal strikes. It makes me realize just how important Cara's become to me over the past four months.

I care about her. A lot.

———————————

CARA

My head is pounding as hard as my heart. I feel drained of the little life I've managed to get back.

I feel filthy. Disgust swallows me in thick waves.

I've been poisoned by the vulgarity and cruelty of the men who raped me, and it's killing me fast.

I'm not going to make it.

The car jerks to a stop, and it only takes seconds for Damian to open my door. He yanks the seatbelt off and then pulls me out of the car. My body feels numb as he holds me tightly to his chest. My arms hang lifelessly next to my sides while his are steel clamps keeping me from shattering to pieces.

"I'm sorry, Cara," Damian whispers as he lifts me in his arms and carries me into the house. He kicks the door shut and then sits down at the bottom of the stairs, cradling me on his lap.

I rest my pounding head against his shoulder, and fresh tears warm my cheeks. It feels like I'm going to explode, but instead, my voice is empty when I whisper, "It never stops."

Damian presses a hand to my cheek, and it feels as if he's trying to engulf me with his body so nothing can ever touch me again.

A sob bursts over my lips as I curl into his warmth. "Make it stop."

"I wish I could. Christ, more than anything, I wish I could," he rasps, sounding just as devastated as I feel.

Damian just holds me until I finally manage to regain control over the tormenting flashes, and I calm down enough to stop the tears.

"Come on. Let's get you in bed." Climbing to his feet, he doesn't let go of me and carries me to my bedroom.

When Damian walks into my room, he doesn't put the light on. The darkness is only broken by the moonlight shining in through the window.

He sets me down on the side of the bed, and then he walks over to the closet. I watch him take clothes out before he comes back.

"Shirt off," he murmurs, his tone nothing but caring.

I take hold of the hem... but then pause.

Damian tilts his head. "Should I leave?"

I shake my head quickly, not wanting to be alone. Closing my eyes, I pull the long-sleeve shirt over my head. Damian holds a t-shirt out to me, and I take it, quickly yanking it on. The fabric falls to just above my knees.

"Are you going to sleep in the jeans and boots?" he asks.

I take off the boots and then shimmy out of the jeans. Standing in front of Damian in only a shirt and panties makes me feel way too vulnerable, and I begin to fidget.

"Get in bed," he commands softly. I sit down on the edge of the bed and then scoot back.

When he takes off his shoes and socks, I somehow manage to squeeze the words out. "You're going to sleep by me?"

"Yeah, move over."

When Damian yanks his shirt off, my breath slams into my throat. Half of his chest is covered with the same tribal marking I've seen on his arm and from his shoulder. The tattoo spreads over his chest as if a claw has ripped his flesh off.

He throws the covers back and sits down, then leans back against the headboard, stretching his legs out over the mattress.

I make sure there's plenty of space between us before I lie down on my side, facing him.

We stare at each other in the darkness, and then he murmurs, "I'm sorry. I shouldn't have taken you out."

Shaking my head, I bunch the covers in a fist.

Seconds pass, and then Damian brushes some hair from my face. "Sleep. You're safe."

I listen to his breathing, focusing on nothing else as the familiar emptiness creeps over me.

My eyes grow heavy from being physically and emotionally drained, and soon I lose the fight against sleep, just like I've lost every other fight in my life.

I wake up in the exact position I fell asleep in, but there's something heavy on me. Somehow Damian has folded his body around mine. I lie with eyes wide open, not knowing what to think about this.

"How do you feel?" he mutters into my hair, sounding a little angry.

"Okay," I whisper.

Damian lets go of me, and getting up, he grabs his shirt, socks, and boots and then leaves.

I pull the covers over me and stretch my body out, going back to sleep.

I finally drag myself out of bed around noon, then take a quick shower before I head downstairs.

When I walk into the kitchen, Damian turns from where he's standing by the back door. I feel his eyes on me.

Only when I'm done making myself some coffee do I hear him leave. Good, I need the silence. I can't deal with anything right now.

The backdoor's still open, and I go sit on the top step, sipping the coffee while my eyes scan over the yard.

It's hard to suppress the memories again. I keep smelling the urine and vomit. I keep hearing the lock clicking open. I keep feeling them, not the punches and kicks – but them groping me. I feel them inside me, and it makes everything in me wither with disgust.

I feel filthy.

"I'm heading out for an hour. Will you be okay on your own?" Damian suddenly asks.

Glancing over my shoulder, I nod. "Sure."

"Call me if you need me."

I nod again, then watch as he walks out the front door.

Letting out a sigh, I stand up and place the empty mug in the sink. I close the back door before I head upstairs so I can shower.

Reaching the hallway, I glance up and noticing the door to Damian's study is open, curiosity gets the better of me.

I sneak up and, stepping inside the office, I take it all in – the maps on the walls, the laptop, the phones, the cabinets, and then I see it – the camera and memory cards.

My body shudders from the sight.

At first, I only stare at the three memory cards, then I step closer, and my hand trembles as I reach for them. They're marked from one to three.

I open the laptop and press a random button. The screen lights up, and then my blood turns to ice.

The screen is frozen on my face. There's blood, so much blood. My eyes skip to the other person on the screen, and I see Steven's revolting face. A strangled whimper pushes its way up my throat as darkness closes in on me.

"Shit, Cara!" I jump back as Damian moves in front of me, blocking my view of the screen. He slaps the laptop shut, and I watch his shoulders heave heavily as he breathes. "Why the hell did you come up here?" he snaps.

He never raises his voice at me – never.

I don't think. I just turn and run.

I run from the room that holds my pain and race blindly down the stairs. I keep going straight out the front door as if I can actually outrun the trauma.

Gravel crunches under my bare feet, and then an arm wraps around my middle, yanking me back. I open my mouth to scream, but instead, a broken cry is all I can manage.

Damian takes me to the ground, and I fall flat on my ass. His arms clamp around me, and he yanks me against his chest. The gravel scrapes at my hands as bursts of panicked air explode from me.

"I'm sorry,' Damian rasps, his voice filled with a foreign urgency while his chest heaves against my back. "I'm sorry," he repeats.

Sobs build in my throat, and no matter how hard I fight, I can't hold them back. They rip through me, and hot tears spill down my cheeks, and then my body sags against his.

Unable to contain the relentless pain, I let out a scream. It's a horrible wailing sound that robs me of my breath.

Damian's arms wrap tighter around me, and I feel his breath warm my hair. "I've got you. You're safe," he keeps repeating the words, holding me as I shatter to pieces.

I lose track of time until lost sobs drift over my lips. Only then does Damian ease his hold on me. Climbing to his feet, he helps me up, and then he frames my face, locking eyes with me.

"Better?"

No.

Never.

I nod, knowing it will set him at ease.

"I'm sorry I snapped at you," he says, his eyes filled with guilt. His thumbs brush the tear tracks away from my cheek. "I forgot to lock the door. That's why I came back."

I should've listened to him and not gone up there.

Pulling my face from his hands, I take a step back.

Damian's eyes scan over me. "You okay?"

I nod again. "I'm going to shower." The horror's too raw in me to talk to Damian any longer.

Walking around him, I head back into the house so I can be alone with my demons.

It feels like every time I manage to take a step forward, I'm knocked two steps back.

There's no escaping this nightmare.

Chapter 14

DAMIAN

Knowing there's no way I can leave now, I wait until I hear the shower running before I call Jane.

"Hey," she answers. "Still coming over?"

"No, something else came up. What do you need help with?"

"My brother owes a drug dealer money, but he's hightailed it out of town, and now they're threatening me," Jane explains.

"What do you want me to do about it?" I ask.

"I'm going to report it to the police but want some kind of protection until the drug dealer is taken care of."

Fuck. There's no way I can protect Jane. Cara needs all of my attention.

"I have a friend. Jeff. He's old, but he'll be able to protect you."

"Why not you?" she asks, disappointment lacing her words.

"I'm busy with another assignment, but Jeff is highly skilled and will be able to keep you safe."

"Okay, fine."

"I'll get Jeff to give you a call so the two of you can make arrangements," I say.

"Thanks, I'd appreciate it."

As soon as we end the call, I dial Jeff's number.

"Everything okay?" he asks, knowing I won't just call for idle chat.

"I have an acquaintance in town that needs protection. She's being hounded by a drug dealer. Can you take care of it?"

"Sure. Send me her details."

"Thanks."

I text Jane's phone number and address to Jeff, then tuck my phone back in my pocket. Hearing the shower still running, I head up to my office, and grabbing the camera and all the memory cards, I shove them in one of the cabinets.

Once I lock the door behind me, I head to the kitchen to grab a bottle of water. Leaning back against the counter, I take a sip, and then I try to figure out where to go from here.

I fucked up. Again.

Christ only knows what damage seeing the footage did to Cara. After last night and what happened today, it feels like I'm back at square one.

Fuck.

My mind starts to race, trying to come up with some way I can undo the damage, even though I know there's none.

I'll just have to be patient and be there for Cara.

Jesus, I fucked up.

CARA

I stand in my room and blindly stare out of the window and into the night.

Once I managed to shove the harrowing memories back down, anger began to grow in me.

Why did Damian keep the camera and memory cards? Why did he watch them?

Did he see when I was raped?

One question after the other only makes my anger grow until I'm trembling from it.

He had no right.

I feel Damian come into the room, the dominance pouring from him, making the air tense.

Not turning around, I ask, "Why did you keep it?"

"Evidence," he murmurs.

"For what?" The words taste bitter as they leave my lips.

I swing around, and he takes a step closer. The air starts to buzz between us as if it's a live wire.

"You kept those memory cards of me being beaten and … and." I can't say it, and instead, I lunge at him. I slam both my hands flat against his chest, but he doesn't even flinch. "Did you watch them?" My voice climbs more, bordering on hysteria.

"I did," he answers, and I hate his honesty. So much.

Shame wraps its claws around my body, ripping the skin off until it feels like I'm bare… broken and exposed for Damian to see every gruesome part of me.

"How could you?" I whimper. I yank my hands back as if the very touch of him burns me. "I trusted you. How could you do that to me?"

"Cara," his voice is tight with tension, "I needed to see what we were up against, to try and get as much information as possible."

Damian takes a breath to gather himself. "The mafia fucking kills. They don't play around, and you should know that. Your parents are dead because your father and uncle got involved with them. The way they work is to take out the smaller dealers until only the most prominent members remain standing. And they take out the whole family. You should've died twice already. I won't risk a third. I need all the information I can get so I can stop them."

My mouth drops open at hearing his admission.

Oh. My. God.

Is it true?

Damian hasn't lied to me before.

Was my father and Uncle Tom involved with the mafia?

Oh, God.

No.

I struggle to breathe through the shock until I finally manage to ask, "Are you saying my father and Uncle Tom are part of the mafia?"

"Yes. I think a deal went sour, and your Uncle made off with money that didn't belong to him." Damian shoves a frustrated hand through his hair, and it's the first time I see him looking anything but sure and deadly. "Everything I have done is to keep you safe. I won't do a single thing differently, Cara." Each word is intense, and it grabs at my heart.

I can't look at him anymore, and I lower my eyes to his chest.

"Now," he continues gruffly, "I understand the past twenty-four hours have been rough, but, Cara," he waits for me to lift my eyes back to his, "you don't disrespect me. Don't ever raise your hands against me again."

I watch him leave, and then I sink to the floor, my emotions a destructive storm inside of me.

I took the pain and fear out on the only person who's been there for me.

What have I done?

———

DAMIAN

I wipe a hand over my tired eyes.

I've failed Cara once, and I'll be damned if I'm just going to stand by and let the fuckers responsible for the hell she's been through get away.

I almost came clean with Cara but caught myself just in time. Hearing her uncle didn't send me might be the one thing that breaks her.

When the door to my room creaks open, my eyes snap up from where I'm sitting on the side of the bed. My body tenses as I watch Cara slowly step inside my bedroom.

When she sees me, she walks closer, stopping right in front of me. Tipping my head back, I look up at her as she sucks in a deep breath.

"I'm so sorry, Damian. What I did was wrong on so many levels," she blurts the apology out and then waves her hand lamely in the air. "I ... I just wanted to apologize."

I raise my hand to her hip, giving it a squeeze, and then I pull her closer until I can wrap my arms around her, resting my forehead against her stomach.

Cara places her hands on my shoulders, her body not stiffening, and I take it as a win after all the shit.

At first, I just wanted to do right by her, but then I watched the memory cards, and something exploded inside my chest. I have to protect her because no one else will.

And then I made the mistake of holding her at that motel, and once she fit so perfectly against my chest, I knew it would be hard to let her go.

But after last night and today, I know with dead certainty I care a hell of a lot for this woman.

If I try to cut her out now, I'll be carving out a chunk of me. She's already in too deep.

"I'm so sorry, Cara." My voice is hoarse with these fucking feelings that have no place being in my heart. Now that she knows I've watched the memory cards, the words I've been wanting to say to her spill from me, "I'm so sorry I didn't get to you in time."

"Bruises heal," she whispers. She gives my shoulder a squeeze. "They didn't kill me. You came in time, Damian."

Me and all my rules, and I was the one who broke them all.

We've crossed a line today. There's no going back. Wanting to even the playing field for Cara, I admit, "I was a coward."

Minutes tick by where neither of us moves. Every day she gets better at the touching thing, but I can see it still makes her uncomfortable.

Pulling back, I lower my hands to my thighs, and then I take a deep breath. I need Cara to trust me again, and the only way for that to happen is if she knows who I am.

"I ran away from home and joined the military, thinking I could get away from my father. I was eighteen and stupid.

175

I threw myself into the military, learning everything I could. I avoided going home."

Cara sits down beside me, and then she surprises me by resting her cheek against my shoulder.

Another win.

"When I didn't feel like a coward anymore..." I pause and suck in a deep breath, "it was too late. I got the call that my girlfriend had committed suicide. I didn't think for one minute when I left, he'd go after her."

Cara keeps quiet, and it makes it easier to say the words. "It was the first time I killed someone. I told myself afterward I'd never take a life in anger again. I killed my own father, and I told myself he deserved to die because he was an animal."

Cara places a comforting hand on mine, and it gives me the strength to continue. "I cleaned up the mess he left behind and disappeared. I tried to make up for failing Leah by helping others. I rid the world of the scum that thrived on preying on others, and if it makes me a monster, then so be it."

When Cara doesn't pull away, seeming to accept what I've told her, I lift an arm and wrap it around her shoulders. Pulling her right against my side, I press my mouth to her hair, taking a deep breath of her naturally soft scent.

Christ, I just want to hold her. I want to keep this fragile woman because she's the only fucking beauty left in this life.

"That's who I am, Cara. Now you know everything about me."

CARA

I don't move a muscle or say a word because Damian's finally opening up to me.

I turn a blind eye to what he is, a cleaner, and to many, it may seem horribly wrong, but to me, it's justice on behalf of those who've been wronged.

When the silence stretches around us, I know he's done talking. I pull back and whisper the words he's said to me countless times before, "I have you. You're safe with me."

It's my turn to be the strong one, and it helps divert my attention away from my own pain.

"Remove the shirt," I order, and I swear I hear him chuckle softly.

I scoot to the side and watch as he pulls the fabric over his head. Then he just sits and looks at me. "Well, you aren't going to sleep in your jeans and shoes, are you?" I repeat his words from last night.

This time he lets out a bark of laughter. It's short and unbelievably hot. I can't help but smile back at him.

Moving to the left side of the bed, I know I'm taking a huge risk, but he's shown me I can trust him by opening up to me.

Damian keeps his pants on as he lies down next to me. He slips his arm under my head and then pulls me closer to him. His body curls around mine just like it did this morning, and then he rests his chin on top of my head.

"Thank you," he whispers, sounding as exhausted as I feel.

Closing my eyes, I absorb the safety I feel when I'm with him.

God, how am I going to make it out there if I have to go out on my own?

Damian didn't say how long I could stay with him.

Also, I'm not sure how I feel about whatever's happening between us. With every passing day, we keep growing closer to each other.

I'm in no way ready for a relationship.

I don't think I'll ever be ready.

It would be unfair for me to stay, knowing there's nothing I can offer Damian in return.

My heart sinks because I know the time for me to leave is drawing near. I'll have to start making plans to leave.

I'll have to hide it from Damian because I'm unsure if he'll just let me walk away.

God, it's going to be hard.

Chapter 15

CARA

I keep myself busy as much as I can. I haven't seen Damian since this morning, so I guess he's up in his office working.

I heat up dinner, but there's still no sign of Damian, so I eat mine while standing at the back door.

I finish up and then head upstairs to shower. I've just changed into a pair of slacks and a t-shirt when Damian knocks on the door.

My heart starts to race suddenly. I don't know if it's from wanting to be close to him or knowing I'll have to leave soon.

I'm confused about what to do.

When I open the door, Damian's eyes scan over me as if he can sense something's wrong. Lifting a hand, he wraps his fingers around the side of my neck, and leaning down, he presses a soft kiss to my forehead... and I cave. I grab hold of his sides as if I might lose him within the next second.

It's because I'll be leaving soon, and the thought scares me half to death.

When Damian pulls back, I see the questions in his eyes, but he doesn't ask them. He just takes my hand and leads me to his room.

We climb under the covers, and again, Damian pulls me to his side so I can rest my head on his chest. I listen to his heartbeat, and long after he's fallen asleep, I still lie awake with my wretched thoughts.

Things are changing between Damian and me. It's too fast and makes me feel panicked that he might expect something from me I'm unable to give.

My emotions are all over the place, and I bite my lip to keep the tears back.

I can't even think of the possibility of a relationship with a man. That part of me was destroyed.

I slow my breathing, willing myself to calm down. I taste blood and let go of my lip, chewing on the inside of my mouth instead.

I'll never be whole again.

The woman in me is dead.

I'm trying to nurse myself with some coffee when Damian walks into the kitchen looking like a lion that's ready to kill.

"I have to head out and take care of a problem. Will you be okay?"

I nod quickly.

"What's that?" Damian asks, and I give him a confused look.

"What's what?"

He moves closer to me, his eyes locked on my mouth. My heart begins to beat faster, and I quickly lower my gaze to his neck, then he lifts a hand and brushes his thumb over the bruise on my bottom lip.

Shit. I forgot.

"I…" I start to sputter against the pad of his thumb. "I… the toothbrush slipped. It nicked my lip," I lie.

I'm terrible at telling lies. He's going to see right through it.

Damian drops his hand to my chin and nudges my face up, then he waits for me to meet his eyes.

Shit, he knows I'm not telling the truth.

"Cara." He tilts his head. "You can talk to me." When I finally meet his gaze, he adds, "about anything."

All the 'anythings' rush through my mind. The horror. The vile things they did to me. My uncertain feeling for him. The life I want. A mundane career. A family. I want to stop thinking about what happened, and I want… normal.

"I'm okay," I lie instead of telling Damian the truth.

He gives me a look I can't quite place before he turns away from me. "I'll be back in an hour."

I watch him walk out of the kitchen, and then my shoulders slump in defeat.

Before I realize what I'm doing, I go to my room and take three sets of clothes, setting them aside on an empty shelf. Only then do I realize that's the clothes I'll be taking with me when I leave.

A numb feeling spreads through my body.

I feel like a zombie as I leave the room and walk up to the office. I can't remember when, but Damian said he had a new identity created for me. I'll need it if I want to disappear. It will also help me get better jobs.

Trying the doorknob, I let out a breath of relief when the door opens. This time there's no sign of the camera and memory cards.

Pressured for time, I quickly look in the drawers, and not finding anything, I move over to a filing cabinet. When

I open one of the last files, I find a passport and I.D card with my photo.

I don't even look at the name as I grab them, shoving both documents into my pocket. I put the file back and make sure I leave everything looking the same as when I came into Damian's office before rushing back to my room.

With a thundering heart, I place the documents under the pile of clothes I've set aside.

I take deep breaths to try and calm down.

Hopefully, Damian won't notice the documents are gone before I leave.

I can't risk leaving now because he might see me next to the road.

Minutes later, I hear tires crunching over the gravel out front. I dart to my bed and quickly climb under the covers. My heart's beating like crazy, and I will it to slow down.

I feel guilty for planning to leave without saying goodbye, but there's no telling what Damian would do if he found out.

Eventually, the afternoon turns gray and night sets in. I stop thinking of the guilt and start reassuring myself I'm doing the right thing by leaving.

Things will only become complicated between Damian and me until he wants more.

I don't know what the time is when I hear my bedroom door creak open and quickly squeeze my eyes shut.

"Cara," Damian murmurs.

I'm hoping he'll think I'm asleep. I hear the door creak again and let out a relieved breath. And then I hear Damian move, and pins and needles flush my body hot and cold all at once.

He didn't leave like I thought he did.

The bed shifts under his weight as he sits down. I stiffen, waiting, but he doesn't touch me.

"I want to help you, but I'll leave it to you to come to me," he murmurs. Then I feel his fingers over my hair, the touch soft and quick before he gets up.

Tears begin to sting behind my eyelids because I know we can't continue down this path.

I want to cry because I don't know what the future has in store for me. There will always be a death sentence hanging over my head. It's terrifying having a faceless enemy, one I can't beat.

I don't know much about the mafia, but I do know they kill. If I stay with Damian, it might end up leading to him being killed as well.

God.

Not after all he's done for me.

I'm so empty and filled with longing for the only place I feel safe that I give up the fight. Wanting to feel safe one last time, I climb out of bed.

When I open my door, it's to find Damian waiting for me.

He closes the distance between us and lifting his hands, his palms are warm on my cheeks. Then he leans down and presses a kiss to my forehead. "I wish you'd talk to me."

I shake my head and, taking hold of his hand, I pull him toward his bedroom.

This is all I'm giving myself, one last night safely in the arms of my protector.

I crawl onto the bed and wait for him to lie down before I snuggle against his side. Once we're comfortable, the silence begins to stretch around us.

"Damian," I whisper, struggling to deal with all the disastrous emotions wreaking havoc in my chest. "Why did you keep me?"

"I'd rather not answer that one," he denies me an answer for the first time.

I pull back so I can see his face better. He's frowning, and the worry muscle in his jaw is jumping again.

"Why not?" I push, needing to know.

"You're healing, Cara." He tries to smile, but it looks like a grimace. "Let's leave it at that."

I lower my eyes to his chest, thinking about what he just said. Why would it have anything to do with my healing?

"Uhm..."

I can feel the frustration begin to pulse off of him.

"Why can't you just leave it?" he grumbles, but after taking a deep breath, he finally admits, "I failed Leah. I left her unprotected, and he beat the shit out of her, knowing it was the only way to get to me. I failed her, and fuck," he hisses, "I failed you, too."

I try not to see the connection - that I'm nothing more than a replacement for Damian's girlfriend he couldn't save.

His voice is nothing but a hoarse whisper as he continues, "When Jeff told me you were being held in that container..." He reaches for my face, but just before his hand touches my cheek, he drops it to his chest. "I just knew I had to get to you. I felt sick knowing they had you."

"Me or Leah?" I whisper, slowly lifting my eyes to his. "Did you go to get Leah or me?" I ask with a quivering voice.

His face darkens, and I see the killer, just like he was that day when he came to get me. He lifts his head slowly, and my heart starts to beat heavily, thumping faster when he sucks a breath through his teeth.

"I dragged you out of that fucking hole," he growls. "I cleaned you, Cara." My name sounds bitter on his lips. He takes a breath, and I know he's not done.

"Don't..." I start, but he holds up his hand, and the gesture alone makes the air crackle.

Then he says, "I feel because of you. I hate because of you. I'm angry because of you. I wish I could go back and torture them, make them suffer, instead of giving them such quick deaths." His voice drops low, and every word is like a punch. "When I watched those recordings they made of you..."

He pauses, and I start to shake my head, willing him to stop.

"That's not what killed me, Cara. Hearing you scream at night for those fuckers to stop is what eats at my fucking soul. Not knowing how to make it better frustrates the shit out of me. Do you know how fucked up I feel because I was too late?"

"Please stop," I croak, my lungs burning for air.

Damian takes a deep, shuddering breath. "I'm not answering your question, though, am I? I kept you because you have no one. There's not a single fucking person out there who cares if you live or die. I saw someone who was shoved into this fucked up world and left to fend for herself, and she couldn't. I saw someone who needed to be protected." He sucks in a ragged breath, and then he whispers, "I see the most beautiful fucked up woman, and you're perfect. You're so beautifully broken, and it makes me want to keep you."

I can't breathe. I can't hear the words he's saying. They hurt too much.

I scramble off of the bed and walk away from Damian and his honesty, unable to process any of it.

I'm not sure what he feels for me. I'm not even sure how I feel about him. But I'm dead sure I'm far from ready for what's between us.

I was right. It's time to leave.

Chapter 16

CARA

It's the middle of the night when I listen for any movement from Damian's room. Not hearing anything, I dart back inside my room and rush to the closet. I get dressed in a pair of jeans, a warm shirt, and sneakers. After dragging a sweater over my head, I grab the passport and I.D.

Unable to find a bag for the rest of the clothes, I shove another pair of underwear in my pocket. I take a deep breath and ignore the sharp ache in my heart as I slip out of the room.

I creep down the stairs and carefully key in the code for the alarm, praying Damian won't hear the soft beeps. I'm careful with the locks on the front door, and when I have it open, I quickly sneak out and pull the door softly shut behind me.

Darting down the steps of the porch, I break out into a run as if my life depends on it.

Bye, Damian.

Thank you for everything.

I run like I should've run back when I met Steven for the first time. When I get to the main road, I head right, not thinking about where I'm going.

I need to get away from my feelings for Damian, unable to deal with them.

This is for the best.

I'll never be whole again. Damian deserves more than my broken, filthy soul.

I hear a car, and soon lights appear, breaking through some of the darkness. Not thinking of my safety, I wave my arms, but the car just keeps going. I'm stupid for leaving in the middle of the night. No sane person will stop for some random stranger.

I quicken my pace to put as much distance between me and the house, just in case Damian wakes up and notices I'm gone.

I've been running for a long while when I hear another car. I wave my arms as it gets closer, praying with burning lungs this one will stop.

Please.

It slows, and bright lights flash over me. Anxiety eats at my insides until the vehicle pulls up next to me. It's one of

191

those homes-on-wheels things. I'm not sure what they're called. RVs?

There's a middle-aged woman behind the wheel, and she's smiling. "Honey," her heavy accent drags the word out, "what's a little thing like you doing out alone in the middle of the night?"

"I need a ride, please." My tone is tense and hopeful. She's a woman, a smiling one – that's a good sign, right?

"Hop on in then," the woman says with a concerned look on her face. I quickly open the door and get in before my fear makes me run back to Damian. Once she pulls back onto the road, I sigh with relief.

"You running from someone?" she asks, without wasting any time.

I stare wide-eyed at her, not sure what to tell her. I didn't think the leaving thing through.

"Don't need to tell me, but a little thing like you running around in the middle of the night, now that's real dangerous. I'm figuring you're running from someone more dangerous?"

"I'm... ahh... just traveling," I blurt out the first excuse that comes to mind. I still have my South African accent, so I'm hoping it will help her buy my excuse.

She gives me a once-over and smirks. "With no bag? You're backpacking through Chesnee with nothing but the clothes on your back? Why would someone wanna see this little old town?" She looks at me as if I'm some escaped lunatic.

I don't even know where I am. How screwed up is that?

"I like quiet places." It's the only reason I can come up with.

"Annie Wilson. That's my name. You can just call me Annie, like everyone else." She starts to ramble. "I'm heading home. Came here for my sister's funeral. Awful bout of bronchitis took her in the end. Told her the weed was no good for her, but she kept smoking that stuff faster than she could grow it."

I tell myself to stop staring - it's not polite, and who am I to judge?

"But no," Annie continues, "she kept saying it was good for her ailments. Well, she ain't got no ailments no more." Annie sighs, and I finally tear my eyes from her rosy cheeks.

"So yeah, I'm heading back home." She glances at me and then says, "It's in Lackawaxen, a small historic town in Pennsylvania. Moved up there when I got married. The old man used to work for the local lumber company, but then he went on to greener pastures. I have a few acres of land outside of town. It keeps me going. I work the ground, or hell, the ground works me." She lets out a bubbly chuckle. "We have an understanding. What I put in, it gives back."

Annie keeps quiet for a moment, and I glance at her. She takes a deep breath, and my stomach ties up in knots. Then she murmurs, "I sure don't know where you're heading, but that's where the road's taking me. You're welcome to tag along."

"You're okay with me going with you?" I ask to make sure I heard right.

"I don't sit in church and pretend to be what I'm not," Annie says. "I believe that the Lord works in mysterious ways. It's not what you give Him between those four walls that matters. It's what you do to his children when they come asking for your help. I'm sure as hell not gonna be saying no to my Lord when He sends me one of his flock to take care of."

All her rambling is oddly comforting.

"I won't be asking what you're running from. You're welcome to come my way. There's work I can give you. You'll feed yourself. Annie sees a lost one, and she sure ain't gonna show you the door."

Oh my god. I've never been lucky in my life. Not until tonight.

"Thank you," I whisper, just grateful Annie stopped to give me a ride.

We've stopped three times for gas before I get out to go to the restroom. I relieve my bladder quickly, and after I've washed my hands, I take the passport and I.D from my pocket so I can inspect them.

I need to know what my new identity is so I can at least give Annie a name. When I open the passport and see the information, I feel a piece of my heart crumble to pieces. The face is mine, but it's a much younger and happier me.

Damian must've gotten it from Uncle Tom.

But the name … Karen Weston. Damian gave me his last name. Back when he hardly knew me. The little card shows my face, my new name, and his address. Chesnee, South Carolina.

I look at the passport, and I swallow hard.

Damian did all of this for me. He was going to take me in and look after me from the start. It wasn't just a fly-by-night, hero trip he was on.

And it only tells me I made the right decision to leave because I can't give anything back to repay all he's done for me.

"Honey, did you fall in?" Annie calls from outside.

"No," I croak and quickly clear my throat. "I'm coming."

I shove the documents back into my pocket and flush the toilet, so Annie will think I was using it all this time. I square my shoulders, and when I walk out, I lift my chin and smile at her. "Sorry I didn't introduce myself earlier. I'm Karen Weston. Thank you for letting me come with you."

"Pleasure meeting you, Karen." Annie smiles warmly while her eyes search my face as if she knows I'm giving her a fake name.

But she doesn't say anything as we head back to the RV.

The road is long, and I can't sleep. We drive forever and then some. Night becomes day, which becomes night again. Time just blurs right by me while I keep staring out the window at the passing scenery.

Annie talks a lot. After a while, her voice is a hum. I nod every now and then to show interest until she hits the palm of her hand on the steering wheel in excitement. My eyes dart to her, and I frown when I see the huge smile on her face.

"Really? You think that would be a great idea? I think so, too," she babbles.

I lift my head from the window and look at her. Her brown hair is graying at the sides, her brown eyes soft and friendly.

"Why did you think it's a great idea?" I try to fish because I have no idea what I just agreed to.

"Well, I've wanted to try the wholesale thing for a while now, but I never had someone to help me work the land. With you there, it might just work," she explains.

"Sounds like a plan," I agree, knowing it will make her smile. I take a deep breath and stare back out the window.

"We're almost there," she suddenly says.

I glance at our surroundings that consist of wide-open fields of green.

When we pull up a dirt road, I get out to open a rusted gate. It rattles as it swings. We drive quite a way up the dirt road before we reach a house. It's simple looking and stands in the middle of a field.

"It's one of those trailer houses. They bring them on wheels when you buy one," Annie explains. I get the feeling talking puts her at ease. "It works for me. Who needs more than two bedrooms and a bathroom? The kitchen's big enough to cook what I eat, and I can rest my old behind in my living room. I don't need something fancy. The land is out back, closer to the river, so I don't have to walk far for water. I'll show you later. Let's get ourselves settled first. My back feels like it's going to break in half."

I follow her into the modest house, not sure what to expect. Her home is… peculiar. But I suppose it's just like her in a way.

Little relics decorate just about every space, and mismatched carpets cover the floor. The two couches are from another era, and I'm not sure they make that kind of television anymore. It still has those knobs you have to turn, and it reminds me of my childhood.

The kitchen is another story. Pots and pans hang from the ceiling, along with dried chili and garlic. A row of little herb pots fill the windowsill, and there are tiny magnets with bible verses decorating the fridge.

"It's home, honey," Annie sighs happily. I smile at her because she's right. "This way," she says, pointing down a short hallway.

The guest room is decorated in shades of purple. I swallow as I take in how pretty it is. A single bed stands in the middle of the room, with a simple chest of drawers against the one wall.

"Thank you for letting me stay," I whisper, the words not nearly enough for how grateful I feel.

"At night, I like to sit outside before I go to bed. I talk to my Lord, tell Him of my worries, and give Him my thanks. I don't know who you talk to, honey, but the stars sure shine bright out here, and they don't talk back like us nosy folk." Annie gives me a warm smile. "I hope you'll feel at home here. I'm happy to have some company."

Annie leaves me standing alone in the room, and I glance around the space.

I've never been the praying kind, but I might just give the stars a try because nothing else has worked so far.

Chapter 17

DAMIAN

I'm up early as always, and walking down the hallway, I glance into Cara's room. When I see her bed's empty, an eerie feeling skitters down my spine.

I search through the rest of the house, and it's only when I notice the alarm's been disabled that the eerie feeling turns to cold, hard fear.

Where the fuck is Cara?

Frustrated, I rub my hand over my beard. I would've heard if someone broke in. I would've heard something if someone came for Cara.

There's no way anyone could've found out where she was staying.

She's been different the past couple of days, but I thought it was from the blows she took.

Worry claws up my spine.

"Fuck!" I race up the stairs to my office and check if anything is out of place, but it's exactly as I left it. I pace the floor, and dark thoughts start to brew in my mind.

Where the fuck is she?

Did something happen I'm not aware of?

My gut instinct tells me to search for the answer so I can fix this mess. I stalk to the filing cabinet, and I take out Cara's file. Maybe there's something I missed about her. I open it, and for a moment, it looks weird, then it hits – the passport and I.D. are gone.

"Fuck," I curse as anger ripples through me. "She's been planning this all along. That's why she's been acting so weird the last couple of days." I throw the file and papers scatter across the floor. "Shit! I should've seen this coming."

One panicked thought after the other starts to slam into my mind.

They'll find her. Fuck, this time, they'll kill her.

I rush to my safe and quickly open it. Taking out my guns, ammunition, an I.D. with the name Damian Weston, and all of the cash and important documents, I shove it all into a backpack.

I spare a moment to set the laptop to default status so it will clear everything on it. I quickly destroy the memory cards, and then, glancing over the office, I make sure I leave nothing behind that can trace to Cara and me.

I rush to my room and pack a traveling bag, the absolute basics, and stop in Cara's room to grab some of her clothes.

It takes me under ten minutes, and then I'm racing out of the house. I throw the bags in the back of the car. I'll get Jeff to torch the place if we've been compromised.

Fuck, Cara. Why did you leave?

I can only think of her as I climb behind the steering wheel.

Her name becomes my every heartbeat. She must've been more affected than I initially thought.

Fuck. Fuck. Fuck.

"Fuck," I slam my fist against the steering wheel when I reach the main road. "Which way did you go, Cara?"

Using only instinct, I turn right, thinking she would've tried to get away from the town as quick as possible.

I take my phone out and quickly dial Jeff's number.

As soon as he answers, I don't give him time to talk. "Put a trace out for Karen Weston. We need to find her, Jeff. She's on the run."

"Christ," he groans grumpily. "I'll get on it. I've found out the uncle, Tom Smith, has put a hit out on her as well.

Be careful. Seems he wants to get rid of her so the mafia can't use her to get him to pay what he owes them."

"It's the last thing we need right now," I bite out. "Let me know when you have a hit on Cara."

When I'm done with the call, I become aware of my heart racing a mile a minute.

Four months... that's all it took for Cara to crawl into the space my heart used to be and make it her own.

CARA

I wake up to The Carpenters harmonizing and shove the pillow over my head. Annie will drive me around the bend with that record player of hers. And she only listens to two records - The Carpenters and the one of Elvis with the scratches on. It hiccups on two of the songs. When she hums along to it, she hiccups with it. It's actually adorable.

The first week I just followed her around like a lost puppy, and she let me. She showed me how to turn the ground, how to plant seeds, and I stared when she began pumping the weird-looking thing that made water come up from the river to the little patch of land.

Some guy named Jason made it for her. She gave me the impression this Jason is like a son to her, but he hasn't been around, which I'm thankful for.

I watched her make bread from scratch, and she pickled some chili. I'll never remember how she did it all, but it was fascinating to watch.

It was also the first time I let myself wonder, why not?

Why can't I just be right here? With Annie.

I miss my parents and Annie doesn't have anyone. She's like a mother hen, and it's precisely what my broken spirit needs.

We could be together out here in the middle of nowhere. No one will ever find me.

"Annie," I call as I walk out of the room that's become mine. I'm wearing one of Annie's old dresses that she adjusted so it would fit me. Some brush the floor when I walk, but most stop beneath my knees. I'm okay with it. It covers everything, and it makes Annie happy.

"Annie, you want me to run up to the patch?"

I find her on the porch, sipping her homemade tea. I won't touch that stuff ever again. Annie drinks flowers. She picks them right out back and lets them dry, and then she drinks them. She calls it her version of Chamomile tea.

I'm not so sure about that because they look like plain old daisies to me.

She started explaining that Chamomile is a type of daisy, and I watered the roses nearest to me with the rest of the tea I had left.

"Come sit next to me, honey." She gives me her all-knowing look. The one I've quickly learned leads to a serious talk.

I sit down on the bench and look out toward the trees to where the river lies.

"Tell me," she starts, "is there something you need from town?" she asks, and I let out a breath of relief. I was expecting questions or worse...

"No, thank you." I smile. She's already giving me so much.

"So you don't need any lady stuff, for you know, down south?"

I flush red at her question, and I start nodding, because duh, I do need those – then the realization slams hard, and the blood drains from my face.

"Oh, God. I haven't had my period in months," I gasp as the horrifying thought settles harshly in my chest.

No.

God. No.

"Oh, dear," Annie sighs.

I shake my head at the shocking possibility staring me right in the face. "I can't be." I jump up and start to pace in front of Annie.

"You're going to make me dizzy. Sit down, child. No need to worry until we know for sure. I'll get one of those tests for you."

Needing a moment to process the awful shock, I mutter, "I... I'm going down to the land. I'll see you later."

I rush away from all the questions in Annie's eyes.

Pregnant?

God.

All the memories flood me, threatening to drown me out in the open. I thought I could run away from the nightmare. I thought if I just ignored it all, then it would be just... a nightmare.

I can't be pregnant. I don't even know which of them impregnated me.

Rushing over the field, I don't take in any of the wildflowers or the sun beaming down. Instead, I gasp for air as the thoughts choke me. My heartbeat speeds up, and a hollow emptiness washes through me.

Stopping in the middle of the field, a sob tears from my tight chest, and I grab at the fabric over my heart.

Pregnant?

"No," I cry, and then I sink to my knees. "No."

Every second will be a stark reminder of being raped, of being beaten – of being degraded.

My fingers dig into the wild grass as my shoulders begin to shudder.

What will I do with a baby? How will I take care of a child? I can't even keep myself safe.

This isn't happening.

Maybe my period's gone because of the trauma?

Maybe when they kicked and assaulted me, it damaged something?

As I desperately try to come up with reasons for my missing period, my gut already knows the truth.

I don't need a test to confirm it.

I'm going to bring a baby into this godforsaken world, and I have no means of keeping the child safe.

"We did that piece already, honey," I hear Annie call. She gave me some time to myself earlier today, for which I'm grateful.

I look over the row I've just done.

We did it already?

I'm so screwed up, I can't even think straight.

"We did it two days ago. Today we plant tomato and potato seeds."

I get up and dust my hands off and then walk over to where all the packets of seeds are.

"Jason," Annie calls out happily.

I glance over my shoulder, and then ice-cold fear ripples through me as I see a man coming toward us.

Shit.

Snapping my eyes back to the packets of seeds, my heart thunders in my chest.

"This here is my Jason," Annie says proudly.

Shit.

For a moment, I wish Damian was here so I could hide behind him. I have to force myself to turn around, my palms sweaty and trembling.

"It's a pleasure to meet you, miss…?" Jason gives me a questioning look.

"Nonsense, Boy. Just call her Karen. The child might as well be from my own rib," Annie steps in for me, and I love her more than ever.

Jason reaches a hand out to me, and I stare at it for too long before I step forward and lift mine. "I'm...sorry," I stammer, and then my mouth grows dry as I take in his uniform. Law enforcement. "Hi," I squeak, and I know – I just know – if I was him, I'd be suspicious of me.

"Jason Williams," he smiles, and my stomach coils into a hard knot.

"Karen Weston." I avoid his eyes and quickly step back, so I'm partially behind Annie.

It feels like my newfound freedom is slipping away.

He's going to take me away from this little piece of heaven.

"I didn't know you had a guest, Annie. Now ain't that something," Jason says, his eyes slowly sweeping over me.

I take another step back, my muscles tightening as if I'm getting ready to run.

"Don't worry, honey," Annie tells me as she takes hold of my hand, squeezing it tightly as if to offer me some comfort. "Why don't you run on up and get me my hat? I feel that ball of fire scorching the gray right into my head."

I nod, and grateful for the escape, I dart off toward the house. I don't know which hat she's referring to, but I take the out she's giving me to get away.

"Annie," I hear Jason ask, and I quicken my pace, "where's that girl from?"

"I told you, Jason," she snaps, "my rib. Now hand me the tomato seeds."

"Shit. Shit. Shit," I chant all the way to the house.

Then Jason's patrol car comes into sight, and it reads State Police on the side.

Oh, God.

It takes everything I have not to break out into a mad run up the road.

Why can't I just have peace?

As soon as I think I've found it, someone comes along to ruin it.

Will this hell ever end?

Rushing into the house, I hurry to my room and shut the door behind me. I gasp for air as I place a hand over my stomach. Panic keeps rippling through me, making one worry after the other bombard me.

What am I going to do if Jason figures out I'm illegally in the country?

What if he finds out my identity is fake?

I hide in my room until I hear his car leave. Then Annie knocks on the door, and coming inside, she opens her arms wide. I rush into her motherly embrace and feel a sliver of relief as she hugs me tightly.

I can't keep all the stress and feelings bottled up any longer. Tears well in my eyes and spill over my cheeks. Gripping hold of her, I cry because I don't want to lose her as well. I don't want to be pregnant with a rapist's child. I just want some peace. Is that too much to ask?

"It's okay," she coos. "It's okay, honey. I should've known better. The boy is as harmless as those pigeons pooping up a storm on the porch. He won't hurt a fly," she sniffs. "We're a family now, and family sticks together."

I hold Annie tighter, her words a soothing balm to my tattered soul that can't take much more.

During the past week, I've come to care for this woman dearly. I really want this to be my home.

Later that night, I'm sitting out on the porch with Annie, worry still gnawing at my insides even though she assured me everything will be okay.

It's a balmy evening, and the stars are clear out here.

For the first time in my life, I feel compelled to share my story with someone, if only to lessen the burden on my shoulders.

"I was eighteen when my parents died. It was a boating accident," I murmur, my eyes locked on the twinkling stars. "We always went out on the dam, just drifting, talking, sleeping. That day I woke up to a loud bang. There was blood, and then the pain came. When I woke up again, my uncle told me my parents were dead. I didn't even get to go to their funerals. The propellers of the boat had sliced through my back. People saw what happened and fished me out. They said I was lucky." I let out a burst of hollow laughter. "Lucky."

I take a shuddering breath before I continue, "My uncle gave me my mother's name and told me to run… and I did."

For a moment, there's only the sound of a cricket chirping nearby.

"I disappeared for so long," my voice sounds hauntingly empty, as empty as my life has been. "For seven years, all I did was run. But then I forgot what I was running from. I was stupid, and they found me."

I hear an owl hoot and listen until it stops.

"Then he found me. He saved me in so many ways, and I felt safe with him."

God, I miss Damian. So much.

Letting out a hopeless sigh, I whisper, "Now I'm just a fading star amongst all the bright ones."

Still, Annie doesn't say anything, and it encourages me to admit, "All I want... ever wanted, is to belong and to have someone who I can call mine. Life really sucks." I let out a bitter chuckle. "All I want is love, and all I get is people trying to kill me and take away what peace I manage to find in between."

For a long moment, silence fills the air, and then Annie whispers, "Sometimes, you just look like a fading star because you burn slower and deeper. You're not an all-consuming star. Your light will shine for longer, and it will shine strong, honey. Yours will still shine long after those bright ones have burned out."

She gets up and places her calloused hand on my shoulder, giving it a squeeze. "We'll keep shining together, you and me, child. Because I have no intention of burning out on you. You find that peace you've been looking for here with me."

Emotions well up in my chest, and biting my bottom lip, I nod at her. Annie heads inside, giving me some alone time, and I sit outside for a while, staring at the stars.

I look for the ones that are the faintest.

Annie's and mine.

Chapter 18

CARA

I haven't even rinsed my coffee cup when a car comes up the road, driving up whirls of dust.

"Don't hide," I hear Annie saying from the porch outside. "You come and rest your behind here next to me. Don't give the boy a reason to ask questions. You hear me?"

"Yes, Annie," I murmur, trying to ignore the fear coiling in my stomach.

I dry my hands and rush outside, then sit down beside Annie. My heart is going crazy as my eyes lock on the patrol car.

"Smile, honey," Annie whispers. "Think of rainbows and butterflies."

I force a smile to my face, but no amount of rainbows and butterflies will stop my stomach from spinning into chaos as Jason takes the two steps up to the porch.

"Annie." He tips his hat. "Karen. How are you two this morning?" He sounds casual, but I'm not falling for it.

"As bright as a sunray, Jason." She nods to the bags in his arms. "Are those mine?"

"Yeah. I think I got everything on the list. I'll just put it in the kitchen." When he comes back out, he takes his hat off and leans against the rail opposite us. He stretches his legs out before him.

His hazel eyes are sharp, and his light brown hair is kept in a neat style. He's tall and lean, and the uniform makes him look threatening.

When his eyes land on me, I swallow hard and start to fidget.

"Out with it, boy." Annie's tone sharpens slightly.

"Karen, I couldn't help but notice you have an accent. I did a search on your name, and it's as clean as a whistle. What I want to know is how someone who was born in South Carolina ends up sounding like you?"

Once again, in the face of danger, I freeze, my mouth going bone dry and my muscles tightening.

"Now, you listen to me." Annie raises herself to her mere five feet, and I quickly grab hold of her hand.

"No, Annie," he cuts her off, "you've been my mother for the past twelve years, and I won't stand by and watch you get used." He straightens to his full height, and it makes me rise to my feet. "I'm no idiot, so don't make me out to be one." Then he turns a look of warning on me.

"Go on inside, Karen," Annie says, her voice dipping low.

Shaking my head, I lift my chin, meeting his angry eyes. "Do you do checks on everyone you meet, Officer?" I take a step forward, and for a moment, my legs feel weak with fear.

I've survived that container. I can damn well survive this guy.

I return his glare. "I have an accent because my mother is from South Africa. My father is American. I was born here. Spent time traveling. Would you like to see my I.D., Officer?" I bite out.

I've built up the story, and he can now do with it what he wants. I don't have to say another word.

"No," he says, and I watch him swallow. "I'd like a moment alone with Annie."

I stare at him for a moment longer, feeling brave that I didn't back down. Giving Annie's hand a squeeze, I head inside but stay in the hallway where I can hear them talk.

"How dare you disrespect Karen?" She launches into him. "She's blood of my blood. You don't come around

217

here talking of her like that. We put my sister in the ground, and Karen is all I have now. We've been through enough to have you kicking up dust all around us."

"Annie," he breathes patiently, "I'm only looking out for you. Something about her just ain't right. You take in lost puppies and kittens –" I hear Annie inhale sharply. "Let me finish," he says quickly, "you don't take in total strangers. You don't know what kind of baggage she's dragging behind her."

"Jason Steward Williams!" Annie breathes his name with indignation. "How dare you!"

"Annie –"

"Don't you Annie me," she fumes.

"It's my duty to look out for you," he grumbles.

That's about all the tension I can take. I stalk back outside.

"Would you both just stop," I say, and I'm surprised at how calm I sound. I level Jason with a look. "You don't know me. You have no right to judge me." Then I glance at Annie. "He only cares. Now let's all take a breather and have some of that awful flower tea."

I walk back into the house to make some of the flower tea Annie likes to drink and coffee for me. Jason can have tea with Annie.

I'm busy arranging everything for the fourth time on the tray when I hear him come into the kitchen. They've been whispering a while, and I've taken my time preparing the beverages.

"She really cares about you," Jason mentions.

"I really care about her," I say as I pick up the tray. It's not even nine in the morning, and I'm tired already.

"I don't want to see her get hurt," he keeps going. "So if there's something, anything that might come to hurt her because she has a kind heart, I'd like to know so I can protect her." I get he loves Annie and wants to keep her safe.

I start toward the door but pause when he asks, "Is there something I should be worried about?"

I don't answer him because I don't know. I was fine until he started digging. I don't know if he triggered anything.

With a sinking feeling, I realize it might be time to run again. But I want to cling to Annie and this safe haven with both hands.

Just for a little while longer.

—————————

DAMIAN

Two weeks. That's how long I've been calling in every damn favor owed to me.

It's been nothing short of hell. Every day, fear grips my heart tighter, and it feels like the very life is being squeezed out of me.

I've tried to figure out if Cara left because of what happened at the bar and the memory disk she saw. Or is it something else? Something I missed.

I thought we were getting closer. She was becoming comfortable and even returning affection.

What the hell did I miss?

What sent her running?

Earlier today, we finally got a lead on Cara's whereabouts. Relief keeps crashing over me, especially because the name Karen Weston popped up. At least she's using the new identity.

I keep driving without stopping to sleep, pushing myself to the limit.

Christ, I hope she's okay.

I just need to lay eyes on her.

The urgency in me keeps growing as mile after mile disappears behind my car.

The lead came from a police station in some town in the middle of bum-fucking-nowhere.

I'm well aware *others* might have caught onto it as well, and if that's the case, Cara's in danger.

Faster.

Not caring about any traffic laws, I press down on the gas.

I just need to get to Cara. I need to see she's okay.

Only then will I be able to breathe freely again.

CARA

I've been living with Annie for just shy of a month. Jason still eyes me warily every time he comes to visit Annie. He doesn't trust me, and I don't trust him.

I started getting sick, especially around two in the afternoon. I don't know why it's called morning sickness if it comes at any damn time of the day.

Annie makes me drink peppermint tea with honey in the morning. It took some getting used to, but it helps a lot. Although the nausea is still there, at least I'm not throwing up anymore.

As I'm waiting on the porch for Annie, I look down at my waist. My hand settles over my stomach, that's starting to swell, and for the zillionth time, I wonder what I'm going to do.

In four months, I'll be forced to push a child into this ugly world.

I'll be forced to give birth to a monster's child.

I always dreamt about getting married, having children, and growing old with the man I love. Now it's the furthest thing from my mind. There's no use in dreaming about something I'll never have.

No man will want a tainted woman like me... and her rapist's child.

My future looks bleak. I don't know how I'm going to do this.

What am I going to do with the baby?

I can't go for an abortion. I just can't. The baby didn't ask to be here.

I could always look at adoption, but that will spotlight the fact that I'm illegally in the country. It might also lead the mafia to me.

What the hell am I going to do?

"No use in stressing over the future, honey. Tomorrow will take care of its own problems. Right now, we have to go work, so we'll have food for tonight," Annie says as she walks by me.

Letting out a heavy breath, I trail behind her, my thoughts refusing to leave the baby growing inside me.

Annie stops and waits for me to catch up, and then she tilts her head. "You've looked like death ever since that test showed you're pregnant. A child ain't a curse, honey."

"I'm not so sure about that," I whisper.

"Now, how can you say that?" We start to walk again, and Annie continues, "It's a blessing to bring a human being into this world. You get to help shape the future."

"You don't understand, Annie," I say, my voice hoarse as I try to hold back the tears.

She stops and gently takes hold of my hand. "Then make me understand."

I shake my head and pull my hand free. There's no way I can tell Annie about what happened in that container.

It's a burden I'll have to carry by myself.

When we get to the patch of land we're working on, I go straight for the plow. It's an old thing Annie's husband made. It has two wheels, with a blade in the middle. You tip the handles up until the blade digs into the earth, and then you push it like a cart. It's hard work, but it makes the time fly by.

An hour or so later, sweat is pouring down the back of my neck. As I wipe it away, I feel an odd sensation tingling up my spine. I haven't felt it in a while.

I used to get that feeling when Damian's eyes were on me.

My head snaps up, and I search the area around us, but there's nothing.

Just my imagination.

I glance around me once more before carrying on with the work that needs to be done today.

My thoughts turn back to my pregnancy, and soon my mind becomes a dark cesspool of disturbing memories and suffocating feelings.

It's been five months since Damian rescued me, but there are still times it feels like it just happened. Some of the memories are starting to fade, like the beatings.

It's the last night I spent in the container that haunts me. I don't think I'll ever forget a single moment of it. But

224

somehow, the harrowing intensity is starting to fade, as if I'm actually finding a way to somehow live with it. Either that or I've managed to switch off the debilitating emotions.

"Honey," Annie calls from the kitchen over Elvis hiccupping, *'You ain't nothing bu-ut a houn-nd do-og.'*

The scratches are getting worse by the day, and soon there will be more hiccups than words.

"Yes, Annie," I pop my head out from my room, holding the towel around myself.

I always shower right after we come up from working the land. Then I put on one of the new dresses Annie made me. The *'sunflower range,'* she calls them. They still reach beneath my knees, and the colors are bright. She says it's to make me shine. I just smile and wear them gratefully.

"I'm gonna head on over to Old Bertha for a quick cup of tea. Just taking her some of the pie I baked. Woman's been complaining about her hips not functioning."

A quick cup means I'll see her much later.

They usually play bridge while finishing the pie between the two of them. Annie tried to get me to go with her once, but I'd rather stay home. It's alone time for me, so I don't mind.

"Take it easy on her," I tease. She winks at me and heads out the front door.

I listen to Annie drive away, and then it's only Elvis and me. I let the record play, so the house isn't too quiet. I sit down in front of the chest of drawers. I started painting it two days ago, lilac with purple butterflies.

Annie loves it.

I get back into stenciling a butterfly when Elvis hiccups, and then the house goes silent.

I wait for the record to go on, but it doesn't, and the second drags out endlessly long. I feel the air shift, the atoms pressing against me, and I know I'm not alone. The paintbrush in my hand starts to tremble, but I don't move.

"If I can find you," Damian murmurs, his voice deeper than I remember, "they can find you just as easy."

I try to listen for movement, but I hear none. I can only feel him.

"Karen Weston," it's a whisper, but it's closer. Really close.

Slowly, I place the paintbrush and stencil down and push myself up. I haven't seen Damian in a month, but his voice has the power to make it feel like it's only been a second.

I try to brace myself for his eyes as I turn around and almost whimper when our gazes lock.

Damian's gaze is emotionless and hard on me.

Somehow he's managed to become harder.

"Damian," I whisper because I still can't believe he's really here. I take in the sight of Damian and notice how tired he looks, and it makes my heart squeeze painfully.

His eyes drift over me, then he says, "You look good, Cara." The compliment catches me by surprise.

His eyes drift over me again, from my bare feet to my still drying hair.

Feeling a little self-conscious, I smooth the dress out in front, and my hand settles protectively over my stomach.

"Annie made the dress," I whisper lamely. Like he actually cares about the dress.

"Who is Williams?" Damian suddenly asks, and my mind scrambles to catch up.

"Who?"

"Jason Williams," he repeats the name. "The man who did the search on you. Who is he?"

"He's Annie's… he's like a son to her. He didn't trust me just showing up here, so he had me checked out. He's a police officer. I don't know him all that well," I answer quickly.

"Really? Because he stops by here a lot," he says, and I hear the warning.

What?

"You've been watching me?" I gasp. "What's it to you, anyway? If he's stopping here for Annie or me, it's really not any of your business, Damian. You have your own life to concern yourself with."

"That's why I'm here." Damian moves closer to me. "I'm not that happy that another man is taking an interest in my life. I damn near went crazy when you just vanished on me." He takes a calming breath. "Why did you leave?"

"Because..." I hesitate, not ready to admit the confusing emotions I have for him. Wetting my lips, I come up with a quick excuse, "Because there will always be someone like Leah. You have a need to save people, and you're done saving me."

"I'm done with you?" Damian says incredulously, then he shakes his head, and his eyes sharpen on me. His voice is a low rumble as he says, "You have to stop comparing yourself to Leah. You're two different people, and in no way do I see you as a replacement for her." He takes a step closer to me, and his earthy scent makes my stomach flutter. "I'll never be done with you, Cara. You remember that before you let that man touch you."

Damian turns, and when it looks like he's going to leave, my body comes to life. I rush forward as the words explode from me, "That's it? You just came here to threaten me?"

Anything to make him stay a minute longer.

God, I missed him so much.

Damian turns back to me, slowly shaking his head. "I'm not threatening you, Cara. The day I dragged your ass out of that container, you became mine. I will never let you go. I'll give you the time you need with this lady, but then you're coming home."

Oh. My. God.

A weird mixture of worry and happiness courses through my veins.

I'm his?

I'm not ready for that kind of relationship. Still, I can't stop the joy I'm feeling from knowing I matter to Damian.

More than I thought.

Needing to come clean with Damian, I let the words fall between us. "I... I..." My voice cuts out from all the emotions waring in my chest. "I'm not ready for a relationship."

Damian's eyes soften on me. "I know, Cara. I don't expect anything from you. I want you as you are. I can't wait."

"What if I'm never ready?" I ask the question that made me run in the first place.

Damian's eyes hold a world of understanding, and I can see the past month has not been kind to him, either.

I didn't know I could hurt him. He seemed so untouchable.

"I'll be okay with that," he replies. "I just want you in my life, no strings attached."

I walk to him and tilt my head back so I can see his face.

I don't remember him being this tall.

"You have to stop growing," I try to joke the uneasiness between us away. "I know I'm unreasonable in my demands of you, but it's one thing to help someone and a totally different thing being in a relationship. I couldn't even deal with the thought of it." I drink in the ink curling up his neck.

I missed you.

"Next time, don't run. Just talk to me," Damian whispers as he lifts his arm. When his palm cups my cheek,

I almost melt into his touch, feeling the safety I missed so much. "Can this woman you're living with make food?"

"Yeah, she whips up bread from scratch," I answer, my voice soft.

"Then eat, baby," Damian leans down and brushes his lips against my temple. "You're fading away. I won't have you starving." Then he steps back and takes a phone out of his pocket. Holding it out to me, he says, "Call when you're ready to come home."

I take it and swallow back the tears because it's too soon to say goodbye to him again, and I haven't even told him I'm pregnant yet.

Damian came to tell me he'd always be there for me, but that might change once he finds out I'm having a baby.

When he walks out of the room, part of me wants to run after him, but knowing Damian has my back while I get to be with Annie doesn't bring the comfort I thought it would.

Instead, it leaves me feeling torn.

Chapter 19

DAMIAN

I drive back to the motel I'm staying at with no intention of leaving this town without Cara.

I just had to see her up close. The month we've been apart hasn't changed a thing. On the contrary, it only solidified my feelings for her.

Deep in my bones, I know if there's a possibility of a future with a woman by my side, that woman will be Cara.

Only Cara.

There are so many reasons why it has to be her, but the main one is because of her inner strength. Every day she wakes up, choosing to live, is a day she won the battle.

She's fighting back and not letting what happened to her beat her down.

It makes my feelings for her grow much faster than I ever thought possible.

Come hell or high water, Cara's mine, and I'll kill anyone who stands in the way of keeping her by my side.

CARA

It's been five days, and I can't stop staring at the phone. It only has one number on it – Damian's – and I know if I press dial, I'll hear his voice.

I know if I ask, he'll come to get me.

I haven't told Annie, but I think she suspects something's up.

It's close to midnight when I sneak outside, shutting the door softly behind me. The stars are clear, and the nights are getting warmer.

I walk a short distance from the house so I won't wake Annie. There's a slight breeze ruffling my hair and the nightgown I'm wearing. Annie insists every woman should have a nightgown. She makes them so big I feel lost in them. They just hang straight down from my shoulders, and most nights, I get twisted up in the fabric.

Suddenly the phone vibrates, and I shriek as I drop it. Stunned, I stare at the glowing screen. Then my heart begins to race as I crouch to pick up the device.

It shows that I have a message, and I press the button to open it.

Go inside.

I read it over and over until the words blur. Then, it vibrates again, and my fingers get all twisted to press the right button.

Go inside before I kidnap you.

My head snaps up as I glance around me.

Damian's here.

It's dark out, and frustration washes over me when I can't see him. I press reply and type as fast as I can.

Where are you?

The response comes seconds later.

Not at home with you.

Closing my eyes, I let out a soft breath as the warmth from his words trickle into my heart.

Another message comes through.

If we were home, you'd be in my arms where you belong.

My breaths hitch, and I glance around me again.

"Damian," I whisper.

I strain my ears to listen for Damian, but there are no sounds. Even the crickets have gone quiet. And then I feel his powerful presence behind me. I take the step backward, right into him, and overwhelming feelings of safety and home spill through me.

When he moves around me, I reach for him, gripping hold of his shirt so he won't vanish into the night. As he comes to stand in front of me, my heartbeat speeds up.

I lift my eyes to his, and for the longest moment, we just stare at each other.

Home. That's what Damian has become to me without me even realizing it.

Suddenly Damian's head snaps up, and then he spins around, his muscles tightening as if he's about to kill someone.

"Stay behind me. Don't get in my way."

The familiar words rip through me, making a gasp burst over my lips.

No.

Damian's hand moves behind his back, and for a stupid moment, I think he's reaching for me, but then the metal of the gun reflects in the moonlight, and my world tilts to the side.

No. No. No.

"Unless one of you gets visitors at midnight I'm not aware of, we might have a bit of a problem," he whispers, sounding way too calm.

Fear ripples through me, and I barely manage to get the words out, "No visitors."

Not again. God, not again.

"Get down." Damian glances back at me. "Fuck, you're wearing white. You're like a damn glowing sign out here."

I crouch down and huddle behind his legs. Then I close my eyes like the coward I am.

I can't handle this again.

A horrible scream echoes through the night, and it has me instantly darting to my feet. "Annie!" I cry, and without a second thought, I run toward the house.

The nightgown flutters around my knees in my sprint to get to her. I'm a coward when it comes to my own life, but not Annie's.

Please, not Annie.

God, I brought death right to her.

I shove the front door open and grab the broom she sweeps the porch with. "Annie!"

I come to a stumbling halt when I see a man and Annie at the end of the hallway. His fingers are wrapped around her throat in a brutal hold as he glances over his shoulder at me.

"Let her go," I whimper, my voice hoarse with fear.

Seeing how much danger Annie's in gives me a burst of courage, and I dart forward, lifting the broom so I can hit him with it.

I slam the piece of wood as hard over his shoulder and head, and it works… he lets go of Annie, and she sags to the floor, gasping for air.

The man swings around, his face is set in a dark scowl as he lifts his arm, and then only do I see the gun.

God.

I hear a shot right outside the house, and I lift the broom to smack the man again.

Then I hear two loud shots.

I hear Annie scream.

I watch as the man slumps to the floor, blood trickling from the wound to his forehead.

I suck in a startled breath as my eyes slowly move to Annie. She reaches for me with a trembling hand, her face a picture of horror. "Honey?"

Pain begins to throb in my abdomen, and my vision blurs. "I'm sorry, Annie," I choke the words out, and then all my strength fades. Arms grab me from behind as my legs give way beneath me.

"I have you. You're safe." Damian's voice comes to me, and then the pain overwhelms me. It feels like something is shredding my insides to pieces. It's a cold, sharp ache that robs me of my breath.

"Call 911!" Damian orders Annie.

"It... hurts..." My body starts to shiver uncontrollably as I'm laid on the floor. "Damian," I manage to gasp, and then his hand presses down on my abdomen.

Damian's features are tight with emotion as his eyes meet mine, and I see my pain reflecting in the icy blue of his irises.

"You're going to be okay," he says, his voice breaking.

I can hear Annie's weeping.

And then my body goes numb, and I can't feel Damian's hands as he presses down on me.

"I... I" I can't get the words out.

I want to tell them I love them.

I want to tell them how grateful I am for them.

But I don't get any of the words out as darkness drags me away from the only people who care for me.

DAMIAN

"Cara!" Her face is ghostly white. I feel her body go limp beneath my hands. "Fuck, did you reach them?" I yell at Annie.

"They're coming," Annie sobs. Sitting down next to Cara, she brushes the hair away from Cara's face. "It's going to be okay, honey," she keeps saying through the sobs wracking her.

I don't dare lift my hands from the wound.

Fuck, she's losing too much blood.

I lower my chin to my chest and close my eyes as the woman who has finally stirred something inside my heart bleeds to death.

Hold on, baby.

Don't leave me.

Minutes drag by agonizingly slowly as her blood seeps through my fingers. With every precious second slipping away, the brutal hold on my heart tightens.

Finally, when I hear the sirens outside, I want to cry with relief but only manage a shuddering breath.

Williams comes in first, followed by the paramedics. I only move back when the one paramedic starts nudging my hands away from the wound.

"Don't let her die," I growl at the man.

Climbing to my feet, I watch as they work on Cara. When they wheel her out to the ambulance, Williams grabs hold of my arm.

"Who are you?" he asks, and I can see the anger burning in his eyes.

"Damian Weston." I yank my arm free from his hold and walk out of the house. "I'm going with my wife. You can find me at the hospital."

Chapter 20

CARA

When I open my eyes, I see white. White walls, white sheets, there's just too much white.

"Where am I?" I croak, but there's no one to answer me.

The fogginess starts to clear, and I begin to remember the shooting.

Annie. Damian. Are they okay?

Gingerly I move into a sitting position. Pain tears through my abdomen as I grab hold of the IV stand next to the bed. Slowly, I force myself to stand, and using the IV as a crutch, I stumble out of the room.

"Mrs. Weston!" someone gasps. "You shouldn't be up." A nurse comes at me, her face tight with worry. "You're so pale," I hear panicked voices join hers, and I see a blur of two figures moving toward me before everything goes dark again.

Hot tears are running into my hair as I wake up. There's an excruciating, piercing pain in my abdomen. I try to move so I can curl up, but the pain intensifies, and I whimper.

"Cara?" A pair of strong hands frame my face, and prying my eyes open, I see Damian. He looks awful, worse than before. "Cara," he says again.

"It hurts," I croak. I don't even have the strength to lift my hands.

"I'll get you something for the pain." There's promise in his voice, and it already makes me feel better.

I hear a beeping start above my head, then Damian talks to someone, but I don't make out the words as I drift off to sleep again.

The next time I wake up, Damian's sitting on the side of the bed, staring down at me.

"Hey, how are you feeling?" he whispers as he brushes his fingers through my hair.

"Alive." It's the only word I can think of. "Annie? Is she okay?"

"She's fine. She went home but said she'd be back soon," he explains.

For a moment, we stare at each other as the horrid incident plays out in my head.

They found me.

Again.

I'll never be safe.

Then Damian's features turn tense, and I figure this is where he lays into me for running into the house to help Annie.

"Cara." Damian leans closer, bracing his hands on either side of my head. Too late do I realize he's trying to give me strength as he says, "The bullet hit low." He pauses as if he's waiting for me to take it in. "The bullet hit…" He takes a breath, and it really sounds like he can't find the words.

I stare at him with confusion.

"There was a lot of damage. You were out of it for a couple of days," he continues, his voice strained. I can see it's hard for him to keep his eyes locked on mine. "The baby is gone."

Gone?

"Oh."

It takes a moment for his words to sink in, and then devastation plows through me.

My baby's dead?

243

"I don't…" The words trail away as the full impact of what he just said hits hard. "The baby… my baby." My voice grows thick with tears. "I lost my baby?" My voice cracks with emotions I wasn't expecting to feel.

I lost my baby.

I didn't even have a chance to decide whether I wanted a baby. It's just another decision forced on me.

Tears spill over my cheeks and Damian's arms slip in under me. He holds me to his chest as I cry for yet another life that was taken from me.

God, I couldn't even keep my baby for five and half months.

It hurts more than anything I've felt before. Too late… I realize I wanted the baby because it would've been mine. Only mine.

Sobs shudder through me, and Damian begins to press kisses to the side of my head. "I'm so sorry, Cara. I'm so sorry."

Eventually, my tears dry up, but my heart keeps shrinking, trying to get away from the unbearable sorrow.

Damian moves a little back, and taking hold of my hand, he doesn't say anything as his eyes stay locked on mine.

The familiar emptiness I haven't felt in a while sinks into my soul. It weighs a ton.

Who would've thought emptiness could weigh so much?

How much pain can one human being take before they just die?

I've been in the hospital for almost a week. I hate hospitals, and I just want to leave.

Annie comes to see me in the early hours of the morning. She holds me tight and then whispers, "Jason's going to ask questions today. I can't hold him off any longer. We told him it was a break-in gone bad. You just tell him that, and everything will be fine."

Annie stays by my side when Jason comes to see me. Damian's with him, and both their faces are set in dark scowls.

"Let me guess," Jason growls, "it was a break-in gone wrong?"

My eyes dart to Damian's, where he's standing behind Jason. He nods at me, and I start nodding too. "Yeah."

"Yeah?" Jason raises an eyebrow, and then he tucks the small notepad back into his pocket. He takes a deep breath, and his eyes lock on mine. "I'll make you a deal." He steps to the side so he can see both Damian and me. "You both leave and never come back to my town, and I'll let it go as a robbery gone wrong. I want you gone."

I open my mouth to protest when Damian moves forward. He comes to stand next to me, and then he gives Jason a look that would scare the bravest of men. "It's a deal. As soon as my wife's ready to go home, we'll leave your town."

"No!" Annie gets up, and her cheeks flush with anger. "You can't tell them what to do!"

Jason shakes his head hard. "Annie, I promised Pete I'd look after you. I won't break my promise to him. Trouble follows these two, and I can't just stand by while your life is in danger. Now, you can be angry at me all you want, but I'm not backing down on this."

Jason nods at us. "As soon as she's released, I want you gone." With his cold words hanging in the air, he stalks out of the room.

I hold onto Annie's hand, and accepting my fate, I put a brave smile on my face. "You've been like a mother to me. Thank you so much for all you've done."

Her chin trembles, and leaning forward, she presses a kiss on my forehead. "Don't listen to the boy." She gives my hand a squeeze.

I shake my head. "He's right, Annie. I'm putting your life in danger. They'll keep coming for me."

"Hush, child," she tries to argue.

"Thank you so much for everything you've done for me," I say, needing her to know how grateful I am for the short time I had with her. "You'll never know how much you mean to me."

She pats my hand. "I'm going to talk to Jason. We'll figure this out." Getting up, I watch as she leaves the room.

"The doctor said you should be able to leave tomorrow or the day after, depending on the wound," Damian informs me.

"What's one day?" I mumble. Turning my head, I look at the only person who's strong enough to face my enemies. "Take me home, Damian."

He rubs a hand over his beard, and his eyes dart to the door. "Let me just get a nurse."

He walks out of the room to go find a nurse while I struggle into a sitting position. There's a hollow pain in my abdomen that serves as a reminder of what I've lost, and it makes a wave of sorrow crash over me.

When Damian stalks back into the room, there's an upset nurse behind him. "Sir, she can't leave without the doctor saying so."

Damian swings back to her, and I see fear flitting across her features, then he orders, "Take out that IV, or I'll do it myself."

Her lips set in a thin line as she comes over to me. I swing my legs off the bed, and then she places a hand on my knee. "Wait for the doctor, please."

I smile as best I can and then shake my head. "I want to go home. Just take it out and leave. Say you didn't see us."

"Just so you know," she huffs, clearly upset with us, "I'm not agreeing with this." She pulls the needle from my arm, and I wince, making Damian take a step closer to me.

"What are you going to wear?" the nurse asks.

Damian takes the blanket from the bed and wraps it around my hospital gown-clad shoulders.

The nurse is just about to open her mouth again when he yanks his wallet out. He throws money on the bed and then slides his arms under me.

Lifting me to his chest, Damian whispers, "Time to go home, baby."

Without sparing the stunned nurse another glance, Damian carries me out of the room.

I avoid any eye contact with the people around us and keep my gaze locked on the ink peeking from beneath Damian's t-shirt.

When we're out of the hospital, it hits me that I won't see Annie again. Another wave of sorrow engulfs me, and I bury my face against Damian's neck.

I'm so tired of losing everything that matters to me.

Chapter 21

DAMIAN

I drive until I feel we've put enough distance between us and that town. I find a motel, and when I switch off the engine, I pause for a moment to take in our surroundings.

It's close to midnight, and the parking area is quiet. There are only four cars.

I hate leaving Cara, but I need to go get us a room. "I'll be right back."

She doesn't answer me, and I quickly get out. I make sure to lock the doors before jogging to the office.

The place is filthy and run down, but it's the best place to hide. People don't notice you around motels like this because they're too busy dealing with their own shit.

The man at reception doesn't make eye contact as he comes to stand in front of the counter. "What can I do you for?" he mutters, either half drugged or half asleep.

"One room for a night."

He checks me in and gives me a key. I rush back to the car and quickly take my bag from the trunk. It has the first aid kit in it, and I'll need it for Cara.

I unlock her door, and when I have it open, I carefully pick her up. Her head falls to my shoulder, and for a moment, I think she's asleep, but glancing down, I see her eyes are open.

The only life in them is the tears shining in the dim light coming from the dingy motel sign.

I walk to our room and let her body slide down against mine. "Just lean into me while I unlock the door," I whisper. Her hands are fisted in the blanket, but she leans into me.

At least she's still with me.

I quickly unlock the door and move us into the room, then immediately lock it behind us. After switching on the light, I carry Cara to the bed, where I gently lay her down.

I close the curtains and, grabbing the first aid kit from my bag, I take a seat on the side of the bed.

Letting out a deep breath.

What a fucking mess.

I have so much cleaning up to do so they won't find her again.

Rubbing tiredly over my face, I take a moment to close my eyes.

"I keep losing people," Cara whispers brokenly. "I just keep losing them like they're a set of keys or a sock." She sniffles, and I open my eyes to look down at her.

The first time I saved her, she was beaten and out of it, but not even that compares to the haunted look staring back at me.

"Let me clean your wound, and then we'll get some rest." I have no false words of comfort to offer her.

We're back to square one, but this time, I can't find it in me to mask my feelings from Cara. I want to wrap her in my arms and hide her from this fucked up world.

I reach for the blanket but then pause. "Is it okay if I clean the wound?" I ask, not wanting to upset her any more than she already is.

She only nods.

The previous time I had to clean her wounds, she would look away and stare blankly at some spot on the ceiling or wall, but now her eyes find mine.

"I'll be quick," I whisper. I pull the blanket down, then push the hospital gown up until I have a clear view of the bandage.

The hospital underwear doesn't look comfortable, but I don't want to push her too hard by having her change into her own clothes.

I open the first aid kit and take out the antiseptic and some wipes. Careful not to hurt Cara, I pull the bandage off and toss it aside. I can feel her eyes on me as I start to clean the area around the wound.

I'll have to take her to a doctor to get the clips removed.

Once I'm done cleaning the wound, I lock eyes with her. "Can you sit up so I can put the fresh bandage on? I'll get some of those stick-on ones tomorrow."

Cara begins to struggle, and I quickly slip an arm around her back. I help her into a sitting position and let her lean against my chest.

She looks away to some spot on the other side of the room. "Please don't be like this," she whispers.

I frown, not sure what she means. "Like what?"

Her chin begins to quiver. "Don't be nice to me. I don't deserve it. Be like you were when you first found me. Just be cold."

I take hold of her chin, lifting her face to mine, but she glances away from me again.

"Look at me," I demand. Her eyes snap to mine. "What the fuck are you thinking up in that head of yours?"

Her hands clutch the harsh material of the gown, and she swallows hard. "It's all my fault," she whispers hollowly.

I frown at her words. "What's your fault?"

"Everything," she whispers, her eyes lowering to my neck. "They found me because I was careless. They beat me... they raped me because I let my guard down." A tear slips over her cheek, and for a moment, I stare at it, thinking how wrong she's is. "I lost my baby because I left you."

"No, Cara," I say. "You might've let your guard down, but it was never your fault that they beat and raped you." I hate the words as they leave my mouth. They're such ugly words to link to her. "It definitely wasn't your fault that you lost your baby."

Cara shakes her head while her eyes stay blankly on my neck.

Fuck, she's losing it.

I wish she would scream and cry. I wish she would show any kind of emotion and just let it all out.

"I... I brought it on myself. I didn't fight hard enough. I didn't... I ran away, and they found me again... I killed my baby," she gasps, every breath coming faster than the previous one.

I frame her face with both my hands, forcing her to keep still. She grabs hold of my right wrist, her nails digging into my skin. "Damian," she gasps.

Watching the pain tear through her is unbearable. I wrap my arms around her, securing her to my chest. "You didn't kill your baby." My voice cracks under the weight of the sadness I feel for her. Pulling back, I press my forehead to hers. Her breaths are heavy with guilt and pain.

"I'm here, baby. You'll get through this, and you'll be so much stronger. I'm here every step of the way."

Cara grabs my shoulder, and I move closer, enveloping her in my arms again.

"I can't, Damian," she chokes on the ache that's eating her alive. "I can't take any more. I'm done. If this is what life is like, then I'd rather die."

I press a kiss to the top of her head and just hold her tight. She's been through so much hell. All I can do right now is to help keep her standing. She just needs time.

It takes a while before she manages to calm down, then she pulls back. "I don't understand," she whispers. "Why do they keep coming after me?"

The muscle in my jaw starts ticking. She can't deal with more shit.

Her eyes search mine, and a slight frown forms between her eyes. "Tell me," she urges more insistent this time.

I wipe a hand over my face and shake my head. This is going to kill her.

"Damian," she whispers, her voice filled with fear of the unknown. Her mind must be conjuring up all kinds of shit.

I can't look at her as the words come. "They know you were with me." I shake my head again, knowing they found her because they traced her through the name I gave her. "They must have people in law enforcement, and when the search for Weston popped up, they went to check if it was you. I was stupid. I slipped up, and you paid for it." The words settle heavy in my gut. Cara got hurt because I led them straight to her.

"Who are they?" She starts to fidget with the hospital gown, and for some reason, the fabric pisses me off. I pull it away from her and, digging through my bag for one of her shirts and sweatpants, I yank the clothes out.

I don't think as I remove the hospital from her body. Pulling the t-shirt over her head, I push one arm at a time through the sleeves. I tug the fabric over her chest, and for a second, I get a glimpse of her breasts.

The first time I saw her, she was naked and beaten. I saw her as a victim who needed saving. I had to get her out of a shitty situation.

Not once did I think of Cara as a woman... until that night she walked into the kitchen wearing those damn tight jeans.

My eyes snap to her face, and I'm not surprised when I see her startled gaze on me, her lips parted with what looks like a mixture of shock and terror.

Fuck, I've crossed the line.

I quickly grab a bandage and start to wrap it around her wound. When I'm done, I tug the shirt all the way down and then keep myself busy with getting rid of the dirty bandage and wipes as I mutter, "Change into the sweatpants so you can get some sleep."

I go to the restroom and splash some water on my face, just needing a moment to myself.

Fuck she has beautiful breasts.

Stop thinking about them. You fucking crossed the line.

I let out a sigh as I shake my head at myself.

When I walk back to the bed, I know I have to say something to break the tension hanging heavily in the room, but I can't think of a damn thing.

"Who?" Cara whispers, reverting back to the conversation we were having before I took it upon myself to dress her.

"The mafia," I murmur, and knowing I'm putting her at risk by keeping her in the dark, I add, "And Tom."

I watch as the information sinks in, and then a distraught expression pulls tightly at her skin. She starts to shake her head but stops and then just stares blankly at nothing.

After a minute or so, Cara wraps her arms around her waist, and it makes my hands fist at my sides. I take a calming breath before I sit down on the bed, but this time I keep my distance.

"I'm sorry, Cara. Tom thinks that by giving you up, he can save his own ass." I shake my head. "He's as good as dead. As soon as you're dead, they'll kill him, too. They're just using him to clean up the last of your family."

"I still don't understand any of it," she whispers so softly I almost miss some of the words.

I thrust a hand through my hair and rising to my feet again, I say, "We can't go home. Now that they know I'm helping you, they'll be looking for both of us."

Cara's head snaps up, and she begins to struggle off the bed. Panic flashes over her face, and then she rasps, "You need to leave." Her skin turns almost translucent as she stares at me in horror. "You need to go. Go… right now!" She loses her voice, and her movements grow more frantic as she stumbles to my bag. Shoving it toward me with her foot, she pleads, "Leave, Damian."

"Cara," I say loud and clear, so she hears every word, "There's no fucking way I'm leaving you."

"Please!" She crumbles to the floor, and that's about as much as I can take. I crouch in front of her, and she grabs at my arms, pulling herself closer to me, and then she sputters against my chest, "They can't get you, Damian. Please go. I can't watch you die. Not you. Please go. Disappear. Just go." Her breaths are way too fast.

Moving my hands up, I frame her face, and our eyes lock. "They won't kill me. They won't find us. I've got you, Cara. You're safe. I'm safe. We're going to disappear. I'll make sure they can't find us."

She tries to shake her head in my hands, her eyes wild with fear on mine, and somewhere deep inside of me, it registers the fear in her eyes is for me.

Cara fears losing me.

She cares about what happens to me.

I stare hard at her as the thoughts sink deep into my heart. She's not as fucked up as I thought. She's just in a world of pain, but we can deal with that, as long as she still cares about something.

"You won't lose me, baby."

"I will," she cries out, and her face crumbles under the weight of her distress.

I sit flat on my ass and pull her body between my legs. Then, leaning back against the bed, I hold her to me while peppering her hair with kisses. When she looks up, one of those kisses lands next to her eye. She doesn't move, and I feel her hair tickling my cheek.

"You won't lose me," I whisper again.

She curls her body against mine and buries her face in my chest. I feel her fingers dig into my shirt. "I lose everyone I love."

The words fold around me like a blanket, giving me warmth for the first time in over a decade.

I've been stuck in a frozen wasteland for so many years, I've forgotten what warmth feels like... until Cara.

"You will never lose me, baby," I promise with steel lacing my words.

God help the person who tries to come after my woman next. I'll fucking kill every single one. There's no way I'm letting them take her from me.

Chapter 22

CARA

I must've fallen asleep on Damian, and when I wake up, I'm groggy and sore.

Damian doesn't say a word as he climbs to his feet, pulling me up along with him. He throws the covers back and then waits for me to climb into bed before he lies down behind me.

His arms come around me, and he curls his body around mine until my back is pressed tightly to his chest. I feel his breath on my hair, and I try to focus on it.

I don't know why I'm still alive. I don't understand how my heart can keep beating when it's been torn to shreds.

This unforgiving world is too much. I want to leave it. I wish I could turn back time to before I was conceived. I want that so desperately – just the nothingness of before I existed.

This life has hollowed me out. I thought I found some happiness with Annie, but no, that was just life giving me the finger... once again.

As my thoughts are inundated with the darkness closing in on me, neither of us goes back to sleep.

The hours creep by, and eventually, my mind turns to Damian and how comfortable I've become with him touching me. Of course, I was shocked when he dressed me, but it didn't make me feel as uncomfortable as I thought it would.

Maybe it's because he's saved my life twice. He's never done anything to hurt me.

As soon as the sun starts to rise, Damian gets up. I glance over my shoulder and watch as he calls someone.

"Jeff," Damian's voice is harsh again. There's no trace of the man who comforted me during the night. "We need to disappear. Burn the house to the ground."

I sit up and watch Damian. "We'll be fine. We go with the retirement plan. I'll check in with you once the dust has settled."

When he tucks the phone back in his pocket, I can't help but ask, "Retirement plan?"

"Yeah." Damian nods as he walks to the window. He peeks through the curtain before he glances back at me. "We have one stop to make before we head south."

Gingerly climbing out of bed, I go to the bathroom, and I cringe when I see the state of the shower. It's filthy.

I turn to the sink and rinse my mouth a couple of times, but it does nothing to remove the stale taste from my mouth.

"Here," Damian says, holding a toothbrush and toothpaste out to me.

Gratefully, I take the items and quickly brush my teeth. I make sure to rinse it properly before Damian takes it from me.

I try to smooth my wild bed hair out, and then my eyes widen as I watch Damian brush his teeth.

I take a step back and just stare because he's using the same toothbrush.

I've been avoiding a relationship with him, but I never considered how he might feel.

Does he already see us as a couple?

At the hospital, he said I'm his wife. Not sister. Not cousin. He chose to make me his wife. Again.

Shit.

I rush out of the bathroom, and the small space of the motel room feels like it's suffocating me.

My mind starts to race frantically. I care about Damian, but I'm a wretched mess. I don't think I'll ever be ready for a relationship, and I told him that.

I need Damian. I know I won't survive this without him, but… what if he changes his mind down the line and wants more?

I can't give him more.

The wound starts to ache, every pulse of pain in rhythm with my racing heart. I sit down on the side of the bed so my body won't take too much strain and then chew on my thumbnail.

Damian comes out of the bathroom, and his eyes lock with mine.

"I… I…" I start to stutter like an idiot.

"I'll be back in a couple of minutes," he grumbles, and then I watch him leave.

I sit frozen, not sure what's happening.

"Maybe it's your imagination?" I try to ease my worry. "You're just friends. Damian knows you can't give him more." I wipe my palms over my sweatpants. "You always wanted a friend, and now you have one." My heart squeezes tightly in my chest.

It feels like I'm detached from life itself. The sun keeps shining. The wind keeps blowing. My body keeps breathing, but I'm drained … just empty, and it's the most lost feeling I've ever felt.

There's nothing left of me to give to Damian even if I wanted to.

DAMIAN

I tuck my hands deep in my pockets as I stalk to the Walmart we passed on the way to the motel.

My mind wanders to Cara and the way she reacted when I used the same toothbrush as her. I know she's not ready for any kind of relationship. That's why I've been so careful with her.

But it's like a fucking car accident. No matter how you try to avoid crashing, it's inevitable. We're going to collide one of these days, and I can only hope we'll survive it.

Walking into the store, I grab a cart and head over to the clothes because Cara needs more than the couple of items I packed. I take the first pair of jeans I see and hold them up.

Yeah, they seem the correct size.

I grab a few shirts, another pair of jeans, and two pairs of sweatpants. Then I come to a standstill in the underwear section.

Fuck.

I grab a box of panties and then sigh when my eyes fall on the bras. I stare at the bras until it's well past the point of weird.

Deciding to just get it over with, I take the first one and then think back to the night before. I only got a glimpse, but the image of Cara's breasts is crystal-fucking-clear.

I search through the row of bras until I find one that looks like it will fit. We can get Cara more when she can pick them herself.

Next, I head over to the shoes and grab a comfy-looking pair. As I walk to the front of the store, my eyes spot the aisle with deodorant and shit. I sniff at a few cans before I pick one that smells fresh.

I also grab a pack of pads and tampons, hoping they're the right ones. I spot some razors and take a pack, tossing it into the cart.

I get a beard trimmer for myself. I've let the beard grow too long and need to change my appearance. I also get Cara her own toothbrush because I don't want a repeat of this morning.

I stare at the hair dye, but I just can't take one. Cara has gorgeous ginger hair. I sigh and glance to my left. There are hats and beanies, and I smile with relief. I get her two beanies, then head for the front of the store again, satisfied that I got the essentials.

After everything's scanned through, I pay with cash and grabbing the bags, I stalk out of the store.

I've taken too long.

Just as I walk across the motel's parking area, four men come out of the room next to ours. They laugh and look casual, but every muscle in my body tenses. I keep my head down as I pass by them, then slow my pace and wait until they get into a car and leave before I open the door to our room.

My eyes immediately search for Cara. She's still sitting on the bed, her hands limply on her lap.

"Got you more clothes and a couple of things you might need," I say, and I put the bag down on the bed. "Want to change before we leave?"

Cara keeps staring at the floor, her face devoid of any emotion. She's got that 'the lights are on but no one's home' expression on her face.

I crouch down in front of her and place my hand on her knee. I catch her eyes, and they seem to come back into focus.

"Time to get dressed," I murmur, and suddenly it feels like there's a fucking rock stuck in my throat.

Christ, I hate seeing her like this.

When Cara finally nods, I rise to my feet and, taking scissors from the first aid kit, I grab the beard trimmer and head to the bathroom.

I cut most of the beard off before using the beard trimmer until there's only a dark dusting of bristles on my jaw.

I'm not fond of a clean shave, and it's easier to maintain this way.

I pack everything away and clean the sink out before I go back to the room. I'm relieved to see Cara changed into a fresh pair of sweatpants and a sweater. She's busy slipping her feet into the shoes.

"Everything fit okay?" I ask as I pack the beard trimmer into my bag. I grab her other clothes and shove them into my bag, and then glance up at Cara.

She's staring at me with her lips slightly parted. She takes a breath and tilts her head. "You shaved," she states the obvious.

"Yeah, time for a new look. Wear one of the beanies to cover your hair."

I leave the room to put the bag in the car and then rush back so I can erase any trace we were here. It's a habit I'll never be able to break. I have to always cover my tracks.

When I'm done, I take Cara's hand. "Let's go."

I open the door and scan the area. When I see it's quiet, I tug her out of the room, then lock it behind us. She stays next to me as we walk to the reception area and placing the key on the counter, we leave without a word.

I open the passenger door, and Cara moves to get in but then stops and glances up at me. It looks like she wants to say something but changes her mind and climbs into the vehicle.

I shut the door and walk around the car to the drivers' side. As I climb behind the steering wheel, I hear her whisper, "Thank you."

Glancing at her, I smile. "You're welcome. We'll grab something to eat on the way out of town so you can take a couple of painkillers."

Cara nods, and then her eyes flutter over my face before she quickly glances out the window. She curls into herself and rests her head against the side of the door.

We have a long way to go, but first, we have to stop at my storage unit so I can get everything we'll need to disappear.

Chapter 23

CARA

I keep my eyes closed and try to get Damian's smiling face out of my head. He shouldn't have shaved. It was easier to ignore the feelings I had for him when he looked like a grizzly bear.

Now... shit, now there's no beard hiding his face.

Those eyes.

That smile.

The look that digs its way into the darkest corner of your soul.

Turns out under all that hair, Damian's dangerously good-looking, and it's messing even more with my head.

A tear sneaks out of the corner of my eye, and I turn my body more toward the door, so Damian won't see.

My emotions are all over the place. One second, I'm so thankful Damian wants to stick around, and the next, I'm swallowed whole by this black hole in my soul. It must be my hormones that are totally messed up after losing my baby.

My mind doesn't stop racing from my parents to Annie, to my baby – to the death sentence hanging over my head – to Damian.

I swear, if I knew what was waiting on the other side of death, I'd end this life in a heartbeat.

But there's no ending this. I'll somehow have to face it.

My whole mid-section is aching, and the pain is spreading into my hips and thighs. After forcing a sandwich and juice down, I took a couple of painkillers, but they haven't kicked in yet.

Feeling nauseous with pain, I bite it back and wrap my arms around myself. The car starts to slow down, and I quickly use my shirt to dry my cheeks.

When Damian brings the vehicle to a standstill, I peek out the window. I can only see rows and rows of storage units. I frown, not sure why we're stopping here.

"Come," Damian says, his eyes already checking our surroundings.

Gingerly, I get out of the car and lean against the door as I wait for Damian, where he's grabbing a bag from the back seat.

He walks to where I'm standing, and lifting his hands, he brushes his knuckles over my cheek. Leaning down, he tilts his head so he can lock eyes with me.

Just like in the beginning, I can't keep eye contact and quickly lower my gaze to his chest.

"How's the pain?" he asks.

It doesn't help to lie, so I grimace. "The painkillers haven't kicked in yet."

He slips his arm around my shoulders and draws me against his side. "I'll get you something stronger as soon as we're done here."

I lean against Damian as we walk down a narrow passage, aware of how his muscles ripple with every step he takes.

There's a flicker of attraction in my belly that's quickly followed by a surge of panic. I swallow hard, forcing the emotions down and focusing on the dim light as we pass a couple of storage units.

We finally stop by one, and I watch as Damian unlocks it. The door rolls up, and he flicks on the light. I'm not sure what I expected to see, but it's not a plain cabinet.

Damian goes to unlock it, and when he opens the door, my eyes widen. There are two guns, ammunition, stacks of cash, and some other items.

I've never seen so much money before.

Damian opens the bag and then empties the cabinet into it. When he glances at me, all I can do is swallow.

God, he's prepared for anything.

He shrugs the bag over his left shoulder and then takes hold of my arm. "Let's go."

Before we can leave, voices echo down the passage. Damian pushes me back and quickly rolls the door shut. He switches the light off, and my heart all but stops.

I gasp as my heart sets off racing again. I open my mouth, but before I can say Damian's name, I feel his arm come around my shoulders. I don't know how he can see anything, but he steers me to the back of the unit.

My back brushes against the cold steel, and my whole body tightens with fear. I grab for Damian, and then his arms fold around me. His body curves over mine, and I feel his stubble scrape against my cheek. His breath is warm on my ear as he whispers, "I know the dark and confined space scares you, but try to stay calm. We just need to wait in case they're from the mafia."

I nod quickly, but wave after wave of fear is crashing over me. My mid-section is aching terribly. I bite at my bottom lip and then let my arms slip around Damian's waist. I hold on to him and bury my face under his chin.

His scent and presence envelop me, and it soothes me some.

"I've got you," he murmurs. "You're safe."

His words sink deep, chasing some of the panic away, but then I hear the drone of voices as men pass by the unit we're in. My anxiety doubles, and it has my midsection aching so badly, waves of nausea and dizziness spill over me.

Damian presses a kiss to my cheek and then another to my neck. "You're doing good, baby."

"I'm going to puke," I whisper, the pain and fear becoming too much.

We stand still and listen as the men roll the door open of the unit next to ours, and then a loud curse makes me cringe as close to Damian as I can get.

Footsteps race by our unit, and then the sounds fade fast.

"Just a little longer," Damian murmurs. "They need to think we're gone."

My legs go numb from the pain, and my body sags against Damian's. "I need to sit," I whimper, feeling terribly weak.

Just like the night before, Damian slides us to the floor and then pulls me between his legs. I curl against his chest and close my eyes, trying my best to fight the urge to cry.

His one hand starts to brush soft circles on my lower back, and it eases some of the pain in my hips. He presses more kisses to the top of my head.

Torturous long minutes tick by before he stirs. "I'm going to go check if they're gone. Stay here."

My head snaps up, and I grab at him. My hands slam into his abs, and I grip hold of his shirt. "No," I shake my head, and even though my body is an aching mess, I struggle to my knees. "Don't leave me here."

Damian hesitates for a second, and my heart stops, but then he pulls me up with him. "Can you walk?"

I nod. God, I'll do anything Damian tells me to do as long as he doesn't leave me in this box.

I can feel his eyes on me, and I wish I could see as well as he does in the dark. "Stay close to me."

"Okay," I reply as we walk to the door.

Damian slides it open, and the light from the hallway spills over us, finally allowing me to take a deep breath of relief.

Damian looks up and down the hallway and then takes the gun from behind his back. Just like that first day when

276

he came for me, he takes my hand with his left one and keeps the gun in his right hand.

"Stay behind me," he orders, and this time the words sound so different from when he first said them to me. There's nothing neutral about Damian anymore. Instead, his tone is filled with warmth and possessiveness.

I stick close to his back as we walk down the hallway, and luckily, when we reach the parking area, there is no sign of the men.

I feel a flicker of hope that we might make it.

"We have to walk up the road. I have a car waiting at a dealership."

"Walk?" I whimper, not sure I can make it much further.

Damian pulls me against his side so I can lean into him, and his arm settles firmly around my shoulders. "We can't take this car." He looks to the one we've been using. "We're leaving it all behind."

"Your house?" I ask, only now realizing what he's giving up for me.

"It was just a safe house." He starts to walk, and my numb legs move sluggishly. With every step I take, I lean more into Damian. Then, suddenly, he stops, and he takes my left arm, pulling it around his waist. His arm goes around me again as he takes more of my weight, which helps a little.

"I'd carry you, but it would only attract unwanted attention."

I can only nod, my mouth filled with thick saliva. My vision starts to blur, and I don't take in any of our surroundings anymore. I only focus on putting one foot in front of the other.

You can do this, Cara.

Just one foot in front of the other.

It feels like the longest distance I've ever walked. When we finally reach the dealership, I can't hold back the bile and quickly turn away from Damian. My body convulses, and it makes the pain blindingly sharp.

I don't know how we get to the car. With blurring sight and a spinning head, I finally get to rest my cheek on the worn upholstery of the back seat, and then I sink away into a bottomless pit of darkness.

DAMIAN

It's been a long day, and it's only early afternoon. When I stop at a drug store, I'm torn in two. Cara's asleep in the back seat, and I don't want to leave her, but I need medical supplies for her.

I'll just have to be quick.

Getting out of the car, I lock all the doors. I rush into the store and grab the strongest painkillers I can find, along with antiseptic and bandages. I also get something for fever and a large first aid kit.

Rather safe than sorry.

I'm in and out in less than ten minutes, but it feels like a year of my life has passed.

I place the stuff on the passenger seat and then open the back door by Cara's head. Placing a hand on her forehead, I feel overwhelming relief when she's cool to my touch. The last thing we need is an infection.

As I brush some hair from her face, emotion for this woman overwhelms me until it's beating strongly in my heart.

I love her.

Christ, I love her so much.

When we leave the busy town behind, I feel a ton of weight roll off my shoulders. I quickly glance to the backseat to check on Cara, then focus on the road ahead.

Now it's just us.

I have Cara all too myself.

I'll help her get through the trauma and give her the life she always dreamt of.

My woman. My love. My life.

My mind goes to the small cabin I have in Southport. I'm so fucking thankful I got a backup I.D made for Cara. With our new identities and the emergency cash, we'll be okay for a while. We'll need to get jobs, but that's a bridge we'll cross when we get to it. The cabin and peaceful atmosphere in Southport will be perfect for Cara to heal.

Every now and then, I glance over my shoulder to make sure she's still okay.

I've put her through hell today, but my girl's a fighter.

I didn't think they'd find the storage unit so fast. Thank fuck I had the other unit under Damian Weston and the one with our emergency stash under Alex Jackson. I rigged the other Weston unit to look like someone had already emptied it out and left, hoping it would throw them off our tails.

Checking the rearview mirror, I make sure we're not being followed and let out a breath of relief when the road is empty behind us.

Chapter 24

CARA

I wake up feeling like a piece of chewed gum, sticky and stretched too thin.

Pulling my face from the leather seat, I wipe the drool from the corner of my mouth. I'm hot, and my whole body's aching.

I sit up in the back and glance at our surroundings, noticing everything's green, and there's a smell of salt in the air.

"How do you feel?" Damian asks, his eyes jumping between the road and the rearview mirror.

"Yucky," I sum it all up for him.

He digs in a bag on the passenger seat and then hands me an energy drink. I take it from him, and as I swallow a couple of greedy gulps, he passes a box of painkillers to me.

"God, thank you." I get excited at the thought of not being in pain. I take two pills, swallowing them down with the rest of the energy drink.

Slumping back against the seat, I stare out the window and the pretty houses lining the street we're driving down. Here and there, someone's working in their garden.

It looks peaceful here.

"Where are we?" I ask.

"Southport," Damian says as he turns down a road. "I have a cabin here."

Here? We'll be staying here?

I feel a flutter of excitement as I say, "It's pretty."

The houses start to thin out, and after a while, it's only trees with a cabin every few miles. "Where's Southport?" I ask.

"It's in North Carolina. I think you'll like it here. It's a small town."

I still smell salt, but I can't see the ocean from where we are. "Is there a beach nearby?"

"Yeah, once you're better, I'll show you around. Everything's within walking distance."

I stare at the trees passing us by, and then Damian pulls up to a weather-beaten cabin. It makes the house we lived in look like a castle.

I push the door open and slowly get out, my midsection feeling tender as hell.

I glance around us, and the peacefulness in the air washes over me.

I hope we'll get to stay here for a while.

Damian grabs our belongings from the vehicle and takes the keys he retrieved from the storage unit out of the bag.

His eyes settle on me, and before he can reach for me, I move toward the front door. I shake the wooden handrail, testing it before I lean on it so I can climb the creaking stairs.

"It doesn't look like much, but we can fix it up and make it our own." Damian unlocks the door as my face flushes from his words. He's using words like '*we*' and '*our*.'

I follow him into a small dusty room. There's only one couch and a tiny TV. Dust particles dance in the air all around us.

It's not much, but it's perfect.

"The bedroom's through here," Damian says, and I follow him into an even smaller room. The furnishings are sparse, consisting only of a bed and closet. I watch as

Damian pulls all the bedding off, then he shakes it all out before making the bed again. "Get in."

He doesn't have to tell me twice, and I don't care what condition the bedding is in. I just want to sleep.

I crawl under the covers and find a comfortable position for my tender body.

Damian takes a bottle of water from the bag and places it on the floor, next to the bed. He leaves a box of painkillers too. "I'll check on you in a while. Get some rest."

"Thank you," I whisper as he turns to leave the room. "For everything."

Damian gives me one of his rare smiles that makes the air whoosh from my lungs, and then he leaves. He doesn't shut the door, so I can hear as he moves around the cabin.

The sound is comforting.

It's quiet out here, and I love it. No people. Nothing but us.

It's my last thought before I drift off to sleep.

The smell of food wakes me. I don't know how long I was asleep.

When I move to get up, pain starts to pulse in my abdomen, and I quickly reach for the painkillers. I down two with the water, then go look for Damian.

I find him in the kitchen where he's stirring something in a pot.

"You're cooking?"

"Yeah, just some chili. I got some fresh bread too, and some other stuff." He points to a coffee pot.

"Always my hero," I joke as I prepare a cup of much-needed coffee for myself. Taking the mug, I walk out onto the small porch, the wood creaking beneath my feet.

I glance over the nature surrounding the cabin, and when I don't see any other homes or people in the near vicinity, I feel a flutter of something close to happiness.

I hear movement inside, and glancing over my shoulder, I see Damian's stripping all the bedding off again.

When he places new bedding on the mattress, warmth trickles into my chest.

I don't deserve him.

I wish I had the energy to help him, but I'm already tired again. It feels as if something is draining every drop of strength from my body.

I finish the coffee and rinse the cup, then go to the bathroom. There's only a bath, sink and toilet. I hesitate for a second before I shut the door.

Panic rises in my chest as I stare at the door.

You can do this.

You have to.

I quickly relieve myself, flush the toilet, and rinse my hands before yanking the door open.

Damian's right on the other side, a smile tugging at his mouth. "You closed the door," he states, sounding proud of me. "That's good."

When Damian walks to the kitchen, I make my way back to the bedroom, and a grateful smile tugs at my lips as I climb under the brand-new bedding.

Letting out a sigh, I close my eyes, and soon I fall asleep to the sounds of Damian moving around the cabin.

DAMIAN

When the chili is ready, I scoop some into a bowl for myself. Cara's still asleep, and there's no way I'm waking her. She needs as much rest as possible. She can eat when she wakes up.

I take my bowl and a bottle of water and go sit on the old beaten-up couch. I have a clear view of Cara, and my eyes never leave her as I enjoy the food.

Once Cara's better, we'll need to talk. The thought of going to South Africa and killing that good-for-nothing uncle of hers has been playing on my mind. I need to put an end to them hunting her before we can build a future together.

The day I got Cara from that container, I never thought we'd end up like this.

God, I never thought there'd be a woman out there who would make me give it all up. Even if there can never be a relationship between us, just having her with me will be enough.

When midnight comes, and it's clear Cara won't be waking up, I quickly bathe. I hate bathing. I need to install a shower.

I pull on a pair of sweatpants and then slip into bed next to Cara. She's lying on her side, with her back facing me. I stare at her silhouette for a few minutes before I move closer to her. I make sure not to jar her as I push my arm under my head, and then I slowly pull her against me.

It feels like I've only been asleep for a couple of seconds when movement wakes me. I open my eyes and see Cara's sitting on the edge of the bed.

As she gets up, I notice she seems sluggish, and her body veers to the left, bumping into the wall.

I quickly get up from the bed, and when I get to her, I notice the tears on her cheeks.

"Sorry," she whispers, "I didn't mean to wake you. I just wanted to get some water."

I take hold of her arm. "Get back in bed. I'll get the water."

I make sure she's sitting down again before I walk to the kitchen. I grab two bottles of water, and when I walk back into the bedroom, she's struggling to open the box of painkillers.

"Here." I open one of the waters, and handing it to her, I take the box of pills. I quickly remove two and give them to her. Her hands are trembling, and it makes me worry. "Is the pain bad?"

She shakes her head and then swallows the medication down. I take the bottle from her and place it on the floor as she gingerly lies back down. Tears keep sneaking out of her eyes.

"Cara, how bad is it?" I ask as I look down at her.

"The pills will take the pain away in a couple of seconds," she whispers, still not telling me how much pain she's in.

Worry seizes my chest, and I quickly switch on the light. "We're up. I might as well change the bandage." I just want to see the wound for myself. She might have an infection, and her stubborn ass won't tell me.

I get the first aid kit, and when I push her shirt up, she doesn't even open her eyes. I slip my arm beneath her shoulders and lift her gently until she's leaning against my chest. I undo the bandage around her waist and toss it to the side, then ease her back onto the mattress.

Removing a couple of wipes from the packaging, I gently clean the wound while inspecting it. It doesn't look infected, and it makes me breathe a little easier.

When I throw the wipe to the side, Cara mumbles sleepily, "That felt nice."

The corner of my mouth tugs up, and I take out another wipe. Then, repeating the process, I watch as the pain eases from her face.

When I go out tomorrow to get supplies for the shower, I'll check where the doctor is. It's been eight days since the surgery, and the clips should be coming out soon.

I'm glad I got the new bandages with some tape. I cover the clips and then stare down at Cara.

Christ, she really trusts me.

The thought shudders through me as I realize Cara fell asleep with her shirt bunched up. She's trusting me not to take advantage of her.

Fuck, that's huge.

I wonder if she even realizes it.

I throw the used bandage and wipes away and then switch off all the lights. When I lie down beside her again, I can't fall asleep.

Instead, I spend the early morning hours taking in every beautiful inch of the woman who's laid claim to my heart.

Chapter 25

CARA

I wake up to find the sun streaming into the room. Sitting up slowly, careful not to aggravate the wound, I have to admit, the pain isn't as bad as it was last night.

I remember how Damian took care of me and how gentle he was. Emotion wells in my heart, and whether I like it or not, I realize I feel more for Damian than just friendship.

Not ready to face my feelings, I climb out of bed and walk to the bathroom, where I find Damian measuring the wall.

"Hey."

His head snaps to me, then back to the wall. He makes a mark on the plaster and then steps out of the bath. His eyes capture mine, and it looks like he's searching for something. "How do you feel?"

Confused as hell.

Miserable.

Damian's fingers brush over my jaw, and he nudges my face up so I'll look at him. "I'm here. Any time you want to talk. I'm here."

I nod and then let my eyes go to the mark he made on the wall. "What are you doing?"

He glances at all the tools lying in the bath. "I need a shower, so I'm installing one. I'll let you have the bathroom before I get to work."

"Thanks." I watch him leave and then shut the door.

I stare at it, and like clockwork, the familiar panic starts to tighten my chest.

I keep my eyes on the door as I quickly relieve myself. When I rinse my hands, I avoid looking in the mirror, not wanting to see the empty shell staring back at me.

After I'm done, I go straight back to bed and pull the covers over my head so it will block out the light.

I don't fall asleep again.

Instead, my growing feelings for Damian keep me wide awake.

Is it possible to love someone but not want to be physical with them?

Can a relationship like that even work?

DAMIAN

When I'm done with the shower, I test it to make sure there are no leaks. I got a white curtain with an imprint of a gray thistle. I hope Cara likes it.

I check the time, and when I notice it's almost afternoon, I decide to warm some chili for her. I butter one of the rolls and then carry the food to the bedroom.

I find her totally under the covers.

"Cara," I say, but she doesn't move. "It's time to eat."

She throws the cover back and slowly pulls herself into a sitting position. "I'm not hungry." Her voice sounds empty, and it chips away at my heart.

I hold the food out to her. "You can't live off painkillers." I know she's in a shitty place, but I won't stand by and watch as she starves herself.

Cara takes the bowl and roll from me, and I watch as she takes a bite before I go to the window to open it so we can get some fresh air in the room.

"I made an appointment for you with the local doctor."

Her head snaps up, her eyes widening. "Why?"

I frown and cross my arms over my chest. "To have the clips removed and the wound checked out."

"Oh." She takes a small bite of the bread roll and takes forever to chew it. I watch her take two more bites of chili before she puts the bowl on the side of the bed. "I can't have more."

She lies back down and pulls the blanket over her head again.

This is not good.

Worry claws at my insides as I take the half-eaten food to the kitchen.

Fuck, Cara's not coping at all.

I can't let her sink into depression.

I stalk up and down, and then it feels as if my blood explodes in my veins.

I have to do something… anything.

I walk back to the room and pull the covers away from her. Pushing my arms beneath Cara, I lift her to my chest.

"Damian?" She startles, but then she quickly wraps her arms around my neck.

I stalk to the bathroom and put her down in the tub. When I open the faucets, Cara gasps as the cold water hits her.

She struggles to her feet and then glares at me. I can see she wants to get angry, but there's just not enough spark.

"I'm not just going to stand by and watch you slip into depression," I warn her. "Clean yourself."

Christ, please let this work. Don't let me fuck things up even more.

I just need her to feel again. Even if it's anger.

I yank the shower curtain closed and then settle with my back against the opposite wall, sending up a prayer that this will work.

Her silhouette doesn't move for a good few seconds, and I worry I won't get through to her. I have to stop this slippery slope she's on before she falls too far, and there's no getting her back.

Finally, I hear a sob, and then she sinks down in the bath.

I close my eyes as her heartbreaking sobs rip my heart to shreds until I can't stand it anymore. Yanking the curtain open again, I crouch down next to the tub and then reach for the plug. I put it in and change the function from shower to bath.

As the water starts to fill the tub, I pull Cara up. "Come on, baby." She doesn't stop me as I begin to undress her. I first pull her shirt over her head and then help her step out of her sweatpants, dropping the soaked fabric to the floor.

I don't put in a lot of water, not wanting her wound to get wet. I peel the bandage off and then reach for the loofah and squirt some body wash onto it.

For a moment, I hesitate, but seeing the heartbreaking tears sneaking over Cara's cheeks, I start to wash her shoulders and arms.

She keeps her eyes trained on the wall behind me as I wash her whole body, except for her breasts, ass, and between her legs.

I've already crossed enough lines for today.

I'm careful around the clips and then gently rinse her body off.

"Lie back," I whisper.

Cara listens, and taking hold of either side of the bath, she slides down.

I'm unable to stop my gaze from drifting over her body, drinking in the breathtaking sight of her breasts and pussy.

Christ.

I harden at the speed of fucking light, my cock twitching with need. My mouth waters at the thought of sucking her pale pink nipples between my lips and thrusting my tongue inside her pussy.

Christ, get a grip of yourself!

Doing my best to suppress the desire, I quickly wet her hair and then squirt some shampoo into my hand. I wash her ginger strands before rinsing the suds out.

When I'm done, I take hold of her shoulders, her wet skin making my fingers tingle and my cock harden even more until it throbs painfully.

I pull the plug and then grab a towel. "Get out," I whisper.

Cara steps out of the bath, and as she moves into the towel I'm holding open, she looks down at the floor. I wrap the fabric around her body. Grabbing another towel, I dry her hair, and when I glance down, the desolate look on her face takes another swing at my heart.

Unable to stop myself, I wrap my arms around her and hold her tightly to my chest. "It's going to be okay, baby. You'll get through this," I say, trying to give her some kind of encouragement.

"You know what sucks?" she whispers, her tone hollow.

"What?"

She presses herself closer to me and then whispers, "It's not being stuck in the darkest hole while the rest of the world is standing in the sun. It's not feeling the cruel bite of loneliness while being surrounded by people. It's not being so exhausted that no amount of sleep helps." Her voice cracks, but she forces the words out, "It's like a cancer eating away at my soul. It's devouring every sliver of light. I can't, Damian. I have nothing left to fight with."

My arms tighten around her. "You have me. Let me help carry the weight. Just don't give up on me."

Her body jerks, and then she presses her face against my shirt, and she breaks in my arms.

"I've got you, baby," I murmur as I press a kiss to her wet hair. "Just lean on me. I'll get you through this."

CARA

The doctor is old, and his touch is gentle as he removes the clips.

"It's healing nicely, Mrs. Jackson. Just keep cleaning it for a while longer. Come see me if it starts to itch or turns tender and red," the doctor says.

"Okay," I whisper as I sit up, pulling my shirt down. "Thank you." I give him an awkward smile and then leave the room.

When I walk into the tiny reception, Damian immediately rises to his feet. "Thank you," he says to the receptionist, and then he takes hold of my hand, linking our fingers.

"Enjoy your day, Mr. and Mrs. Jackson," the receptionist calls out cheerfully.

I'm now using the identity of Nina Jackson while Damian's Alex Jackson. Once again, we're married.

"It feels weird being called Mrs. Jackson," I say as we climb into the car.

Damian steers the vehicle onto the main road before he says, "We need to practice the new names. We don't want to slip up in public. So you have to call me Alex, and I'll call you Nina."

"So we're married... again?" I can't help but ask.

"Yeah." His eyes flit to mine before he continues, "I thought it would be safer to just make us a married couple."

"Oh." I slump back against the seat, not sure how I feel about it. "So ... do we have a real marriage certificate?"

"As real as our I.D. cards," he says. I'm surprised when he doesn't turn back onto the road that leads to the cabin but instead drives past it.

I let the subject of our fake marriage go and ask, "Where are we going?"

"I want to show you something."

Silence fills the cab until Damian pulls the car into an empty parking area. He gets out, walks around the car, and opens my door. "Come on."

Again he takes my hand and links our fingers, and then he tugs me toward a stairway carved out of a rock. Reaching a stretch of beach, waves lazily roll to shore, and the sight makes some of the tension leave my body.

"It's so beautiful," I murmur. "And peaceful."

"I thought you'd like it," Damian says, and then he pulls me closer to the water. Crouching in front of me, he slips my shoes off and rolls my pants up to my knees before he does the same with his own.

When we step into the cold water, I give him a look, silently asking what now?

He turns his gaze to the horizon. "I know you feel lost in an ocean of pain, but just for a minute, I want you to focus on what I say."

I feel uncomfortable with the direction the conversation is heading in, so I glance at the ocean as well.

"Do you feel the cold water lapping at your legs?"

I frown but answer anyway, "Yeah?"

"That means you have legs to be grateful for. You can walk."

Emotion trickles into my heart as I brush some hair from my face.

"Do you feel that breeze?"

"Yes," I whisper.

"Do you feel the sun on your face?"

I pull my hand free from his as the word drifts over my lips, "Yes."

"Do you see the blue of the ocean?"

It becomes too much, and I turn around to walk back to the car, but then Damian says, "There are hundreds of people who would've given anything to see it one last time. There are many who would've done anything to take just one more step."

I swing back to him. "Why are you doing this?"

Damian steps right up to me, and his eyes are blazing with emotion. "You're alive. Fuck, Cara. Your heart is beating. You still get to see all this beauty. You get to feel that breeze. You get to walk." He wipes a hand over his face, then says, "You're alive. There are so many who die young. So many lose so much, but they don't give up. They fucking live every day to the fullest. Cara…" He sucks in a deep breath, his features tense. "You're given one fucking life, and it might have been a fucked up one so far, but you get to decide how it will end. Are you going to let a bunch of fuckers ruin your entire life, or are you going to fight back and take control of what's left?"

My throat feels thick, and I swallow hard on the threatening tears.

I know he's right, but…

"I don't know how," I whisper.

"That's why I brought you here. All you have to do is look at the ocean and see the blue. Feel the breeze and cold water on your skin. For today…" His eyes are stormy with emotions, and I'm scared if I stare any longer, I'll get caught up in them. "Just do that. Nothing more. Just feel, Cara."

I walk back into the water and focus on the cold waves splashing around my legs. I feel the breeze play in my hair, and I look out across the ocean, taking note of all the shades of blue.

I am grateful to be alive, and I'm so thankful I have Damian. I just wish I could shake this heaviness that keeps weighing me down.

Chapter 26

DAMIAN

It's been two weeks, and every day I take Cara outside and make her list something she sees, feels, and one of her body functions she's grateful for. It's a long process, but I'm seeing the difference it's making in her.

I'm going to fucking win if it's the last thing I do. I won't lose her to depression. Not after everything she's survived.

Cara comes out onto the porch, and I glance up at her. "You ready for our walk?"

She doesn't look at me as she nods. "Let's go."

When we head down the stairs, I notice she has more energy. She hasn't been taking any painkillers for the past couple of days, and she's eating more. It's making my worry ease a little.

I catch up to Cara, and before I can say anything, she says, "I saw something yesterday. It's this way."

I follow her deeper into the trees, and we walk for a while in silence before she points to something. "Over there."

I follow her until she stops and crouches down. There's a bunch of dandelions. She plucks one and then blows on it, making the tiny seeds waft into the air, and then she fucking grins up at me, and the sight makes me almost cry with relief.

That's my girl. I knew you could do it.

Cara plucks a few more and then hands me one. "Make a wish when you blow on it."

I watch her blow two more before she gives me an expectant look.

I wish you'll fully heal and learn to love me back. I just want to make you happy, baby.

I hold it in front of my mouth and slowly blow at the seeds. Watching as they float away, I pray the wish will come true.

Cara gives me a pleased smile, and then she takes the stem from between my fingers, tucking all four into her pocket.

Today was a huge win. Cara made a choice and did something she wanted to do.

"Thank you," I murmur as we begin to walk back to the cabin.

Cara nods, glancing up at the sunrays filtering through the treetops. "I'm sorry things have been so difficult."

I wrap an arm around her shoulders and tug her to my side. "You've been through hell. It's expected. I'm just glad you're fighting back."

Cara turns her gaze to me, a soft smile curing her lips. "Just following your lead."

CARA

At first, going on walks with Damian took all the strength I had, but not anymore. Now I enjoy them.

It's been two months since we moved to Southport. Gosh, it feels like years have passed since I lost my baby and Annie, but at the same time, it feels like it all happened yesterday.

I want to reach out to Annie, but I'm scared it will put her in danger, and that's the only reason I haven't tried to contact her.

It's not so dark anymore… in my mind. There are moments when I'm actually happy.

I still don't understand why all these bad things keep happening to me, but I hope life will take a break from shitting on me.

Damian and I have fallen into a routine where we take turns cooking. Every day he's busy around the cabin, slowly making it home.

Our home.

Standing in the kitchen, I open one of the cupboards and take out a cup to make myself some coffee. As I close the cupboard and place the cup on the counter, the door suddenly comes loose. Letting out a startled shriek, I try to catch it, and the corner of the door slams into my hand. I cry out from the bite of pain, and then the door falls to the floor, taking the cup with it. Ceramic shards shatter around my bare feet just as Damian rushes into the kitchen.

"Don't move," he says, and stalking over to me, he effortlessly picks me up and carries me out of the kitchen. Only when we're in the living room does he place me back on my feet.

I watch as he walks back into the kitchen to clean up the shattered pieces of the cup. He takes hold of the door and inspecting it, he mutters, "It needs new hinges. Damn thing stripped right off. I'll get some and then check all the doors."

Damian places the door on the counter and then walks back to where I'm still standing. "Are you okay?"

"Yeah." I look down at my right hand. "It slammed into my hand, but I'm okay."

He takes my hand in both of his and inspects every inch of it. There's a small blue bruise where the corner hit, and he brushes his thumb lightly over the tender spot before pressing a kiss to it.

My eyebrows lift slightly as my stomach flutters.

Lifting his gaze to mine, our eyes lock, and it only makes the fluttering increase until I slap my hand over my stomach.

Scared of what it might mean, I pull my hand from his. "I'm just going to mop the floor to make sure there are no pieces we'll accidentally step on."

Rushing away from Damian and how he makes me feel, I keep myself busy, cleaning the cabin from top to bottom.

Damian got us the necessities, and I'm thankful a washing machine was one of those things. He also put up a washing line in the back where I can hang our clothes to dry.

I usually do the laundry on Sunday mornings. The first few times, I quickly realized there was no underwear for Damian. He goes commando, and the thought only makes me more aware of him as a man.

It's not Sunday, but I do the laundry, adding the towels, so the machine is full. Then, I keep busy outside, working on the small garden I'm trying to make until it's time to hang the clothes.

Anything not to face the fact that I'm falling in love with my protector.

After I'm done with everything, I glance over my shoulder at the little piece of ground I've managed to clear of weeds when I walk right into Damian. I bounce back. "Sorry."

"I'm just going to the hardware to get some supplies. Do you need anything?"

You.

The word vibrates through me, and like a deaf-mute, I can only shake my head. The second he leaves, I slap my hand over my mouth.

Oh. My. God.

Yes, Damian's attractive and any woman's dream come true... but I'm not ready. It's only been eight months.

I don't understand where the attraction is coming from, because how can I want something I fear?

I'm not afraid of Damian, not at all. I'm scared of intimacy. I've been ruined when it comes to that part of life. The thought of ever having sex again makes me spiral into a panicked mess.

There's no way I'm ready to even deal with what was done to me, never mind thinking of ever being intimate with a man again.

I brush a trembling hand through my hair, feeling hot and cold all at once. Taking a couple of deep breaths, I calm my racing heart.

Is it possible because it's Damian?

I know I'm safe with him, and he's done nothing but take care of me. He's attractive and strong, and… perfect.

He's the kind of man I used to dream about before everything happened.

I understand why I'm falling for him, but having sex? Shaking my head, I head into the house and grab clean clothes from the closet.

I stare at Damian's clothes next to mine, and then I glance at the bed we share every night.

God. We're already living like a married couple.

The thought doesn't send me into a state of horror-stricken panic, and it makes me frown.

When did things change?

Stunned by the revelation, I walk to the bathroom so I can wash the sweat off from all the gardening and cleaning I did.

I shut the bathroom door behind me and begin to strip out of the clothes. The panic I feel when I shut the door has also lessened with time, and now I just feel a twinge.

The corner of my mouth lifts as I realize how much I've healed without even noticing. Hope explodes in my chest, and I let out a burst of thankful laughter, my body trembling as positive emotions wash over me.

God. Thank you.

Knowing things won't always be dark makes excitement for what the future might hold trickle through me.

"Slowly but surely, I'll get there," I whisper. "All because of Damian never giving up on me."

My heart fills until it feels as if it might burst because without Damian, I wouldn't be here. I wouldn't have survived.

It's okay to love him.

My eyes drift shut as I finally stop fighting my feelings, accepting it's a good thing. It's safe.

For the first time since the container, I don't feel completely broken, and the dead weight that's been wearing me thin lifts a little.

I can't stop smiling as I open the faucets, and then I step under the water and let it wash over me. I feel free from the constraints that have been suffocating all the joy out of my life.

Picking up the loofah, I squirt some body wash onto it and work it into a lather.

But… what about the physical part of a relationship?

I quickly shake my head, not wanting to sour my happiness.

Don't think about it.

One step at a time.

I start to wash my body, and when I clean between my legs, my body jerks from how sensitive it feels.

My eyebrows dart up as I freeze, waiting for the demons to creep from the cracks.

Instead, an image of Damian shirtless as he hammers nails into the porch flashes through my mind.

My eyebrows lift even higher when there's a flush of heat in my abdomen.

God, I can't remember the last time I masturbated, and as the thought crosses my mind, I feel unsure of what to do.

I stand still as the water pours over me, and then I allow myself to recall the sweat glistening on Damian's golden skin, his muscles straining as he works.

A needy moan drifts over my lips, and then I close my eyes, losing myself in how manly and attractive Damian is.

My stomach flutters and my abdomen tightens.

His eyes.

The curve of his lips when he gives me a crooked smile.

The strength in his body.

The gentleness in his touch.

Slowly I start to move the loofah between my legs, and again my body jerks, the friction sending pleasure instead of fear through me. A gasp bursts from me, and pressing my other hand to the tiles, I imagine Damian's arms around me.

There's a trickle of fear, and I breathe through it, focusing harder.

I remember the predatory heat in his eyes when he saw me naked, and instead of taking what he wanted, he buried his own need and focused on mine.

I love him. It's okay.

My hand begins to move, brushing the loofah against my sensitive skin, and it makes pleasure tighten my abdomen.

I've given myself an orgasm before, but this time it's different. The other times the guy was always faceless. But this time, it's Damian, I see.

I imagine his muscled body brushing against mine. I feel his fingers trail over my jaw. I feel his mouth on my skin.

I start to rub the loofah faster, and as I picture his mouth curving into a hot grin, my legs tremble as the orgasm tears through me. The intense pleasure spasms through my body, my breaths bursting over my parted lips.

The instant the last tendrils of ecstasy drift away, my mind clears.

For a moment, I try to process how I feel, but when dark thoughts skirt around the edges of my mind, I turn off the faucet and quickly dry myself. I pull on the clean clothes, and avoiding the mirror, I rush out of the bathroom.

Don't think about it.

Chasing all thoughts of love, sex, and the trauma from my mind, I rush out of the cabin and head toward the ocean.

I force myself to see the green of the leaves, the brown of the bark, and the blue of the sky. I listen to the sound of the ocean, and when I reach the stretch of beach, I kick off my shoes and walk into the water.

Focus on the good.

Just like Damian taught you.

Focus only on the good.

Chapter 27

DAMIAN

Cara's been weird around me the past couple of weeks. She hardly makes eye contact and almost seems shy, which I don't understand.

I walk out onto the porch and search the surrounding area. She went for a walk quite a while ago, and I'm worried that she's not back yet. With the sun setting, I start to walk in the direction I saw her head in.

After a while, the trees begin to thin out, and about ten minutes later, I reach the beach.

I scan the stretch of sand until I see her lone figure, sitting with her knees drawn up against her chest.

I slowly make my way over to where she's staring out over the ocean, and then I hear a sigh escape her lips.

She gets up, dusts some sand from her ass, and then turns around. When her eyes fall on me, they widen before she lowers them to the sand.

I walk right up to her, and taking hold of her chin, I lift her face to mine. I wait for her eyes to meet mine before I ask, "What's going on?"

She pulls her chin from my fingers and looks back out over the ocean. "Remember you told me not to ask you questions unless you were prepared to hear the truth?"

"Yeah," I reply, my eyes searching her face. She's been doing so well, and I don't want a relapse.

"The same counts for you, Damian. Don't ask me something unless you're sure you can handle the truth."

Cara starts to walk away, but I grab hold of her hand, tugging her back to me. "What's that supposed to mean? You can't tell me why you're acting so weird around me?"

She looks at our joined hands, and then her eyes slowly drift up the length of my body until they lock with mine. She clears her throat and then squares her shoulders, raising her chin an inch. "I'll make you a deal, Damian. I'll answer your question if you answer one of mine."

I look for any sign of what might be going on in that head of hers, but not finding any answers, I murmur, "Deal."

Cara nods and takes a step closer to me. She looks up at me, her eyes drifting over my face. "I'm confused about us."

Her tongue darts out, nervously wetting her lips, and then she lowers her eyes to my chest. "I… I feel something for you, and I don't know what to do with it. I'm scared to death of where it might lead. I don't understand how I can feel attracted to you after what happened. Any other man …" she shakes her head slowly, shutting her eyes tightly, "I'm repulsed by the thought of any other man. I hate them with this burning rage that keeps flowing through me like lava. I just…" she lowers her head as if in defeat. "I'm just trying to process my feelings."

Her shoulders slump, and I watch as she sucks in a deep breath. Whatever's happening between us is scaring the living hell out of Cara.

Sucking in a deep breath of air, I take a step closer to her, and wrapping my arms around her, I pull her to my chest.

Cara tenses and tries to pull back, mumbling, "Don't feel sorry for me."

I tug her back against my chest and lock my arms around her. Lowering my head, I press a kiss to her temple and then another above her ear.

My lips brush against her skin. "I'm not sure what's happening between us, and I understand you're scared, but

318

you're safe with me. I'll never do anything to hurt you or expect more than you're willing to give."

I pull back slightly, and lifting my hand, I brush some strands of hair away from her cheek. Cara's eyes dart up to my face, then away to the ocean, before coming back to mine.

Slowly the atmosphere between us begins to change, and soon anticipation builds between us.

The corner of my mouth lifts as I admit, "You're fucking gorgeous, Cara. Any man with warm blood pumping through his veins would be crazy not to want you." I see fear creep into her eyes at the mention of other men. "Maybe you're okay with me because I was the one who helped you, and if that's the case, we'll just let the feelings pass. Being grateful is not a reason to want someone, and we'd be stupid to act on it."

She turns her face away from me, a hurt expression tightening her features.

Fuck, she thinks I'm rejecting her.

"If you really feel something for me, then only time will tell," I continue. "We'll take it slow."

Cara nods, still looking dejected. I brush my fingers over the curve of her cheek, and her eyes jump to mine.

There's a world of pain shimmering from them as she says, "I'll understand if you don't want me." She pauses, taking a shuddering breath. "I mean... it's okay. I just wanted to tell you how I feel."

"Why would you think I don't want you?" I move closer until our bodies brush against each other. I watch her cheeks grow pink, and it stirs something inside of me.

"Because of what happened," she whispers. "Because a man like you wouldn't want something that's been used."

A hot flare of anger surges through me.

Fuck.

I tilt my head, my eyes narrowing on her. "That's what you've been thinking?"

"It's okay," she says, trying to take a step away from me.

I frame her face with my hands so she can't look away, and I press my forehead to hers. "Don't think that. You're not used, baby." I pull slightly back and lock eyes with her. "Don't let them make you feel worthless because, to me, you're fucking priceless."

Cara's fucking beautiful as her eyes light up, and a slow smile begins to tug at her lips. "You think I'm priceless?"

"I risked my life twice for you, Cara. I'll keep risking my life until I die if it means I can keep you safe because to me, you're everything good in my life."

Cara brings her hands to my chest and slides them up to my shoulders. Then, cautiously, she lifts herself to the tip of her toes and presses a soft kiss to my lips.

For a moment, I keep still, not wanting to do anything that will spook her. Her lips are soft and full against mine, tentatively moving as if she's asking if this is okay.

My heart swells impossibly for this woman, and unable to hold back, I wrap a hand around the back of her neck and brush my tongue over the seam of her lips.

Cara instantly opens for me, and when I taste her for the first time, everything around us fades to background noise.

Holy fuck.

She's fucking intoxicating. My tongue explores her mouth, and when the hunger inside my chest keeps growing, my teeth tug at her bottom lip.

Slow down.

I manage to pull back a little, so I can see her eyes, and when I don't see any fear in them, I ask, "You okay?"

As she nods, my hold on her tightens, and then I claim her the only way I know how. I fucking devour her, and it doesn't take long for our breaths to grow ragged.

I brand every part of her mouth, and it creates a wildfire in my chest when she kisses me back with the same passion.

Christ, baby.

Cara's body melts against mine, and her fingers weave into my hair at the nape of my neck. Then a soft moan drifts into my mouth, and I fucking breathe it in as if it's my last breath.

When she moans again, I know I'm reaching my limits, and breaking the kiss, I pull back, putting a safe distance between us.

With swollen lips and eyes filled with desire, Cara looks like a fucking wet dream.

I suck in a deep breath and take another step away from her.

"I'm okay with more," she says, taking a step toward me.

I shake my head hard. "I'm not."

Worry tightens her beautiful face, and then hurt flickers in her eyes.

Needing to explain, so she won't misunderstand, I say, "Once I claim you, there's no way I'll ever let you go, and I won't settle for just a kiss."

I expect to see fear, but instead, heat flares in her eyes, and it almost makes me take her right here in the open.

Christ, give me strength so I don't lose control over the situation.

CARA

I'm having a sensory overload. I can still taste Damian. Kissing him was unlike anything I've ever experienced before.

Hot. Intense. Empowering.

God was it empowering.

I take a step closer to him, but then he takes one backward... away from me. He shakes his head again, and it confuses me because I can see the desire in his eyes.

Am I reading him wrong?

"Not now," he grumbles. "I'm struggling with my control."

My lips curve up, knowing I'm responsible for his iron-clad control slipping.

Damian stares at me, and when his eyes lower to my smile, he lets out a groan, and then he moves fast.

His body slams into mine, and his fingers wrap around the back of my neck, his thumbs keeping my jaw in place so I can't move.

When his mouth takes mine, I can't keep the moan from slipping over my lips. The kiss is hot and heavy, filled with feelings I didn't even know I had for him.

Yes, there was love, but now there's actual desire... for him.. for Damian.

And it still feels safe.

Just as quickly as Damian grabbed hold of me, he pulls back again, but this time, he presses his forehead to mine. His voice is low and deep as he says, "I want you so fucking bad, Cara, but we can't."

Only then do I feel his hard-on pressing against my stomach, and it makes a sliver of fear ripple through me.

Damian instantly picks up on it. "See, you're not ready." He pulls his body away from mine, letting go of me. "You still have so much healing to do. The day we fuck, you have to want it as much as I do."

Frustration washes over me, dousing the heat flowing through my veins.

I want Damian.

I really do.

He's all man, hard and rough, and those eyes – they've seen all my horrors and not once has he looked at me like I'm less... like I'm broken.

I want Damian.

I let my eyes caress his face, taking in the rugged beauty of the man in front of me.

But... I'm not sure my want for him is stronger than my fear of being intimate again.

Clearing his throat, he wipes the pad of his thumb over his bottom lip, then asks, "You had a question?"

I clear my throat, as well, then tuck as a strand of hair behind my ear. "Yeah, I did."

We start to walk back to the cabin, and I'm highly aware of every step Damian takes.

For a moment, my thoughts turn back to the kiss, and my cheeks heat up from how intense it was.

I liked it.

I really did.

It was perfect as far as kisses go.

"What did you want to ask?" Damian breaks through my thoughts.

Right. Focus, Cara.

"I was wondering, since you're Alex Jackson now, is Damian Weston your real name or just another alias?"

He doesn't answer me immediately, and only when we're halfway to the cabin does he say, "After Leah died, and I killed my father, I had to disappear. Jeff is retired FBI and Leah's father. I did him a favor by taking out my dad, so he did me one by getting me a new identity. The only reason I've been able to get away with my job as a cleaner is because of Jeff. He covers our tracks. It's weird because he didn't like the fact that Leah and I were dating. He didn't trust me one bit. But after she died and I killed my father, he stepped right in to help me." Damian pauses, and when he looks at me, he murmurs, "My name is Sam Rees."

Sam Rees.

Such a normal name for such an extraordinary man.

I reach my hand out to him. "Hi, Sam."

He takes my hand and smiles as he says, "Hi, Cara."

Chapter 28

DAMIAN

Since our kiss on the beach, it's been getting harder with every passing day to keep my hands off Cara.

I've been waking up with a raging hard-on every morning, and just like every other day, I grab clean clothes and go to the shower.

The first couple of times, I felt guilty for picturing Cara while I jerked off, but not anymore. I open the faucets, strip the sweatpants from my body, and step under the warm spray.

I grip my cock hard and bring up the image of Cara's breasts and pussy that's been fucking engraved in my mind ever since I bathed her.

As I imagine taking bites of her soft skin, my fingers tighten around my thick shaft. My pumps grow faster, and I place a hand against the tiles, swallowing the groan building in my chest.

I watch as my cock thrusts through my fingers and picture Cara's mouth taking me, her wide green eyes staring up at me as I slam against the back of her throat.

Christ.

The image changes to her pussy wrapping tightly around my cock as I sink balls deep into her, her lips parting on a cry of ecstasy.

Fuck. Take all of me, baby. Jesus, I'm going to explode.

My breaths rush from my heaving chest, and then my teeth sink into my bottom lip as I hammer into my fist, thinking how I'm taking Cara hard and fast, making her pussy mine.

Motherfucker.

The orgasm hits hard, ripping a growl from me as I come against the tiles in spurts of ecstasy.

As I come down from the high that the mere thought of Cara took me to, I let out a soft chuckle.

I didn't even last five fucking minutes. Taking a deep breath, I reach for the body wash.

Knowing Cara needs time, I'll just have to suck it up until she's ready for a relationship.

Yeah, it will be me and my right hand until she's ready.

When I come out of the bathroom, I hear Cara in the kitchen. Her sexy ass looks fucking amazing in the pair of leggings she's wearing.

The sight makes my cock stir as if I didn't just jerk off, and I keep a safe distance from her.

"I advertised in the local newspaper," I say, my voice hoarse with unadulterated lust. I clear my throat before I continue, "I need to keep busy, so I'm going to do odd jobs. Repairs."

Cara takes a sip of coffee and then smiles at me from over the rim of the cup. "Always the fixer."

"Yeah." I force a smile to my face. "I have a job today. I don't know how long I'll be."

She places the cup on the counter and walks closer to me, making my muscles tighten. "Does that mean I can go look for a job too?"

"Sure," I say, and my voice goes hoarse again as she moves into my personal space. "Just remember to go by your new name, Nina Jackson. If we're going into town more, we'll have to start calling each other Alex and Nina."

"Sure, Alex," she says, a sexy smile playing around the curve of her lips, which makes me stare at her mouth for a moment too long. "Are you leaving now?"

How's it possible that this woman has reduced me to a walking hard-on?

"I am." I take a step away from her. "I've made an extra set of keys for you. If you do decide to go somewhere, just lock the door."

I begin to walk toward the front door, but then remember the phone I got her. Turning back, I head to the kitchen and open the cupboard that's become a little storage space for my tools. I take the cheap phone out and hand it to Cara. "Same thing as before. Use it only to phone me. Don't give the number out to anyone."

"But..." She takes the phone from me, and our fingers brush, sending electric pulses straight to my cock that's once again ready for action. "What if I need to give a number to an employer?"

"Shit, you're right. Just don't go giving it to everyone."

She glares at me, and it makes her look cute. "I'm not stupid, Mr. Jackson. Go to work." She starts to walk toward the bedroom but then stops and turns back to me. "It has your number on it, right?"

"Yeah." I can't keep from staring at her. "Call if you need anything."

She smiles and nods. "Great, thanks." She walks into the bedroom and then calls out, "Have a nice day, hubby."

A grin forms around my lips as I head out the front door.

———————————

CARA

After Damian leaves, I quickly shower and get ready to head out myself. I'll go crazy if I have to sit around doing nothing all day. I need something to keep myself busy.

When I'm ready, I make sure all the appliances are off, and all the windows are closed. I lock up behind me and then walk in the direction of town.

I love Southport. The fresh ocean air is calming.

My thoughts turn back to this morning when I walked past the bathroom on my way to make some coffee, and I could swear I heard Damian growl.

Did he..."

Nah?

But it sounded like he was orgasming.

Just the thought of his strong hand stroking himself makes my body grow hot and bothered, but there's a pang of sadness at the same time.

I might've masturbated to the image of him, but I don't know if I'll be able to have actual sex with him.

We haven't talked about us or what we are since the kiss. We also haven't kissed again.

Damian's actually more careful around me, not touching me unless he has to – which sucks. It feels like we've taken a step backward instead of forward.

Maybe I scared him off?

When I reach the town, I shove the thoughts of Damian and me to the back of my mind and glance up the main road.

Here goes nothing.

I try Pete's Place first, the local diner, but there are no vacancies.

This is going to be harder than I thought.

When I try the supermarket, the cashier there tells me to try the hardware.

I cross the road and walk into the small hardware store. It's hot and stuffy inside as I head to the dark wooden counter. There's a bell on top, and I hesitate to ring it. I tap it quickly, and the soft ping makes me cringe.

"Back here," a man calls from one of the aisles.

I walk closer and stop when I see a middle-aged man sitting on a crate. He's busy stocking the shelves.

"Hi... uhm." I clear my throat. "I was wondering if you have any jobs available... for me? I mean, I'm looking for any kind of work."

The man rises to his feet and looks me up and down. I take a step back just to be safe. Not that he looks threatening, but seeing as I'm a piss-poor judge of character, I'm not taking any chances.

"I have an opening, but not for someone like you," he says rudely.

I lift an eyebrow and cross my arms over my chest. "Someone like me?"

"Yeah." He waves a hand at me. "You're too small. I need someone with muscle. You'll have to carry heavy boxes, stock the shelves, sign for stock as it's delivered, and carry it to the storeroom. You're too small."

In other words, I'm a woman.

My mouth drops open in surprise that he's discriminating against me.

Is this man from the middle-ages?

"I'm strong," I argue. "I'm a hard worker, too. What would you rather have, some guy who hasn't worked an honest day in his life or a woman who doesn't have a lazy bone in her body?"

The man stares at me, and it looks like my smart mouth just lost me any chance of getting the job.

Shit, you should've kept your mouth shut, Cara.

I turn around to walk away when he says, "Fine, I'll give you a week. The pay's not great, but it will take care of the bread and milk. There are no benefits. You work from eight a.m. until five p.m., and you get an hour's lunch."

He points to the box he was busy unpacking. "You can start with that. You'll find more boxes in the back. I don't want to lose a sale because you didn't keep the shelves well-stocked. Also, make sure we have stock in the backroom. If we run low on something, tell me, and I'll place an order."

He starts to walk by me, and I quickly give way. "I'm Nina Jackson. Don't you need any of my information?"

He keeps walking. "I have your name. I'll be paying cash, so I don't want to know any of your shit."

I frown at his rudeness but still call after him, "Thank you for the chance."

Taking a seat on the crate, I continue packing the nails, screws, and bolts where they belong. I'm so damn thankful I've worked in a hardware store before. I'm going to make this man eat every one of his words.

Chapter 29

DAMIAN

I drive away from Mrs. Perry's house after fixing her fish tank. She got new lights, but they didn't work. The problem was with the switch. A wire came loose, and it only took a minute to fix, so I didn't charge her.

I think about the other job I have. It'll take up most of my time for the next couple of weeks. Mr. Taylor is wheelchair-bound, and they want me to add a ramp for him at the back of the house. I also have to maintain the other ramps around and inside the house.

I stop at the hardware store so I can order some lumber and get other supplies. Walking in, I see Joshua behind the counter.

"Hey, Joshua," I say as I take the measurements out of my pocket. "I just need a couple of things."

"Sure," he smiles at me.

"I'll need these measurements in treated lumber for a wheelchair ramp over at Mr. Taylor's place."

Joshua takes the piece of paper I wrote all the measurements on and checks it. "I'd suggest you use screws. Nails will pull loose."

That makes sense. I nod at him. "Yeah, you're right. Let's go with the screws."

"I have some medium-length boards in the back, two by four. They should work well." He starts to walk toward the back, then asks, "What are you going to use to make it non-slippery?"

"I was thinking grit tape. You have any?"

"I don't have enough for this size ramp. I'll have to order." He stops in the back of the store, inspecting the lumber. "You're going to need some thinner pieces for hand and guard rails."

"Yes, you think you can get it all ready for me? Just give me a call, and I'll swing by to pick it up."

"Sure thing," he grins, walking back to the counter. "Just write your number here." He shoves a piece of paper my way, then yells, "Nina!"

I write down my name, Alex Jackson, along with my phone number and push the piece of paper back to him.

"Yes," I hear a familiar voice behind me. Turning around, I frown when I see Cara.

What is she doing here?

"Go check how many packs of screws we have," he barks at her, making my eyebrow dart up.

What the fuck?

Cara's eyes dart from Joshua to me, and then she quickly disappears into the back.

"So," I turn back to Joshua, "she's working for you?"

"Who?" he asks, looking confused for a second. "Oh, you mean the woman? Nah, not for long. She came in here earlier asking for a job. Said she could do anything a man could." He chuckles, and I don't like the sound of it. "We'll see how long she lasts."

I don't want to mess things up for Cara on her first day at a job, but I want to give Joshua a subtle warning. He better not mess with my woman.

Cara comes back, looking nervous, and she stays a safe distance from the counter. "Fourteen," she says, trying to sound sure of herself, but the uncertain look in her eyes doesn't escape my watchful gaze.

"Get back to work," he barks at her again.

"Nina," I say before she can dart to the back of the store. I walk right up to her, and taking hold of her chin, I watch her eyes widen. I press a kiss to her lips and then smile at her. "What time do you get off?"

"Five," she squeaks.

"I'll be outside." I give her another kiss and then let her go. "We can grab something from the diner to celebrate your job, baby."

"Okay," she grins, and her eyes dart to Joshua, and the smile quickly fades before she darts to the back of the store.

"Later," I say to Joshua, who's gawking at us.

Let him try and fuck with her now.

CARA

It's funny how nice people can be if they're scared of your husband. Not that Damian is really my husband, but Joshua doesn't know any different.

Joshua did a total one-eighty after the stunt Damian pulled, kissing me in front of him. So at least I'm not being treated like shit anymore, which is always a good thing.

I've worked my butt off, making sure there's nothing Joshua can complain about.

The last thirty minutes really drags, and every time I look at the clock above the counter, only a minute has crawled by.

Having worked through my lunch hour because I started late, I'm hungry and tired.

I glance at the clock again, and a wave of relief washes over me when I see it's one minute to five. I watch the seconds tick by and then walk to the front of the store.

"Bye," I say uncomfortably, not sure if I can call Joshua by his first name.

He smiles at me, but the smile doesn't extend to his eyes. "Bye, Nina. Have a good night."

"Thanks… you too," I almost sputter, and then I rush out of the store.

Damian's parked right out front, and he's leaning against the driver's door with his arms crossed over his chest. When his eyes land on me, he pushes away from the car and walks toward me. "Hey, gorgeous."

Lifting a hand, he reaches for me, and wrapping his fingers around the back of my neck, he pulls me into a hug.

We're standing in front of the hardware store.

My boss can see us.

Everyone can see us.

My eyes widen as Damian leans closer to me. I feel his breath on my cheek. His eyes flick over my shoulder at the entrance to the hardware store, and then they flick back to me, and oh my freaking word, it's the hottest thing I've ever seen.

When Damian's mouth brushes over mine, I forget to breathe. I'm still stuck in a trance as he guides me around the car, and opening the passenger door, he waits for me to climb inside before he shuts it behind me.

My eyes follow him as he walks around the front of the vehicle, and I watch as he waves at Joshua, who's been staring at us from the doorway.

Seeing Joshua snaps me out of my stupor, and I realize Damian's just acting like we're a married couple for appearance's sake.

I wouldn't have minded if it weren't an act, though.

Letting out a sigh, I pull on my safety belt as Damian slips behind the steering wheel.

Starting the engine, he asks, "How was your first day?"

"I think I did okay," I mention.

"How did Joshua treat you?"

I slant my eyes to Damian. "After the stunt, you pulled he was sweet as pie."

"Good," he chuckles while steering the car toward the diner. "Let me know the second anyone gives you trouble."

I can't stop a smile from forming around my lips. "Always the protector."

Damian shakes his head. "No, just taking care of my woman."

His words make a flush of heat spread through me, and then happiness bursts inside my chest.

I love the sound of that.

His woman.

Damian glances at me, catching the smile on my face. "You look happy."

"I am," I murmur as I lean my head back against the headrest.

"Yeah?"

Nodding, I wish I could explain how good it feels to be happy because I thought it wasn't in the cards for me.

Feeling overwhelmed, I turn my gaze to the window.

I'm really happy.

Damian's hand covers mine, and he gives me a quick squeeze before he places it back on the steering wheel.

"Another win, baby." Hearing the pride in his voice makes a tear escape and brush it quickly away.

"Another win," I chuckle.

Chapter 30

DAMIAN

I wipe the sweat from my forehead and then secure the last of the screws for the landing. Once I'm done, I stand back and look at what I've achieved this past week.

The ramp is perfect. I've given Mr. Taylor enough elbow space as well. At the rate I'm going, I'll complete the job sooner than I expected.

I pack up my tools and then walk into the house. "I'm heading home, Mr. T."

"Would you like to stay for some coffee and cookies?" Mrs. Taylor asks from the kitchen. She baked today, and it smells mouthwatering.

"No thanks, Mrs. T. I have to pick up Nina from work."

"Of course. I'll keep some for you for tomorrow. You have a good night, dear. Send my regards to Nina."

I rush to the car, not wanting to be late to pick up Cara. I have a little surprise for her. The drive into town is quick, and as I stop in front of the hardware store, Cara comes out.

My eyes drift over her face as she walks toward our vehicle. She looks a little tired, but she smiles happily when she sees me.

The work is good for her. It's not the job I would've chosen for her, but it keeps her busy.

Cara gets into the car, and I lean over, pressing a kiss to her lips. "Hey, gorgeous. How was your day?"

It's becoming routine, the hello and goodbye pecks. I tell myself it's only for appearances, but yeah, that's total bullshit. I'm stealing every touch I can get from her.

"It was good. The rest of your lumber order came in. You can pick it up when you drop me off tomorrow morning."

"Great, just in time," I say as I drive us to the local car dealership.

"I'm trading the car in for a truck. It would suit our environment better," I tell Cara.

"Okay." When I stop in front of the dealership, she scrunches her nose. "Can I wait outside?"

"Sure." I go inside and find Ben, the sales guy I spoke with about the trade-in. "You have it ready?" I ask, hoping this will be a quick transaction.

"Yeah," Ben points to the table that's overflowing with paperwork. "I just need to make a copy of your license while you sign a couple of papers."

I take a seat, and then he hands me the documents with a pen. "Just sign where I've marked with an x."

I hand him my driver's license for Alex Jackson, and I make sure to sign in that name too. One screw-up and our lives could be at risk.

The whole transaction takes about fifteen minutes before I get the keys. "You'll see it parked out front. I had it washed, but you'll have to put in some gas."

"Sure." I smile and reach out my hand to him, "Thanks for all your help."

Cara's standing outside, just staring off into space. I take her hand and point to the truck. "There's our new ride."

I open the door for her, but instead of getting in, she tilts her head and glances up at me. "Does it come with a ladder?"

Laughter bubbles over my lips, and I take hold of her hips, lifting her into the truck.

"Oh, that works too," she says, sounding a little breathless, and I don't miss the flush on her cheeks.

She's definitely not scared of my touch. If anything, she likes it, and I'm totally taking it as another win.

Climbing behind the steering wheel, I start the engine and drive toward the gas station.

While I'm filling the tank, Cara glances around the inside of the cab. "Oh, look, there's space behind the seats for your toolbox."

My lips curve up, and for a split second, it feels real. *Cara's my wife. We're starting the rest of our lives in Southport.*

It's only for a moment, though, before reality sinks in. *Cara still has a long way to go.*

With the truck filled up, I steer us in the direction of the diner, and when I stop outside it, Cara gives me a confused look. "Again? We were here Tuesday."

"Just stay put. I'll be back soon." I run into the diner and get us ice creams.

When I come out of the diner, Cara smiles widely. "Yes! I swear, sometimes it's like you can read my mind."

After handing her one of the cones, I watch her take a lick, and it has a direct link to my cock, which hardens instantly.

I drive to a quiet spot where we have a nice view of the ocean, all the while trying to get rid of my hard-on. We get out of the cab, and I lower the tailgate before jumping onto the cargo bed. Holding a hand out to Cara, I help her up, and then we both take a seat, leaning against the back of the cab.

The view is stunning, and just sitting like this is relaxing.

We should do this more often.

"That was so good. Thanks," Cara says as she finishes the last of her cone and licks her fingertips. I watch every one of those tips slide between her perfect lips. I hear every tiny pop as she pulls that same tip out again.

Fuck.

Her eyes meet mine, and she freezes with a finger in her mouth. I reach for her hand, and pulling it toward me, I bring the still wet tip to my mouth and then close my lips over her skin.

Cara's tongue darts out over her bottom lip as her eyes zoom in on her finger in my mouth.

I suck gently and then watch as heat flares in her eyes. I'm playing with fire, and we could both get burned, but fuck, I can't stop what's happening.

Cara shifts onto her knees and moves closer to me. She pulls her finger from my mouth, and then her eyes search mine as she slowly leans in.

It takes everything I have to keep still and to give Cara control.

Hesitantly, she keeps coming closer until her breath flutters over my lips. When her mouth touches mine in a soft kiss, my hands fist for restraint.

Cara pulls a little back, searching my eyes again, and when I tilt my head, giving her a reassuring look, her mouth crashes against mine.

Thank fuck.

Unable to keep back any longer, I grab hold of her hips and guide her onto my lap. She straddles me, her arms wrapping tightly around my neck. Her tongue plunges into my mouth, and I'm surprised by the passion she's kissing me with.

Suddenly she pulls back again, her eyes wide. "Are you okay with this?" she asks, motioning between us with the same finger I had in my mouth only seconds ago.

I slip a hand around the back of her neck and pull her back to me. "Just fucking kiss me already," I growl.

When our lips touch again, it feels as if something explodes between us, blowing all our self-control to hell. I stroke her tongue hard with mine, sucking the taste of ice cream from her tongue while taking bites of her bottom lip.

Christ.

I've wanted to do this for so fucking long. I break the kiss and then continue pressing kisses along her jaw and down her neck, finally getting to taste her silky skin.

Cara's head falls back, giving me full access to her neck. I kiss and suck, leaving my mark all the way down to her collarbone.

I'm so fucking hard my cock is going to tear right through my jeans.

With the air bursting from my lungs, I grab hold of the hem of her shirt and shove the piece of fabric up until I can see her bra. I pull the flimsy lace down, exposing her plump flesh and pale pink nipples to me, and then go in for the kill.

I take one of her nipples in my mouth and suck at the soft flesh before gently biting down on it. Her hips jerk against my cock, and I let go of her breast.

Locking eyes with Cara, I see the shock on her face. She's confused because she wants me, but there's still a fuck-ton of hesitation.

I cover her breast with my hand, soaking in the feel of her soft skin, and gently begin to massage her.

There's no way I'm stopping this. It will do more damage than good. Cara needs to feel desired, and I plan on doing just that.

"Fuck, baby, you feel so good," I praise her, and it makes her cheeks flush the same color as her nipples. "So fucking beautiful."

I watch as desire wins out over her hesitation, and bringing her mouth to mine, I whisper against her hot breaths, "Ride me, Cara. Make yourself come."

I take her mouth, thrusting my tongue inside her warmth, and show her exactly how I want to take her.

My other hand slides down her side to her hip, and gently, I thrust up against her hot center.

When a soft moan drifts from her into my mouth, I dip my hand beneath her slacks and panties. The second my fingers brush over her pussy and I feel how fucking wet she is, a growl ripples from my chest.

She's fucking burning up for me.

I press my palm against her clit and circle her opening with the pad of my middle finger. Her nails dig into my shoulders, and I can feel I'm losing her attention. I pull slightly back and, locking eyes with her again, I murmur, "Focus on us, baby. Just me and you."

If I can just get her past this point so she can experience intimacy as something good, I know it will help her heal a hell of a lot more.

"Fuck my hand, gorgeous," I encourage her, my eyes never leaving hers. With my other hand, I take hold of the side of her neck and stare deep into her eyes. "I want you, Cara. Only you."

Cara looks at me with so much trust, it overwhelms my heart, ruining me for any other woman.

Heart, body, and soul, I'm hers whether she wants me or not.

Cara's cheeks flush as she begins to move. I rub her gently, teasing her, and soon, her body takes over. Her breaths begin to come faster, matching every jerk of her hips. She presses down harder on my hand, and her movements grow slower. She's so fucking close.

I push my finger inside her and watch as her eyes glaze over with pleasure. Her mouth opens, but no sound comes out as her body begins to convulse.

Lifting my hand from her hip, I wrap my fingers around the back of her neck and yank her to me as she comes apart. I crush her lips beneath mine and fuck her mouth with my tongue, wanting to devour her orgasm.

Cara's body jerks against mine, matching my pace as I keep thrusting my finger inside her. Her breasts push against my chest, and it takes every last bit of strength I have not to strip her down and fuck her right here on the back of the truck.

"Christ, baby, I've never seen anything more beautiful than you. You own me."

CARA

Hearing the words from Damian as his hand works me into a frenzy of pleasure, emotion overwhelms me.

Shit. Shit. Shit.

It's all I can think of as wave after wave of ecstasy pulses through me. It makes my toes curl and my skin tingle.

"Damian," I breathe as my orgasm crashes through me, causing my body to convulse. His mouth crashes against mine, and his tongue and teeth make the orgasm last longer. His finger thrusts in and out, and his rough palm presses hard against my clit with just the right amount of pressure.

A moan drifts from me as I tighten my hold on his shoulders, soaking in all the pleasure he's giving me.

Again he's made me feel something I've never felt before. It's the first time I've orgasmed with a man.

The pleasure begins to fade, and my body stills against Damian's as he slows the kiss while he pulls his hand out of my pants. His mouth breaks away from mine, and then he sucks his middle finger into his mouth.

Holy hotness.

Settling both his hands on my hips, he just stares at me, his icy blue eyes filled with the intensity of what we just shared.

What we just shared.

Ahh...

Damian's not saying anything, and I begin to feel awkward. I let go of his shoulders and quickly straighten the fabric around his neck.

Then it sinks in – in broad daylight, I just jumped Damian on the back of his truck. I rubbed myself shamelessly against him.

I actually initiated intimacy between us even though I thought I wasn't ready, and... it confuses me.

"Look at me," Damian murmurs softly.

I shake my head and start to get up, but his hands tighten their hold on my hips, and he yanks me back down against his still hard cock.

My eyes dart to his, and it makes my cheeks flame even more.

"Talk to me," he says calmly.

"I don't understand how you can be so calm about this. Why would you even want me?" I try to get up again, but he won't let me up. "Sam," I snap, using his real name to show him I'm serious. "Let go of me."

A predatory look shadows his eyes, making them look like frozen ice. "Don't you fucking Sam me." He yanks me closer until our chests are flush against each other. "I kissed you, Cara. I touched you. I want to fuck you, but you're not ready," he spells the words out to me. "I wanted this. I want you."

Damian shakes his head and then pushes me off of him. We both stand up, and I watch as he jumps from the back of the truck. I hurry to the tailgate and slide down.

He starts to walk away from me but then stops and swings back. "You have got to stop thinking I wouldn't want you," he snaps, clearly upset.

I don't think I've seen him upset before, and it makes me realize this is hard for him as well. Damian is always so calm and strong I tend to forget he can hurt as well.

He stalks toward me, and grabbing hold of my hand, he presses my palm to his hard-on. "You feel that?"

I nod quickly, unable to form words as my mouth goes dry.

God, he feels huge.

"That's me wanting you, Cara. I want you every fucking day. I jerk off like a fucking teenager in the shower. Every. Fucking. Morning." He lets go of my hand and then stalks back to the truck, climbing in behind the steering wheel.

I stare down at my hand, his words playing over and over in my mind.

Damian wants me.

I know he's right. I'm the problem. It's hard to believe someone like him would ever want someone like me.

Feeling confused, my emotions are all over the place. I don't get back in the truck.

"I'm going to walk home," I say, and then I head toward the beach.

I don't hear the truck start as I get lost in my turbulent thoughts.

Damian wants me.

I was able to be intimate with him.

Yes, there was panic, but when I looked into his eyes, it faded away. There was only him and how he made me feel.

No demons.

354

Does it mean my feelings for Damian are stronger than my fears?

Is there hope for me to be whole again?

I have to think this all through and make sure I'm ready. I don't want to mess up my chance with Damian. He's too important to me to risk losing.

My feet stop, and with the ocean to my left and a lining of trees to my right, I admit for the first time that I'm ready.

I love Damian, and my biggest fear is that I'll lose him.

If that ever happens, I won't survive, and it makes all my other fears pale in comparison.

Chapter 31

DAMIAN

Things have been awkward between us the past couple weeks. Cara's quiet, only talking to me when I ask her something.

We work. We eat. We sleep.

It sucks, but I'm determined to give her the time she needs to process what's happening between us, even though it's the hardest thing I've ever had to do.

It's eight on a Friday night, and she's in bed pretending to be asleep.

Sighing, I get up and walk into the bathroom to brush my teeth. When I reach for the toothpaste, I notice it's finished. I crouch down, and opening the cupboard under the sink, I grab a new tube.

Something catches my eye, and then I'm surprised as I stare at the contraceptive pills.

Cara's on the pill? When did she start?

Fuck that!

More importantly, why did she start?

I brush my teeth and then stalk to the bedroom.

Tonight I'm getting some answers.

I flick on the light. "We need to talk," I say, sitting down on the side of the bed.

Cara opens her eyes and watches me warily as she scoots to the middle of the bed. "About?"

"I won't let us fall into some fucked up routine where we ignore each other when we're home. If you feel you have to leave and find your own way, I won't stand in your way. But, if you're going to stay with me, then we need to talk about us."

Cara swallows hard. "I don't want to leave."

"Why?" I ask. This is one of the most important questions she'll ever have to answer.

She starts to fiddle with the covers and whispers, "I want to stay with you because..." She swallows again, looking nervous as hell. "You're my life now."

Thank fuck.

Hearing her answer, a smile tugs at the corner of my mouth. We would've had a problem if her answer was because I kept her safe. We can't build a relationship on that. Then, it would be better if we stayed friends.

But she didn't say that. Instead, she said I was her life, and that makes a huge difference to where we go from here.

CARA

The past few weeks have been agonizing, not knowing where I stand with Damian. Not knowing if I've ruined my chance with him. It's been killing me, but I've been too scared to ask him how he feels.

If I'm going to share my future with a man, it can only be Damian. Not only because I feel safe with him, but because he really has become my entire world.

He kept me standing when I had no strength to stand on my own.

Not once did he give up on me.

When I was blinded by my trauma and pain, he showed me there's still beauty in life.

And I've come to the conclusion I won't know if I'm ready for sex unless I actually try. It's just... the word sex brings up images of pain and despair.

I really want this. I want a future with Damian so badly it hurts. He's the only person who's survived my enemies. He's the only one who's strong enough.

More importantly, Damian has seen me at my worst. He's seen my ugly, my dark, my broken parts – and he's still here. Not once has he looked at me like I'm a mess.

I scoot closer to where he's sitting and glance up at him, my heart beating wildly in my chest. I swallow hard, then admit, "I really want to try with you."

Damian's eyes are intense as they bore into mine. "You have to be sure, Cara." I can hear the concern in his voice, and it melts my heart.

"You saved all of me, and I want to give that to you."

He lifts his hand and gently cups my cheek. His touch is filled with comfort and strength. It doesn't make my skin crawl but instead makes me feel priceless.

As I take a deep breath, Damian begins to lean in toward me. His lips brush softly over my forehead.

"I want to fuck you, but more than that, I want you to be sure you're ready for it," he says, his breath warming my skin.

I've already put myself out on a ledge here, and I might as well jump.

"I'm ready," I whisper, my heart leaping to my throat.

I feel his hand move to my side, and his fingers brush over some exposed skin.

Damian lifts his other hand to my face and tucks some of my hair behind my ear. His eyes are intense as they scan my features.

"You sure?" he asks.

I glance away, out the window at the dark night and then back. I see the muscle start to jump on the side of his jaw.

It's just us here.

Damian and me.

It's safe.

"Yes."

Damian leans closer to me until I feel his breath fan over my lips. I let out a groan, and he takes a breath as if he's breathing in the sound, tasting it.

With my need for Damian becoming an overwhelming force, I beg, "Will you make love to me?"

Damian's eyes drift over my face, and the corner of his mouth lifts into a hot grin. "You have no idea how long I've waited to hear those words from you."

He takes hold of my shirt, and as he pulls the fabric over my head, my heart rushes up along with the material. Lowering his mouth to my neck, his lips brush over my racing pulse. I close my eyes when he presses his chest against mine, pushing me back onto the bed.

When Damian's body covers mine, and I feel his hardness press against my core as he rocks his hips forward, a breath explodes from my lungs.

Damian grabs hold of my thighs, and he rubs himself against me again, his eyes locked on my face.

The air crackles around us, the moment filled with intensity, anticipation, and need.

There's only him.

My protector.

My love.

Leaning down, his teeth tug at the sensitive skin beneath my ear. I gasp when his fingers tighten around my thighs, bunching some of the fabric of my sweatpants together. Suddenly he moves away, yanking my pants down my legs. When both his hands settle low on my abdomen, right over my panties, there's a spike of anxiety in my chest.

My heartbeat changes, going from fast to erratic.

Damian doesn't remove my panties but instead crawls over me again. His expression is serious as he locks eyes with me. "We need to clear one thing," he says, and I take a breath as I try to brace myself for whatever he's about to tell me. "We don't do I love you's and shit like that. The day that starts, things just go bad. We trust each other."

Taking a deep breath, I nod.

He lowers his head and presses a kiss above my right breast. "We respect each other." His voice is much softer when he kisses me above my left breast. "We'll have sex." I flush, but I keep my eyes on him as he moves to press his lips between my breasts. "And we will always…" he takes hold of my panties, and my heart explodes through my chest as he tugs the fabric down my legs, "have each other's back."

Damian's mouth burns a hot trail over my breasts and down to my abdomen. Goosebumps spread over my skin, and when he comes up to cover my body with his again, I realize he's still fully dressed.

Damn, he's good.

I'm really starting to think he can read my mind because a smile tugs at the corner of his mouth as I lay naked beneath him.

"Now that I have you where I want you," he murmurs. The look on his face turns predatory, and it makes me want to squirm – with need. "What will I do with you?"

His teeth scrape over his bottom lip, and it sends a flash of heat through me.

God, I'm going to go up in flames just from him looking at me like that.

Damian lifts his hand to my face and brushes a single finger over my lips, then down my neck and over my breast.

My body starts to quiver with want, and I feel no fear.

He continues down to my stomach, I close my eyes.

All of a sudden, he takes hold of my thighs, opening my legs. He leans into me, and his breath rushes over my ear as he nips at my earlobe. "Eyes on me at all times, baby."

Opening my eyes and wanting to seem braver than I feel, I lift my hands to his sides and slowly move them up the wide expanse of his back. I soak in the feel of his muscles rippling beneath my fingertips and wish he'd remove his clothes.

When Damian's hand moves down between my legs, I grab fistfuls of his shirt and gasp at the tightening it causes in my abdomen. His finger pushes inside me, and it makes the blood rush faster through my body. A soft moan drifts over my lips.

This is good. This I can do. I like this.

"I want to hear more of those moans," Damian growls possessively in my ear, and my body shudders beneath his.

He continues to thrust his finger inside me, making my hips swivel for more friction. Instead of getting what I want, Damian pulls free from me, leaving me a quivering mess at the loss of his touch.

As he starts to unbutton his shirt, I lift myself on my elbows, so I can see every inch of him. When he removes his shirt, my eyes drink in his hard chest and abs. I take in the tattoo, now understanding what the claw marks over his heart means. It must represent how he felt when he lost Leah.

Then Damian undoes the button of his jeans and pushes the pants down his thighs.

I begin to blink, and my lips part in shock.

Now I also understand the meaning of well-endowed.

Everything about Damian is hard.

Every. Single. Inch.

My mouth dries right up at the sight of his cock, and it feels as if my tongue has turned to stone.

I dare a tentative glance at his face. His eyes are on mine as the bed shifts under his weight, watching closely for my reaction as he moves closer.

I have a sensory overload as he lies down on top of me, covering me with his warmth. He places an arm on either side of my head, and a blush pushes up my neck.

The memories are threatening to break through the walls I've built around them as I give him a trembling smile. "Hi."

"You still okay?" he asks.

I nod quickly, wrapping my arms around his neck.

Damian presses a tender kiss to my forehead and against each of my cheeks. And then he dips his head to my neck, and I lose him to my breasts.

At first, I feel the sting of loss because I want him to kiss me senseless. Instead of this moment being romantic or hot, it feels like Damian is focused on removing any other man's touch from my body and replacing it with his own.

He presses a kiss to my breast and then asks, "Are you sure?"

Am I?

I think...

Shit, I'm at least ninety percent sure.

"Uh-huh," I mumble.

Damian settles his elbows on either side of my head again and stares down at me. He tilts his head, and then I feel his hard length pressing against my opening.

My whole body stills as fear flutters through my chest.

"I need to hear the word 'yes' from you," he whispers, his eyes searching mine.

I wet my lips and open my mouth, but nothing comes out.

This is Damian.

I love Damian.

Damian will never hurt me.

I'm safe.

"Yes," I croak through parched lips.

His eyes soften on me. "It's just us here, baby. You're safe."

I nod and then manage to sound sure of myself when I say, "I want this. I want you."

Damian adjusts himself over me, taking some of his weight from my chest, and it allows me to see him better. Then I feel him better, too, as he positions the head of his cock at my entrance.

Oh, God.

I take a deep breath, my eyes glued to his as my heart beats wildly.

When Damian thrusts forward, I have to fight the urge to not move away from him. He enters me just an inch, and his hand moves down, grabbing hold of my butt to keep me in place.

Then he keeps still, except for his eyes searching my face. "Breathe, baby."

I take a deep breath and shift my hands to his shoulders because I need something to hold onto.

"Are you ready?" he asks again.

I nod. My gaze skips from his eyes to his mouth and then back. I keep nodding. "Yes," the word rushes from me.

Damian's hold on my butt tightens, and then he enters me another inch. Slowly, he keeps going watching my reaction like a hawk until he's finally sheathed all the way.

I feel impossibly full, and there's discomfort. I just focus on my breathing until I grow accustomed to his size.

Damian stills over me, and I feel his breath on the corner of my mouth. The teasing is painfully sweet.

He pulls out, and when he thrusts inside me again, my fingers dig into his shoulders, and our breaths mingle as they rush over our lips.

And then it sinks in – We're naked, and Damian's inside me.

As he withdraws, I feel something pull deep within me. He lifts his head to look at me as he thrusts harder than before. A strangled moan gets lost in a gasp, and I tilt my hips up to give him better access. His breathing falters, and when I drag my nails down his back, a deep groan rumbles in the back of his throat. "Christ, baby."

Instead of pulling back, he slams in deeper, shifting my body up, and I gasp loudly against his neck.

"You're so fucking tight around my cock," he says, his voice hoarse with the desire he feels for me.

Pulling out, he thrusts even harder inside me. "Jesus," he breathes, and then he frames my face with both his hands, and his eyes burn into mine. His breath is hot on my lips, setting them on fire, and I whimper because I want him to kiss me so badly.

"Only me," he growls and bites my bottom lip while filling me once again.

My body trembles beneath his with want.

There is no fear, no shame – just us.

"No one else touches you ever again," he breathes into my mouth, and I inhale all of him. He slams back into me, and I cry my pleasure out.

And then Damian's lips devour mine, biting and nipping, and it drives me wild. His thrusts become fast and hard until all I can do is hang on for dear life as he dominates me.

The man fucking me is everything but sweet. He's exactly what the ink on his skin represents.

He's predatory.

He's dangerous.

He's mine.

I smile against Damian's mouth, and he increases his pace even more until the sound of our skin meeting fills the air.

The force he takes me with wipes the smile right from my face, and my body tenses beneath his until it feels like I'm about to snap.

Damian keeps his eyes on mine. "So fucking perfect."

He holds my attention with every thrust.

"You're mine." The words seep into my bones.

His.

Only his.

My body tenses even more until it feels as if I'll explode into pieces. Damian's body claims mine in every way, and his hard thrusts send me spiraling over the edge with a cry. I begin to convulse as intense pleasure, unlike anything I've felt before, spasms through me. "God, Damian."

Damian wraps his arms around me, pinning me to his body as he keeps filling me with every inch of cock. "That's it, baby. Come for me."

The orgasm rips the air from my lungs, and Damian's tight hold on me keeps me from shattering into a million pieces.

His mouth finds mine, and he devours me as I ride the wave of pleasure, almost feeling delirious.

"Fuck, Cara," he growls, and then his body jerks against mine as he finds his own release.

I hold him as tight as I can while he slams into me one last time, and in this moment, it feels as if he's trying to become one with me as he empties himself inside me.

His breaths are harsh as they burst over my ear before he lifts himself on his elbows. Then he just stares down at me.

Damian said there won't be any I love you's, but the look on his face tells me differently.

"You're mine, Cara Ellison," he says my full name, and it makes tears form in my eyes.

"I'm yours, Sam Rees," I whisper because my heart is too full.

This is the only time we'll get to be ourselves. This is the part of us no one else will ever see. This is what makes us one.

Chapter 32

DAMIAN

Since Cara fell asleep, I've been staring at her. We've finally taken the final step, and now there's nothing that can take her away from me.

She's mine.

Forever.

I'm glad I was able to hold myself back. If I had fucked her the way I really wanted to, I probably would've scared the hell out of her. Once she's used to us being intimate, it will be a whole different story.

I've spent many mornings picturing how I'd take her, but all those fantasies pale in comparison to finally being inside her. Her body's reaction to me was hot. Her moans drove me wild, and the way she looked at me with trust and desire claimed every inch of my soul.

And her body. Christ, her body.

Fuck, it's making me hard again just thinking about it.

Cara stretches out and turns on her side, her back facing me. I want her again, and I want her now. Reaching for the blanket, I pull it back, exposing her sinful body to me.

I move closer to her, pressing my chest against her back. I push her hair away from her neck and press a kiss to the soft skin, right where her neck curves into her shoulder. Her body jerks and I take it as a sign that she's waking up.

Feeling her heat, smelling the fresh scent that always clings to her skin, makes me rock my hips against her ass.

"I just want to fuck you all night long," I groan in her ear.

A sound ripples up Cara's throat, and it pours ice through my veins. I've heard that sound before. It was on the memory disks. It's like a broken whimper, but it quickly turns into a feral growl, and she swings her arm back. Her elbow connects with my chest, and then she darts forward.

Her eyes are still closed as she falls off the side of the bed. In a stunned stupor, I watch her head slam against the corner of the bedside table, and then she darts up and runs out of the room.

Only then does life return to me.

What the fuck have I done?

I jump out of bed and quickly pull on my pair of jeans that were still lying on the floor.

I can hear her yanking at one of the doors, and then her desperate cries reach me, and I run for her. Coming out of the room, I'm just in time to see her pull the front door open.

"Cara!" I yell as she darts into the night.

Running out onto the porch, I see her slam full-on into a tree.

Fuck, that's got to hurt.

"Cara!"

She bounces back and then darts around the tree.

I jump over the railing and set after her. We're both barefoot, so it's not one of the easiest runs I've ever had.

She's fucking fast, not even the branches lashing at her slow her down. I don't think she's feeling any of the pain in her shocked state.

Her body must've gone into survival mode, and it's killing me that I was the one to trigger it in her.

Cara's heading in the direction of the beach. I start to catch up with her, and as I reach for her, she ducks and lets out a terrifying scream.

She darts forward again, and for a moment, my heart stutters with pain.

Christ, seeing her like this is killing me.

We reach the slight hill that leads to the beach, and in horror, I watch her take the leap. Her body slams hard into the sand, and then she struggles back to her feet.

Fuck, my heart.

I take the leap, and my legs shudder with pain as I hit the sand, so I can only imagine how much it must've hurt Cara.

I get up and go after her again as she starts to wade into the ocean. Her shorter legs make it hard for her to run in the water, and it slows her down enough for me to catch up. I slam into her, and wrapping my arms around her, I lock her arms to her sides.

As I yank her out of the water, she starts to scream and struggle against my hold.

Once I have us back on the stretch of sand, I take her down. I lock my legs around hers and move a hand up to her forehead, securing her against my chest so she can't hurt herself any further.

"You're safe," I rasp the words out, but it doesn't do anything to calm her.

I take a couple of deep breaths before I say in a neutral tone, "Cara, you're safe. It's me, Damian." She growls at me, thrashing like she's possessed.

Panic flares through me, and I gasp, "It's Sam. You're safe. It's Sam." I say the words until my voice cracks with the heartache I'm feeling for her. "It's Sam, baby. It's Sam."

Finally, Cara stops her wild thrashing, and for a moment, all I can hear is the ocean and her feral breaths racing over her lips.

She starts to tremble in my arms, and then her body jerks to the side. She heaves, and I quickly roll her over, so she's on her hands and knees. It's just in time as she vomits.

I quickly gather her hair behind her neck, and I wish there was more I could do right now.

"I'm so sorry," the words tear from my chest.

I sit on my knees next to her until she starts to jerk with dry heaves and sobs. I can't hold back my own tears. Seeing her broken like this shreds my heart to pieces. I hated it the first time, and I hate it now.

I sit flat on my ass and pull her into my arms. The emotions swarming inside of me are just too much.

I feel rage toward Tom Smith for fucking up Cara's life. All for fucking money he stole from the mafia. I feel a deep craving to kill every single person who's ever hurt her.

My heart breaks for her, and my soul screams for revenge for what's been done to her.

Cara's gasping for air through her panic, and I know I have to do something to calm us both.

Before I can think of anything, she starts to pound her fists against her chest. "I feel them all the time," she rasps between heartbreaking sobs. "It never stops."

"Tell me, baby," I whisper hoarsely. It will haunt me forever, but I need to know what happened so I won't trigger a panic attack like this ever again. "Tell me what they did, Cara. Let me share it."

She shakes her head, and for a minute, I think she's not going to open up, but then the words start to spill over her lips. I'm bombarded with image after gruesome fucking image.

There's so much that the memory cards didn't show, and it guts me open until my heart is nothing but pulverized meat.

Certain words hit harder, embedding themselves into my soul.

'They shoved me face down every time.'

'I was breathing in chunks of vomit, and still, they wouldn't stop.'

'It felt like I was being stabbed, over and over and over.'

'It hurt so much.'

'I feel defiled ... just ruined beyond repair.'

Sitting on the beach in the middle of the night, Cara's trauma becomes mine. She gives me all her pain and sorrow, and it takes all my strength to bear her burden.

When she slumps against my chest, I press a kiss to her hair. "Never again, baby. I'll kill anyone who tries to hurt you. I promise. I'll kill every last person on this fucking planet to keep you safe."

All of the pain for one man's greed. I channel all my rage into one thought – I'm going to fucking kill Tom Smith.

He's a dead man walking for fucking with the woman I love.

CARA

It feels as if it just happened again, every single revolting second.

I can't remember much of what actually happened the past few hours – only the horror I suffered in the container.

Damian says I took off running through the trees and into the ocean.

I'm sitting in the bath, staring down at all the scrapes over my chest and arms. My feet sting, but I grit my teeth as Damian pulls thorn after thorn out of my soles.

"What about your feet?" I whisper.

"Don't worry about me. Let's just get you cleaned up and in bed."

As he continues to wash my feet, I just sit and stare at his face. That worry muscle is jumping over time. He looks like he did back when he found me... like a killer.

He rinses both my feet off and then grabs a towel. "Come on," he says gruffly.

It feels like a freight train plowed over me. I move gingerly as I get out and then step into the towel.

I look up at Damian and whisper, "What are you thinking?"

I need to know he's not angry with me.

I need to know I haven't pushed him away with the panic attack from earlier.

Damian swallows, and then his gaze meets mine for the first time since we came home.

Seeing the heartache and anger on his face, tears rush to my eyes, clogging up my throat. It makes him look wounded, and it hurts so much to see him like this.

"I'm going to kill him," he says, his voice laced with the promise of death. "We're going to fly to South Africa, and I'm going to kill Tom."

The words shudder through me, cold chills racing up my spine.

I shake my head and take a step back from him. "N-no. I don't want to go back there." I wrap the towel tightly around me and then grip it hard to my body. "Can't we just forget tonight and go on as if nothing happened? We're just starting to make a life for ourselves here in Southport."

"Forget what happened?" he snaps. An enraged look tightens his features, and then he growls, "I can't forget, Cara. You... the sounds you made. What you told me... fuck no, he's dying."

I rush by him and go to the bedroom. I grab a clean shirt and leggings and quickly get dressed. Damian comes to stand in the doorway, and he crosses his arms over his bare chest, the jeans hanging low on his hips.

"You need to shower, and then let me look at your feet," I say, hoping he'll drop this insane idea of his.

"Cara," he says, sounding calm again.

379

I start to straighten the sheets when he closes the distance between us. He takes hold of my arm and turns me to face him. When his hands frame my cheeks, his palms are cool on my hot skin.

His eyes lock on mine. "Your uncle took out a hit on your life. He wants you dead, so the mafia won't use you to get the money from him that he owes them. We have to finish it. We either keep running or fight back and put an end to it. I can't run. It's not in me to hide. I have to do this. I have to kill him for what he's done to you. It's the only way I'll be able to live with myself."

Oh my God.

Uncle Tom wants me dead?

My face crumbles as the blow of betrayal hits.

"You lost your parents because of Tom. He's put you through fucking hell. Let's just put an end to this nightmare, baby."

"I'm not as brave as you," I whisper, and then the stupid tears come again, making me look as weak as I feel. "I'm not like you, Damian. I'd rather run."

He shakes his head and presses his forehead to mine. "You're so fucking strong, baby. You've survived so much, and you keep coming back from it all. You're not a quitter, and that's how I know you can do this with me."

He presses a soft kiss to my lips and then locks eyes with me again. "We promised to have each other's back, Cara."

I nod, unable to come up with any more excuses.

"Let's take this war to him and finish it so we can build a life here for ourselves. Let's close the door on your past."

I nod again, and then Damian pulls me to his chest, wrapping his arms tightly around me.

"You're everything to me, and I need to do this to make sure you're safe."

I nod again as I soak in the safety I feel in his embrace, and closing my eyes, I whisper, "Thank you for coming for me back then." I tighten my arms around the man I love more than anything in this world. "Thank you for never leaving me. If it weren't for you, I would be alive today."

I have to bite the rest of the words back, but they lie heavy on my tongue.

I love you, Damian.

Chapter 33

CARA

The following week is pretty much uneventful after all hell broke loose Friday night. I go to work as if nothing has changed. Damian said he's been in contact with his friend Jeff to get us visas so we can travel.

I'm still processing the fact that Uncle Tom wants me dead, and everything happened because of his greed and selfishness.

At first, the news threw me off balance, but I'm starting to realize it's either Uncle Tom or me. Unfortunately, one of us will have to die for this madness to end.

It hurts, but I've come to terms that Damian is right. We have to end this nightmare.

It's a typical Thursday at the hardware store. I'm checking to see what we need to order for the following week while wondering why Thursdays always feel so long. It's like two days got shoved into one.

I hear voices from the front of the store, and it sounds like Damian. I slowly make my way up the aisle with the list of stock we have to order.

Sure enough, Damian's talking with Joshua. When they both look at me, I force a happy smile around my lips.

I hold the piece of paper out to Joshua, "Here's the order for next week."

He takes it and then looks at me with sympathy, which confuses the hell out of me. "I'm just telling Alex it's okay for you to take some time off."

"Huh?" the word pops from me. Now I'm even more confused.

"Yeah, babe, so we can go to your uncle's funeral."

The half-stunned expression drops from my face, and I'm glad Joshua mistakes it for grief.

"You can go now, Nina. I'll get the Jameson boy to help out after school for the next week."

Mutely, I nod as Damian takes my hand. He pulls me to his side and then reaches a hand out to Joshua, "Thank you so much for understanding. She'll be back in a week."

Joshua shakes Damian's hand. "Sure thing."

I feel like a robot as Damian tugs me out of the hardware store and then helps me into the truck. I look down at my hands all the way home, not sure how I feel about going to South Africa.

I understand this has to be done, but the last time I was there, my parents were killed.

Because of Uncle Tom.

When Damian parks the truck in front of the cabin, he opens his door, then says, "We'll meet Jeff tonight before driving through to the airport. He has the tickets and documents."

"What about transport once we're there? What about a place to stay? How will we get close to my uncle? How will we get back? What if we get caught?" The questions pour from me in a desperate attempt to find a reason to stay here... where we're safe even though I know we have to go.

Damian takes my hand and brings it to his mouth. His words are hot on my skin, "We won't get caught. I've done my homework. South Africa has a high crime rate. Thousands of people die every day, and the killers are never found. I'll hire a car under our fake names, and we'll stay at some cheap motel." He presses another kiss to the back of my fingers. "We'll be fine. I'll keep us safe."

"But... but." I swallow hard. There's just no way for me to suppress the fear. "I'm scared."

"Don't be," he whispers. "I know you'd rather stay here, but then you'd be unprotected, and I can't risk it. We'll only be there for three days. Remember what I told you? We make people look the other way. Make them not notice you. You can't look scared, because that will draw attention to us. We're just two normal people going about our business." He gives me a reassuring look. "Trust me."

Trust Damian.

He's never given me any reason not to.

Slowly, I nod, then he continues, "You'll be doing all the talking. People will notice my accent, but you will fit right in. I need you to have my back with this one."

I start to nod my head again as I try to focus on what he's saying. I swallow down the fear and then frown. "I have to do the talking? What if they ask me something I can't answer?"

"We're going to go over every detail on our drive up to Charleston, where Jeff will meet us. We'll be flying from there. Everything is going to be fine."

DAMIAN

The flight was fucking long. My legs were starting to cramp. The fact that we're both exhausted from the flight counts in our favor. We look the same as all the other passengers, sweaty and wrinkled.

The man at customs hardly looks at our passports, and soon we're waiting for our luggage, which is only one bag. I didn't bring any weapons because... well, that would be a fucking stupid move on my part.

I got us simple names for this trip. Mike and Sonja Durant. I grab the bag, and then, holding Cara's hand tightly, we make our way over to Avis car hire.

Cara takes a deep breath as we near the counter and then smiles at the woman behind the counter. "Hi, we'd like to hire a car for a few days."

The woman smiles professionally. "Are you here for holiday?"

Cara freezes suddenly, then mutters, "Give us a moment." She grabs my hand and pulls me away from the counter. When we're out of hearing distance of the woman, she whispers, "Neither of us has a license. We can't hire a car." Her eyes dart around us to make sure no one hears her.

Fuck, I totally forgot about that part.

"Wait." She points outside. "We can get one of those taxis. It looks safe enough... I think."

She's pointing to a beaten-up white car. "Yeah, let's do that."

When we get to the car, a man smiles at us. "One-stop taxi service with a smile. Where can I take you?" he says in a funny-sounding accent.

"Thanks, uhm..."

Cara glances at me, and then the man starts to ramble in a language I know abso-fucking-lutely nothing about.

"Ooo... julle's Afrikaans. Jammer man. Waar wil mevrou-hulle gaan? Ek kry julle daar in 'n jiffy."

Cara starts to laugh, and she shakes her head. "My Afrikaans sucks. Let's stick to English, please. Uhm... could you take us to a cheap hotel close to Bedfordview?"

"Oh, sorry, man," he laughs and then opens the back door. "Sure, there's one in Edenvale. It's close to the shops."

I keep the bag with us as we climb into the back, and soon we're on our way to the hotel. I don't know what I expected to see once we got here, but it all looks pretty normal.

Cara nudges my arm, and I glance at her smiling face. "Did you expect to see wild animals roaming the streets?"

"Of course not," I chuckle.

"The only animals here are the people. Trust no one."

The smile drops from my face as I'm reminded of why we're here.

When we reach the hotel, Cara deals with the cab driver. Once we're settled in a tiny room, I take a deep breath. The first stage has gone down okay. It sucks that we don't have a car, and it makes moving around harder because this country's public transport is almost non-existent.

We'll manage.

Cara sits down on the bed and then stares at the floor. I crouch in front of her and catch her eyes. "What's going on in that mind of yours?"

She shrugs and gives me a sad smile. "I'm thinking about the last time I was here." Her eyes meet mine, and I see the sadness. "Every Sunday, my parents and I used to drive out to the Vaal dam. We'd spend the day there... just the three of us. I was so happy back then, Damian. I loved my parents so much, and they were just ripped from me. I didn't even get to go to their funerals. Uncle Tom just shoved money at me with the stupid passport and told me to run. I was only eighteen. I didn't know any better. I didn't understand anything back then, and I still don't."

388

I brush the palm of my hand over her cheek and press a kiss to her lips. "Let's just get this over with so we can get our assess back home."

"Sounds good." Her teeth tug at her bottom lip as her eyes dart shyly to my face.

I tilt my head and take hold of her chin, so she has no choice but to look at me. "What's that look for?"

"Uhm..." she bites at her bottom lip again, clearly nervous about something. "I was just wondering if... uhm... did I ruin things between us with the panic attack?"

Fuck. Cara thinks she scared me off?

I shake my head and smile at her. "Never. I'm just taking things slow with you."

She stands up, pulling me up along with her. Her hands settle on my chest, and she tilts her head back to meet my eyes. "So... you still like me a little bit?" She pulls the cutest face ever, and it makes my heart melt.

"I more than like you a little bit," I murmur, but then I get serious. I've never told Cara how I feel about her, and that's probably why she's unsure of us. "It's not just about the sex, Cara." Her eyes dart away from my face.

She's obviously very uncomfortable with the word sex, and I make a mental note not to use it again.

Her hands start to slip from my chest, and I quickly grab them, holding them in place. "I live you."

Her eyes dart back to mine, and then I see the confusion wash over her features, which has me explaining, "Love is too much like hate. They're emotions that come and go. Life, now that's a different ball game. You only get one life." Leaning a little down, I stare deep into her eyes. "I live you, Cara. You're my life."

Her chin starts to tremble, but a smile still breaks through. "I am?"

I press my lips to her mouth and whisper, "You are."

She makes the first move, reaching for my shirt. I let her pull it over my head, and then she presses a kiss to my shoulder. "Will you show me?"

"Hell, yeah," I growl. Grabbing hold of Cara's hips, I lift her off the floor and throw her onto the bed.

She takes hold of her shirt and tugs it off. I watch as she strips until she's naked, and then my eyes devour every inch of her creamy soft skin.

She scoots to the edge of the bed and takes my belt off, and then my jeans drop to the floor. I step out of them and watch for her next move, every muscle in my body tensing.

Cara leans forward and presses a kiss to my abs. When her fingers wrap around my cock, I grab hold of her hair.

Her fist begins to pump me, and it makes it impossibly hard to keep still.

Her eyes lower to my cock, and I watch her expressions closely.

"I'm done being scared. They were the ones who hurt me, not you." And then her mouth closes over the head of my cock, and my eyes drift shut from how fucking good it feels.

Fucking, nirvana.

Cara sucks me deep, making my balls tingle, and then she pulls the heat of her mouth away from my cock and crawls up my body, pressing kisses all the way up my abs and chest until her breasts presses against my chest.

Her lips brush over mine, and then she whispers, "Fuck me, Sam."

That's all the encouragement I need. "Lie down," I order.

A seductive smile I haven't seen before curves around her mouth, and she quickly lies down.

Taking hold of her thighs, I yank her closer to the edge of the bed. I step between her legs, forcing them open with my body, and then lean over her.

When my fingers stroke over her clit and opening, and I feel how wet she is, satisfaction fills me.

As I take hold of my cock, her eyes dart down, and she watches as I rub the swollen head against her pussy. "That's right, baby. Watch me fuck you."

Positioning myself at her entrance, it takes all my strength to ease gently into her. My body's screaming for hard and fast, but it's still too soon for that.

I watch as Cara's lips part on a silent moan, her back arching from being filled with my cock.

My muscles strain, and clenching my teeth, I take hold of her hips so I can hold her in place as I start to move. I keep the pace as slow as I possibly can, my control paper-thin.

"Don't hold back," she murmurs.

My eyes snap to hers, and I shake my head.

"I want you, Sam. Don't hold back," she urges, a feverish look tightening her features. "Please.

Christ.

My control fucking vanishes, and I slam hard into her, sending shivers of pleasure down my thighs. Pulling only halfway out, my ass clenches as I begin to take her fucking hard and fast, the strokes short and powerful.

It only takes a couple of thrusts for Cara's body to submit to mine. She grabs hold of the covers and lifts her ass off the bed, giving me better access, and it rips a pleasure-filled groan from me.

I keep driving into her, intoxicated by the feel of her clamping around my cock.

When she begins to moan, my eyes lower to where her pussy is wrapped tightly around my thick length, and I watch as I own her.

Cara tilts her head back, letting out a needy moan, and then her body starts to convulse. The sight makes me fuck her with every ounce of strength I have. A gasp explodes from her parted lips as she starts to come undone. Her whole body tenses, her eyes find mine, and then I watch as ecstasy washes through her.

I slam as deep as I can into her, the slap sending a mixture of pain and pleasure sizzling through me, and then my cock swells and pulses as I empty myself inside her.

"Fuck, baby," I growl, keeping myself buried in her, my muscles tensing to breaking point.

Sweat trickles down my back as our eyes lock. There's no fear but only satisfaction relaxing Cara's features, and it makes my cock jerk one last time.

As soon as the ecstasy fades, I slip an arm beneath her, and picking her up, she quickly wraps her legs and arms around me. I walk us to the bathroom and straight into the shower with me still buried inside her.

I press her back against the wall and murmur, "Drop your legs for me, baby."

She slowly slides them down, and it makes my cock slip out of her.

I turn on the faucets and then grab the soap. I work it into a lather and then slip my hand between her legs. I gently wash her, and it doesn't take long for her hips to start grinding down on my fingers and palm.

I press Cara against the tiles with my body and slam my mouth down on hers. She moans on my tongue, and I fuck her with my hand and tongue until she's gasping in pleasure, and I'm hard again.

This is how I want to see her all the time, lost in ecstasy because of me.

I grab hold of her thighs and lift her against me, and when her pussy wraps around my cock, I begin to move slow and deep.

I've never been one for making love… until now.

I want to feel every inch of Cara as she takes all of me. Every time I sink deep inside her, she clenches around me as if she's trying to keep me from pulling out.

"Sam," Cara whimpers, and it makes me smile that I'm driving her so wild she's reached the point of begging me for her orgasm.

I keep going slow and deep until her nails dig into my skin, and she drags them down my back to my ass.

"Fuck, I love that. Brand me, baby."

Adjusting my hold on Cara, I slam deep inside her once again. A grin spreads over her face as I quicken the pace, and after a couple of hard thrusts, her nails dig into my skin, and she buries her face against my neck.

"Shit. Shit. Shit," she chants, and then her pussy clenches hard around my cock as her orgasm hits.

I follow close behind her, and this time my legs almost give out from the intense ecstasy unraveling in me.

Cara's legs slip down, and she leans back against the tiles, her breaths rushing over her parted lips.

I reach for the soap, but she grabs hold of my wrist to stop me. "No, wait."

She pushes me slightly back and then looks down at her legs. I frown, not sure what she's doing.

Did I hurt her?

"You okay?" I ask, still slightly out of breath.

She looks up at me, and a smile spreads around her lips. "I just wanted to see your cum run down my legs."

Holy fuck.

Possessiveness fills every inch of my chest as I lower my eyes to her legs.

"You've branded me, Sam. Now you only have to fuck me from behind, and then I'll feel you everywhere on my body. I want you to replace every image until all I see, all I smell, and all I feel is you."

I frame her face, overwhelmed by the love I feel for this woman flooding me. "I live you, Cara. So fucking much."

Her smile turns tearful, and she just looks at me with something akin to awe all over her face. "I live you more than anything, Sam."

Chapter 34

CARA

We go to bed early, wanting to get a good night's rest because jet lag's a bitch.

I wake up to find Damian staring at his phone, and I take a moment to just look at him. I drink in the slight stubble on his strong jaw, his full lips, and straight nose, and then his sharp eyes that never miss a thing.

"Morning," he murmurs, and then a hot grin tugs at the corner of his mouth. "I can feel your eyes on me."

"Just enjoying the view," I chuckle.

Damian leans into me and turns the phone, so I can see it. He's looking at a map. "Tom has a strip club here." He points to a street name and then looks at me. "Do you know the area?"

I look again and notice it's not that far from the street I grew up on. I point to Kloof street and say, "That's where I lived. It's not that far from there, maybe five minutes by car."

Damian frowns and then looks at me. "I wonder what happened to your house. Surely your parents had a will?"

I never even thought of that. "I don't know," I whisper, a pang of sadness rippling through me. "Uncle Tom must've taken it all."

Damian climbs out of bed and then glances around the space. "We need to clean every inch of this room. Make sure we leave nothing behind. We'll have to steal a car."

"I can't drive," I tell him, worry spinning in my stomach. "In South Africa, you have to be eighteen before you can get a license. I never got mine."

"It's okay, I'll drive. We'll get a car, head to the club, and I'll kill him there. We'll have to leave the car there and make a run for it. I'm thinking we could find our way to the nearest gas station and call a cab from there to take us back to the airport. We can sleep at the airport and then leave tomorrow."

"Damian." I crawl to the edge of the bed and climb off. Standing in front of him, I give him a pleading look. "We can still go home. We don't need to do any of this. Just… let's just go."

His eyes search my face, and then he shakes his head. "It's the only way you'll be safe. We need to finish this war, Cara."

DAMIAN

I stole the ugliest piece of shit I could find. Driving on the opposite side of the road, I have to focus as Cara gives the directions.

When we reach the club, I feel her tensing beside me as I park the car near a row of dumpsters. We quickly wipe the car down, making sure we don't leave any fingerprints.

"Don't lock it and leave the keys," she whispers. "With a little luck, someone else will come along and steal it."

"Good idea." That would totally work in our favor.

She shrugs. "It's normal around here."

As we walk to the entrance, an African man waves at us and yells something I don't understand. Cara waves at him and pushes me forward. "He's offering to watch the car."

"That sucks," I mutter.

"Don't worry, he's going to sit on his ass and get drunk. He won't stop a thief. The car's fine where we left it."

Cara pays the cover charge, and we head inside the club. I'm instantly on guard as I start to search the place for any sign of Tom.

Now that we're here, nerves tighten in my gut. I've avoided thinking about it, but tonight's going to turn out shit for me, one way or another. I lied to Cara, and she might just find out the truth that Tom never hired me.

Hopefully, she'll give me a chance to explain.

I glance at her and notice she's just as tense as me, and then I spot Tom at a table in the back. He's not alone, sitting between two scantily dressed strippers with guards flanking the table.

Taking a deep breath, I link my fingers with Cara's. "Just play along."

"What?" she whispers, and then her eyes grow huge as I start to walk toward Tom. "You're just going to walk up to him and kill him in front of all these people?"

"No," I hiss. "Just look scared as fuck and do what I tell you."

"No problem there," she snips at me. "I'm about to wet myself."

Tom glances over the floor and to the half-naked women dancing on a nearby stage before his eyes finally settle on us. Shock registers on his face, and then he waves at the people around them. They get up in a hurry and scatter in all directions, leaving Tom alone at the table.

When we're close to the table, he slams a fist down on it, making the glasses rattle. "What the fuck is this?"

"Is there somewhere private we can do this?" I growl, jerking Cara closer. "You've put a price on her head, and I'm here to claim it." She stumbles over her feet and almost loses her balance, which makes for a good show.

"Fuck... we could've done this somewhere else." Tom gets up and, looking pissed, he snaps, "This way." He leads us down a dimly lit passage, and I check behind us to make sure no one's following. The guards stay at the end of the hallway, glancing at the patrons.

Idiots.

Once we're in the office, I shut the door behind us.

I can't even look at Cara as the words leave my mouth. "Seeing as the bounty said you want her dead, I thought I'd deliver an up, close and personal service and kill her right here for you."

"Damian?" Cara whimpers, her voice tight.

Tom's eyes flick from me to her, and then he starts to ramble, "Sorry, Cara, I can't have you running around. I thought I could, but they'll keep using you to draw me out, and I can't have that. It's a fucking headache." He looks around the dingy office. "I can't risk losing all of this, and it will prove my loyalty to Tredoux." Tom gestures at me. "He'll make it quick. You won't feel a thing."

Disgust wells up in me as I stare the man down. The fucking bastard.

His eyes snap to me. "Just do it quick. I don't want her to suffer."

Letting go of Cara's hand, I walk to the desk. I grab a pair of scissors, and just as Tom's eyes widen, I lunge at him, burying the scissors in his gut. Slowly he drops to the floor, his eyes filled with shock.

I yank the scissors out, and as I crouch in front of the fucker, I catch his horror-stricken eyes and say, "I'm a cleaner, Tom, not an assassin. I rid the world of filth like you. It was pure luck that I stumbled upon Cara before they could kill her. She's mine now, and for her, I'll kill every fucking bastard who tries to hurt her, just like I'm going to kill you."

"Wait," he gasps. "Wait."

I plunge the scissors right under his ribs, praying I hit a lung. "Fucking hurts being stabbed over and over, doesn't it?"

He tries to say something again, but it comes out garbled, blood spilling over his lips.

All the rage I've felt for what was done to Cara goes into my last swing as I bury the scissors in his ear, and then I watch as the light dims in his eyes.

They say hell is where you relive your worst nightmare, over and over. I fucking hope it's true for this bastard.

CARA

I stare at Uncle Tom's body, a turbulent mess of sadness and relief swirling in my chest.

I watch as Damian uses Uncle Tom's shirt to wipe the blood from the scissors before he tucks them into his back pocket.

My mind can't get past what Uncle Tom said, that he would pay Damian to kill me.

I thought Uncle Tom hired Damian to help me?

Damian just said it was pure luck he stumbled upon me.

So... Uncle Tom never hired him?

Damian turns to me, and avoiding my eyes, he glances around the office. "Did you touch anything?"

"You weren't hired by my uncle, were you?" I ask, still trying to make sense of the truth I just learned.

Damian doesn't answer me but instead grabs hold of my hand and drags me out of the office. He closes the door behind us, and we walk down the dark hallway toward the back of the club. He shoves a heavy emergency door open, and we slip out into the night.

Damian keeps walking, just pulling me behind him. We head toward the nearest gas station, and when we reach it, I have to order an Uber to come pick us up.

When I'm done, I walk away from Damian, needing some space to think.

Damian wasn't hired to rescue me.

"Cara," he whispers harshly, quickly catching up to me.

When we're out of the light and direct view of people putting in petrol, I turn back to him. "You were never hired to rescue me?"

"No, I wasn't," he finally admits.

"You didn't know me. Why did you save me?"

"I told you I'm a cleaner, Cara. I was already watching the group when they brought you there."

Oh my God.

"So the four days I was in that container, you knew about me?" The words taste vile on my tongue.

404

Damian takes a step closer, and lifting his hand, he wraps his fingers around the back of my neck, and only then does he explain, "We couldn't just barge in, Cara. We had to gather enough intel and secure the safest possible exit for you." He swallows hard. "If I had known..." He takes a second to breathe. "If I had known they'd rape you, I would've risked it all to get you out sooner."

Damian came for me out of his own free will. I wasn't just a paid job.

His admission and my realization make tears spiral down my cheeks, and I shake my head, wanting to tell him I don't blame him for what happened, but I can't find my voice.

Damian takes another step closer to me, and I quickly wipe the tears away.

"I lied to you about Tom hiring me so you would trust me. I just needed to buy myself some time until you were comfortable with me."

Just then, a cab pulls into the gas station. I make sure my cheeks are dry as I gesture to it.

"Cara," Damian murmurs, his voice tight with worry.

"Not now," I manage to whisper past the lump in my throat. "We can talk about this when we're home."

I should feel something after seeing my uncle being murdered by the man I love... but instead, I feel nothing.

But when it comes to Damian, the new realization leaves me feeling... wanted.

Damian took me out of that hellhole and kept me because he wanted to.

Chapter 35

DAMIAN

It's been three days, and the news shows the authorities have no suspects for the murder of businessman Tom Smith but that he was linked to a crime syndicate. His death has been attributed to a deal gone bad.

I ditched the scissors in a trashcan right at the airport. There should be no way for the police to trace the weapon to Tom's death if they find it.

Everything should be fine, but it's not. Things feel shaky between Cara and me. I want to hold her. I want to tell her everything will be fine now that the bastard is out of her life, but I know she needs time, and I'm giving her as much space as she wants until she's ready to talk about it.

At least she doesn't seem to be angry with me.

I've been keeping busy with odd jobs, but as day four rolls by and Cara remains quiet, I'm worried she'll sink back into depression.

When Cara walks out onto the porch, my eyes snap to her. She gives me a smile that doesn't reach her eyes before she heads toward the beach.

Seeing her out and about eases some of the worry. At least she's not holing up in our bedroom.

"Take all the time you need, baby," I whisper as my eyes follow her through the trees.

CARA

I'm not angry. It just hurts so much that my own blood wanted me dead. Damian was right when he said he saw someone who was alone in this world when he saw me.

It's a scary thought... being alone. Now that I can finally stop running, everything I lost rushes to the surface.

My parents. My baby. The hell I've been through.

All my loss and horror were for one man's greed.

There are still so many questions that I know will never be answered. The thoughts weigh heavily on me as I lie awake next to Damian.

Damian.

Why do I keep calling him that?

He's not Sam to me. Sam will always belong to Leah.

Damian... The man who saved me. The predator who kills. The cleaner who found me beaten and raped... and kept me.

Alex... The man who's supposed to be my husband. The handyman who loves fixing things.

Who is the real man lying next to me?

I hear him move, and I whisper, "Why did you really keep me?"

It's quiet for a while, but I know he's awake. I can feel his energy buzzing around us.

"You had no one and needed to be saved."

"Because you couldn't save Leah?"

"No. There was just something about you... even though you were broken, you were still the most beautiful thing I'd ever seen. I couldn't let you go."

I absorb what he's telling me and then turn onto my back. I stare up at the dark ceiling.

"Why are you staying with me now?" I close my eyes, scared of what his answer might be.

"I've never met anyone as strong as you. Normally, people are scared shitless of me, but you never backed down, although you were afraid initially. You were at your lowest, and you still stood your ground in front of me. I've never seen such strength in anyone. It's rare. Life just keeps taking blows at you, and you just keep getting up. I admire you, Cara, and that's why I fell so hard for you."

"Life hits like a bitch," I try to joke, and we both chuckle, even though we know it's not the truth. Life hits hard, so fucking hard.

I feel Damian move closer to me, then he murmurs, "I'm staying with you because you've become my life."

I swallow hard on the emotions welling in my chest. "You didn't have to save me." Turning onto my side, I meet Damian's eyes. "You didn't have to do any of the things you did." I lean forward and press a tender kiss to his mouth, then whisper, "You came for me."

He moves closer to me, and then his fingers brush over the curve of my cheek. "I live you, Cara. I live for you, and I'll die for you. There's nothing on this godforsaken planet for me but you."

"I live you, Alex," I whisper, and it makes him pull back so he can see my eyes.

"Why Alex all of a sudden?"

"Sam belongs in your past. I'll never get to know him. I think he died with Leah, and I'll let her have him to keep her safe wherever she is. Damian is a cleaner who saved my life, but Alex… he's is my husband, and he pieced me back together. Alex is my family."

From now on, that's all he'll be to me. Alex Jackson… my future.

He presses a kiss to my lips again and then murmurs, "I live you, Nina."

A grin tugs at the corner of my mouth as I tease him. "Why Nina all of a sudden?"

"Cara's an eighteen-year-old girl who died in an accident with her parents. I think we should let her rest in peace with them. Karen suffered so much heartache. No one can possibly survive everything she's endured. I think it's best we let her go." He presses a kiss to my forehead. "But Nina, she's this kick-ass woman who works down at the hardware store, and I really want to build a life with her."

Laughter bursts from my lips, and I roll onto his chest. "Alex." My eyes drift over his face. "So you're okay with being my husband?"

"Hell, yeah," he growls, his hands slipping over my hips and gripping my ass tight.

I push off of him and tease, "Then you better put a ring on my finger, Mr. Jackson."

I hear him chuckle as I walk to the kitchen to make myself some tea because lately, coffee's been messing with my stomach. I think it's from all the stress, so I'm just taking it easy.

Stirring the liquid in the cup, I glance over our modest home.

I finally have a place I can call home.

ALEX

It's been a week since we talked. Things feel better between us, and those deafening silences are gone.

I'm leaning against the truck, waiting for Nina to get off from work. I'm forcing myself to think of her as Nina because she's fought so hard for that name. It will also reduce the risk of one of us slipping up.

Jeff's been keeping tabs on the mafia, and after I killed Tom, they seemed to have gone quiet. Nina's practically disappeared off their radar, so I feel confident they won't continue to look for her.

It's time to put the past behind us and to focus on our future, the one neither of us thought we'd ever have.

I hear Nina say goodbye to Joshua, and then she comes walking out of the store. Her eyes find me, and she smiles happily.

I drink in the sight of her – the woman who changed my life, who gave me a reason to live.

I grin back at her. "Hey, beautiful." I push away from the truck when she's within reaching distance of me. Wrapping my fingers around the back of her neck, I pull her to me and press a tender kiss to her mouth. "How was your day?"

"Good." She grins up at me. "Yours?"

"Too long," I grumble. "I missed you."

The grin transforms into a happy smile. "I missed you, too."

Dropping my voice low, I ask, "Want to get ice cream?"

Desire instantly darkens her green eyes. "Hmm. Sounds like a good idea."

Tugging her against my body, I lean down to reach her ear. "I plan on fucking you on the back of the truck."

Nina makes a needy sound in the back of her throat.

"Would you like that, baby?" I let out a breath over her skin, and it makes goosebumps form.

She nods, and pulling back so she can lock eyes with me, she whispers, "Skip the ice cream."

Letting out a chuckle, I hurry to open the door and bundle her inside, then I rush around the truck, my cock straining against my pants.

I drive us to the same spot we parked when I made Nina come for the first time. I help her onto the back, and after I sit down, I pull her onto my lap so she's straddling me.

"Fuck, this is all I've been thinking about all day long," I mutter as my eyes rake over her. "Walked around with a hard-on."

"Yeah?" she murmurs as she leans closer, placing a kiss to the side of my neck.

"Yeah. So fucking hard for you, baby." My hand slips between her legs, and feeling the heat from her pussy has satisfaction rippling in my chest. "You wet for me?"

She grinds down on my hand for more friction. "Always."

"Fuck," I groan. "How wet?"

"Soaking." A mischievous light shimmers in her eyes, and as I lean in for a kiss, she darts up. I let out a chuckle when she jumps off the back of the truck, making a run for the beach.

Oh, my woman wants to play.

I get up and run after her. Nina runs into the water and lets out a burst of bubbling laughter. "Cold! God, it's cold."

As she turns around to see where I am, I lunge at her, and it makes her cry with laugher as we hit the water. I quickly turn us around, so she's on top.

"C-cold," she shivers.

"Want me to warm you up?" I tease her. I stare up at her, and she takes my breath away. Her hair is wet, and as my eyes travel lower, I see her hard nipples straining against her shirt. "Christ, you look hot all wet."

She lets out a chuckle, and with a seductive look in her eyes, she presses a kiss to my jaw. "Not half as hot as you look right now."

"Can I tell you a secret?" I whisper, and she nods quickly. "You're the only woman I'll allow on top of me, but we're going to drown if we don't get up now."

"Ass!" Nina shoves me under the water and gets up. I watch her as she stalks away from me and then call out to her, "You love my ass."

"Lucky for you," she calls back."

I get up and follow her to the truck. We're both soaked. We might as well take this party home.

We don't even make it to the front door before I peel off her shirt. If we had neighbors, they'd be getting a show right now.

Slamming Nina against the nearest wall, my mouth burns a hot path down her neck. We fight to get all our wet clothes off, and the moment we're naked, I fill her with a powerful thrust.

My body keeps Nina pinned to the wall, my eyes locked on hers with a burning intensity as I own every part of her.

The broken, the beautiful... and most importantly... the survivor in her.

NINA

Two months later...

I'm biting my nails as I leave the hardware store, my stomach a tight bundle of nerves.

Shit.

I get in the truck, bracing myself to face Alex. But, before I can say anything, he presses a kiss to my mouth and then steers the vehicle down the road.

Smiling at me, he asks, "Did you have a good day?"

I bite my bottom lip and then blurt the words out, "I'm pregnant."

He quickly moves the truck to the side of the road and then just stares at me.

"Did you hear what I said?" I ask nervously, and I go back to biting my thumbnail.

Slowly, he nods, a stunned expression tightening his features.

"Alex?" I whisper when the tension becomes too much.

"We're pregnant?" he asks, and I watch as emotion washes over his features. A second later, he grabs me to his chest and kisses me hard. "We're pregnant?" he asks again.

"Well, I don't know about the 'we' part. I'm the one doing all the work."

"My sperm had to swim its ass off for that egg. Give it some credit," Alex says, all serious, but I see the smile tugging at the corner of his mouth.

"Your sperm didn't take my egg on a date. Your sperm is so in the doghouse," I tease him, relieved to see he's okay with the news.

A huge grin spreads over his face, and then he turns the truck around and drives back down the road.

"Where are we going?" I ask.

"The sperm is taking the egg to dinner," he mutters playfully.

I burst out laughing as he stops in front of the diner. Getting out, Alex jogs around the front of the truck and opens the door for me. He helps me out, letting me slide down the front of his body, and then his eyes start to shimmer with tears, and it instantly makes me want to cry.

"I'm taking my beautiful pregnant wife to dinner," he whispers, and a tear slips down his cheek.

All choked up, I whisper, "Why are you crying?"

"Because I'm so fucking happy. I'm so happy you chose to stay with me, and we're going to build a family together."

"I'm happy, too," I whisper, and then I stand on my toes so I can reach his lips. "Thank you for making every one of my dreams come true."

"I did?" he asks, holding back on the kiss.

"Yeah." I inch a little closer to his mouth. "I just wanted a husband who loves me and a home filled with kids. That's all I ever wanted."

418

He presses a tender kiss to my lips, and I smile against his mouth. "I'll have to build onto the cabin to make space for all those kids."

"I'd like that."

Taking my hand, he links our fingers and leads me into the diner. "Time to feed my wife and kid."

His wife.

His kid.

I place my other hand over my stomach and swallow back the emotions.

My husband.

Our child.

"Do you think at some point I could reach out to Annie?" I ask after we've taken a seat at one of the booths.

Alex's eyes jump to mine, and then he says, "Yeah, I'm sure you can call her. I'd like to wait another six months at least, just to make sure the dust has settled and there's no one sniffing around. Also, you won't be able to visit her, but she can always come here. We'll figure something out that's safe for everyone."

"Really?" I ask to make sure before I get my hopes up.

"We'll just need to explain everything to her so she knows not to call us by our old names."

"I can do that." A wide smile splits over my face.

"Just give it six months. Okay?" Alex gives me a comforting smile, knowing how much Annie means to me.

"Thank you."

We look over the menu, and I'm overflowing with gratefulness for Alex and another chance at being a mother. And soon, I'll get to see Annie again.

My little family.

Glancing up from the menu, I stare at the man who changed my life. God, he's given me so much. Most importantly, a sense of belonging.

It was a long and hard road to get here, but it led me to Alex Jackson.

I'd walk that road again if I had to, but only for him.

The End.

JUST A NOTE FROM ME...

This book is so close to my heart.

I got to deal with a lot while writing it, and years later,

it's still special to me.

If you're in a dark place, I hope it will offer you some

sense of comfort.

Please, stay strong. It will get better.

Love yourself because you are priceless, and don't let

anyone ever make you feel worthless.

Hugs,

Michelle.

Published Books

STANDALONE NOVELS
Mafia / Organized Crime / Suspense Romance
(Can be read in this order or as standalones)

MERCILESS SAINTS
Damien Vetrov

CRUEL SAINTS
Lucian Cotroni

RUTHLESS SAINTS
Carson Koslov

TEARS OF BETRAYAL
Demitri Vetrov

TEARS OF SALVATION
Alexei Koslov

Beautifully Broken

Organized Crime / Suspense Romance
(Can be read in this order or as standalones)

Beautifully Broken
Previously published as Predator

Beautifully Hurt
Previously published as Redemption

Beautifully Destroyed
Previously titled as Legacy

Enemies To Lovers

College Romance / New Adult / Billionaire Romance

Heartless
Reckless
Careless
Ruthless
Shameless
False Perceptions
(Spin-off Military Romance)

Trinity Academy

College Romance / New Adult / Billionaire Romance

Falcon
Mason

Lake
Julian
The Epilogue

The Heirs

College Romance / New Adult / Billionaire Romance

Coldhearted Heir
Arrogant Heir
Defiant Heir
Loyal Heir
Callous Heir
Sinful Heir
Tempted Heir
Forbidden Heir

Stand Alone in The Black Mountain Academy Series
Not My Hero
Young Adult / High School Romance

The Southern Heroes Series

*Suspense Romance / Contemporary Romance /
Police Officers & Detectives*

The Ocean Between Us
The Girl In The Closet
The Lies We Tell Ourselves
All The Wasted Time
We Were Lost

Connect with me

Newsletter

FaceBook

Amazon

GoodReads

BookBub

Instagram

Acknowledgments

This was my first book to break through the top 100 on Amazon back in 2016. I've rewritten and edited it, and after all these years, it's still close to my heart.

To my alpha and beta readers – Leeann, Sheena, Sherrie, and Allyson, thank you for being the godparents of my paper-baby.

Candi Kane PR - Thank you for being patient with me and my bad habit of missing deadlines.

Yoly, Cormar Covers – Thank you for giving my paper-babies the perfect look.

My street team, thank you for promoting my books. It means the world to me!

A special thank you to every blogger and reader who took the time to participate in the cover reveal and release day.

Love ya all tons ;)